Uncle Jack,

Some fun stories 🙂

a quick break in your day.

Hope you enjoy!

Love you,

Martha June

MIDNIGHT

MIDNIGHT

JOHN M. FLOYD

DOGWOOD PRESS

Library of Congress Control Number
2008929285

Printed in the United States of America

Jacket design by Bill Wilson
Author photo of John M. Floyd by Carolyn Floyd
First Dogwood Press edition: October, 2008

**DOGWOOD
PRESS**

DOGWOOD PRESS
P.O. Box 5958 • Brandon, MS 39047
www.dogwoodpress.com

For Michael, David, and Karen

ACKNOWLEDGMENTS

As always, I'd like to thank my friends and fellow authors for their kind support and encouragement. Names that stand out are my longtime writing buddies Ben Douglas, Janet Brown, Carole Bailey, and Susan Weatherholt—I certainly appreciate you folks. And sincere thanks once again to Joe Lee of Dogwood Press, a good friend who has continued to believe in me and my "second career."

I'm especially grateful to my wife Carolyn, for putting up with my blank stares and marathon writing sessions. Being married to a storyteller is a challenge, and I'm fortunate that she seems somehow able to overlook most of my faults and quirks.

The stories included in this book first appeared in the following publications:

"Midnight," "Word Games," "Dooley's Code," "Eyes in the Sky," "Speed Dial," and "The Winslow Tunnel"—Amazon Shorts, 2005-2007; "A Place in History"—*T-Zero,* 2003; "The Pony Creek Gang"—*Reader's Break,* 1998; "A Thousand Words"—*Pleiades,* 1995; "Nothing But the Truth"—*Yellow Sticky Notes,* 2001; "Ladies of the North"—*Phoebe,* 2002; "Silent Partner"—*Crimestalker Casebook,* 2004; "The Garden Club"—*Eureka Literary Magazine,* 1995; "Button's and Bo's"—*Thou Shalt Not . . .* anthology (Pittsburgh, PA: Dark Cloud Press), 2006; "Break Time," "A Little Knight Music," "Good Samaritan," "Dry Spell," "Name Games," "Batteries Not Included," "Diamond Jim," "Old School," and "Elevator Music" (four of which were first published under different titles)—*Woman's World,* 1999 and 2005-2007; "The Moon and Marcie Wade"—*Just a Moment,* 1994; "One-Way Ticket"—*Dogwood Tales,* 1997; "Greased Lightnin'"—*The Atlantean Press Review,* 1995; "Illumination"—*Futures,* 2001; "Clara's Helper"—*Thema,* 1996; "The Wading Pool"—*Spinetingler Magazine,* 2006; "Knights of the Court"—*Red Herring Mystery Magazine,* 1996.

CONTENTS

MIDNIGHT

On a hot June day in 1959, two weeks after my twelfth birthday, I fell in love for the first time. And even though it happens to most of us sooner or later, my experience was a little different. Cupid's arrow, when it found me, was aimed high: I was sitting six feet above the ground, in the branches of Leland Stallworth's pecan tree.

And I wasn't up there because it was a good day for climbing. I was there because I had no other choice. In fact, on two separate occasions—once just before going up the tree and once just after coming down—I came close to dying a gruesome death. It was a memorable day.

And it all started because of a tractor part.

***

Early that morning, Deborah Jo Hardin and I were, as usual, playing cowboys in the back yard of her folks' farmhouse out on Barfield Road. She was Annie Oakley and I was Roy Rogers, and the two broomhandles we used for transportation were named, appropriately, Target and Trigger. By the time the sun peeked over the barnyard fence we were engaged in our daily gunfight with a pair of Mattel sixshooters she had inherited from her older brother.

And I know what you're thinking: In modern times, twelve years of age is a little old to be playing with cap guns and stick-horses. But these weren't modern times, or even modern places. This was rural Mississippi in the fifties, and children then were blessed with a quiet, happy innocence. Simply put, we were content with what we had and unaware of what we didn't have.

We were also blessed with a disregard for logical thinking, since Annie and Roy—both of them Good Guys—were trying to shoot each other. At any rate, that day's showdown never took place. As I was creeping toward her spot of ambush, Miss Oakley's mother stuck her head out the back door and called to her. I dropped to the ground and took aim; when my opponent came out to answer I intended to pop her one. But Deborah Jo (D.J., for short) knew that, and kept quiet. After a moment Mrs. Hardin called again, and again, and on the fourth attempt I heard an unpleasant note in her voice. Enough was enough, it seemed to say.

"Here I am, Mama," D.J. called, rising from her hiding place. No gentleman, I shot her in the back.

"Gotcha, Annie," I said.

She turned and gave me a dark look, then said sweetly, "What is it, Mama?"

"Your daddy and I are going into town awhile, honey."

Even though D.J. had her back to me, I knew she was frowning now. "But it ain't Saturday."

"Isn't Saturday, you mean."

"Right." And Saturday was grocery day, everybody knew that. "So why—"

"The John Deere place got that part in, your daddy ordered. He's dropping me off at your Aunt Lettie's for a visit." I noticed, for the first time, that Mrs. Hardin had lipstick on. She almost never wore lipstick. "The thing is, I need you to watch your little brother while we're gone."

I still couldn't see D.J.'s face, but I could see her shoulders sag. We both knew what this meant. Our game was over. Nobody could play while little Davey was around. He was always pointing out our hiding places and chewing on our horses' tails and wandering into the field of fire.

Reluctantly I leaned Trigger and Target against the wall in the toolshed while D.J. took our pistols and gunbelts into the house. She returned a moment later leading her four-year-old brother by the hand and grumbling. The three of us met at her playhouse underneath the fig tree, where we sat down in the dirt to make new plans. Or at least she and I sat down to make plans. Little Davey ran to the door of the playhouse and tried to stand on his head in their dog's water bowl.

And then it hit me.

"Why don't we go exploring?"

"Exploring where?" D.J. growled. As she was in no mood for stupid suggestions, I picked the most interesting place I could think of.

"The beaver dam. The one in the creek behind the Sullivan place. Tommy Westmoreland told me about it." It was a ways from here, sure, but that was the whole point. Exploring was no fun close to home.

"What about the Sniper?" she said.

I swallowed. All of a sudden the summer wind seemed to turn cold. "That's way over in Lake County," I said.

"That's just ten miles, Jimmy. Mama said we should stay close by, till they catch him."

My folks had told me the same thing. And it was scary, I'll admit. For weeks now, somebody had been terrorizing families east of town, mostly shooting out house windows and car tires in the middle of the night. Several pigs had even been shot, in broad daylight. It had begun when the union tried to move in at the big lumberyard near the river; my dad said whoever it was had probably been hired to put pressure on protesters. The only progress the sheriff had made was to recover some of the bullets, which eventually narrowed the mystery down to one person—or at least to one rifle. Finding that person (the newspapers had quickly named him the Sniper) was proving more difficult.

"Even if we ran across him," I said to D.J., "he wouldn't hurt us. We're just kids."

She seemed to give that some thought. "Daddy says anybody who'd shoot a pig would shoot a human."

"Your daddy, and mine too, kills pigs every year. Where do you think pork sausage comes from?"

"That's different and you know it."

Of course it was, and I did, but I didn't give up. I really felt, in my heart, that the Sniper was no threat to us. Neither we nor our folks had anything to do with the lumberyard. And most of those shootings were in the dead of night, and a long way from here. Besides, I really did want to see Tommy's beaver dam.

D.J. did too. Which made it easier, after a few more minutes, to get her agreement.

"We need to be back by noontime," she said, with an uneasy look.

"Deal." I got up and dusted off the seat of my pants. "We can pull Davey along in his wagon."

"No wagon," she said, lacing her shoes. "Road's too rough for that. He can walk."

"What if he gets tired?" I knew about little brothers. I had one too, and he was almost as big a pain as Davey.

"Then I'll carry him," she said.

"And what if you get tired?"

She finished tying her shoes and looked up at me. "Then you'll carry him."

Our travel arrangements finalized, we waited until her parents' pickup sputtered out of the driveway, then set out on our journey. Davey wasn't too thrilled by all this. He had already told us, his lower lip poking out at least an inch, that he'd rather play in his sandpile. He moped along with his hands in his pockets the first hundred yards or so, stopping now and then to examine a bug or a rock in the road. But when we passed my house without turning into the drive, he realized this was something out of the ordinary. He stopped and stared at us.

"Where we goin', Debba Jo?" he asked.

I grinned in spite of myself. He was sort of cute, standing there looking up at us.

"On an adventure," she said. "We'll be back by lunchtime."

She was right, I realized. We weren't just playing around anymore. This *was* an adventure.

"Wait here," I said to her. I jogged down the driveway to my house. A few minutes later I was back, and feeling a little embarrassed. "Now I'm ready."

"What was that all about?"

"An explorer never goes unarmed into the dark unknown," I said. With a flourish, I reached into my back pocket and took out my weapon.

It was a slingshot. And no ordinary slingshot, either. It was a Bullseye Special, with an oak frame and a leather pouch and a thick rubber sling. And I didn't use it to shoot pebbles, or marbles, or acorns—I used pellets. Daisy all-lead .177-caliber pellets. I had once put a hole all the way through a Campbell's soup can at thirty yards, something my dad would have had trouble doing with his .22 rifle.

If the Sniper took a shot at us, I thought, he better be good and he better be out of my range. Otherwise, he might be the one getting sniped.

I tucked the slingshot back into my pocket but left my hand on it. Just touching it made me feel safer. Besides, I was a Boy Scout; I believed in being prepared. Who knew what unseen dangers might lie between us and our destination?

"I can't tell you how relieved I am," D.J. said, rolling her eyes. "Can we go now?"

We went. She took the lead, Davey scampered along at her heels, I brought up the rear. And after twenty minutes I saw that she was right once again: Pulling the wagon would have been hard work. The dirt road was badly rutted in places, and was uphill almost all the way to the edge of old Leland Stallworth's property, where it turned south, toward the county line.

We finally reached the bend in the road. D.J. stopped in the middle of the turn, looking up at the barbed-wire fence that marched along the top of the ridge dead ahead. From here, we couldn't see what was on the other side. In fact, the posts and strands of bobwire looked a little spooky up there, silhouetted against the blue sky. It was easy to imagine them as some kind of warning to the unsuspecting traveler, a barrier marking the edge of a forbidden land.

All it marked, of course, was the west edge of the Stallworths' cowpasture. And if there was anything evil lurking about, it was well concealed. The place was as quiet and peaceful as a churchyard. A hundred kinds of flowers grew wild along the ridge, and pine trees shaded the grassy slope between the fence and the roadway. The wind whispered in their branches.

D.J. still hadn't moved, so Davey and I passed her and continued down the road. It had leveled out now, and ran along parallel to—and ten feet or so below—the fenceline. When she didn't follow us, I turned and looked back. "You coming?"

She was still watching the ridge. "Let's cut across," she said.
"What?"
"The road'll take us a mile out of the way." She nodded

toward the line of fenceposts above us. "That's old man Stallworth's place. Let's cut across his pasture."

Without waiting to hear what I thought about that (D.J. never waited to hear what I thought about much of anything), she strode up the slope to the fence. Little Davey, noticing right away that climbing a hill looked like more fun than walking along beside it, took off after her. I followed them, and a minute later the three of us stood together and stared at what lay beyond the fence.

On the other side of the barbed wire was a bowl-shaped pasture almost half a mile across. On closer inspection, it was more of a scoop than a bowl, with three sloping sides funneling down into a long valley that rounded a corner and vanished far to the north, where the ramshackle buildings of the Stallworth homestead lay hidden behind the summer foliage. A deep ravine snaked along the east side of the field for a ways, then flattened out halfway down the valley. In the very center of the pasture was a single pecan tree, tall and sturdy and bright with new leaves. From our vantage point it looked like a stalk of broccoli standing upright at the bottom of a green dish.

We looked down at it awhile without speaking. Even though I lived less than two miles away, I had somehow never before been to this spot. The discovery gave me a pleasant little tingly feeling—a feeling made even more intense because the place was so . . . different. It was pretty, yes, in the midmorning sun—but a lot of the countryside around here was pretty. This place was unique. In a world of small hills and valleys, we had stumbled upon some really *big* hills and valleys. The vast rolling scoop of the pasture was like a mini-Grand Canyon, filled with grass instead of rocks.

"Well," I said, "if we're going, let's go."

With that, I ducked between the middle two strands of bobwire, stepped through, and (gentleman that I am) held them apart for D.J. She didn't seem to like that much, but she didn't say anything, and stepped through also. Then I raised the bottom wire so Davey could crawl under, and as I did I saw he hadn't moved a muscle. He was just standing there with a solemn expression on his face, staring past us at the field.

"Come on, Davey," I said.

"Don't want to," he murmured.

We studied him a moment. "Why?" D.J. asked. "What's the matter?"

He shook his head. "Don't like it."

D.J. and I exchanged glances. Then she knelt and reached through the fence to caress his cheek.

"C'mon, Peanut. It'll be fun. We'll see if we can catch some grasshoppers."

He still didn't look convinced, but the mention of grasshoppers helped. Finally he nodded and wriggled under the bottom wire, and the three of us set off like Musketeers down the long hill toward the middle of the pasture.

Within two minutes Davey seemed to have forgotten his misgivings. Dozens of butterflies flitted in the grass and wild-flowers, and he happily chased them all, his little legs churning like pistons. "Stay close, Davey," D.J. called. "There's a big ditch over there. And watch for snakes." Both of us hated snakes.

We continued down the hill. Idly I studied the far side of the pasture, marking the point where we should exit the field. The fence on that side ran along a ridge much like the one we'd just left, and the open country beyond should lead us to the creek and the dam. For the second time that day I realized D.J. had been right in her view of our route. We were saving a lot of time by not continuing on the road. Besides, if we had stayed cautious we would never have seen this little corner of the world.

I took in a long, deep breath. This really was fun. The sun was hot but not yet uncomfortable, the sky was a hard, pure blue, and the grass smelled sweet and fresh and clean as we trudged along. I felt good. I glanced over at D.J. and saw that she was grinning, and I grinned back.

We were halfway across the pasture when we saw the bull.

We heard him, actually, before we saw him. He must have been hidden in the shade of the hardwoods that lined the fence on that side. Wherever he had been, he was now charging straight at us.

For a moment we stood frozen, staring at him. D.J. was the first to recover; she turned and screamed to her brother, who was ahead and to our left, between us and the big pecan tree, then took off toward him. I followed an instant later. Neither of us bothered looking back over our shoulder the way they do in the movies—what we had seen already was enough. The thing coming down the hill after us was Death Itself, and if we were to live we had to run.

The tree was our only chance.

The thunder of hooves behind us seemed as loud as a cotton gin at full tilt. D.J. slowed for an instant to scoop Davey into her arms, and I streaked past them, heading for the tree as fast as I could go. The bottom limb was maybe six feet above ground. I jumped for it at full speed, caught it, and swung myself up.

When I looked around, D.J. and her brother were twenty feet away and coming fast, and the bull was right behind them. Without even thinking about it I wrapped my left arm and leg around the branch and leaned down, holding out my right hand. "Grab hold!" I shouted.

There would only be one chance. With Davey held tight under her left arm she would be able to offer me no help in pulling her up, and I prayed she'd see what had to be done. She did. Even as she reached for me with her right hand, she leaped up and planted her left shoe in the rough bark of the trunk.

With a slap my hand grasped her forearm, and hers found mine. I pulled with all my might, and while I pulled she practically ran up the side of the tree. Below us the bull flashed past, so close I could smell his breath. With a grunt D.J. piled on top of me, and for a second I thought all three of us were going down. But she let go of my arm long enough to grab a second limb just behind us, and somehow we stabilized. I hauled myself back up and grabbed a handful of Davey's shirt to ease her load. Suddenly everything was quiet, except for the whooshing of our breaths and the pounding of my heart in my chest.

We were still alive.

Clinging to them both, I leaned over and looked down.

The bull was going crazy. He pawed the ground, ran in circles, and hooked viciously at the tree trunk with his horns. Finally he stopped and looked up at us, blowing and snorting.

I was still trembling. Carefully I shifted my weight on the branch, and soon found I could lean backward onto the second limb without falling off. That made things easier. After a few minutes D.J. turned to look at me. Her face was white as powder. "Where'd he come from?" she asked.

I glanced up the hill to the south, and swallowed before I answered. I wasn't at all sure whether any words were going to come out, but they did. "He was in the trees, I think. We're lucky he waited long as he did."

I looked at her again, then at her brother, then back at the bull. My heart was at last beginning to slow down. "Question is," I said, "what do we do now?"

But there wasn't a lot we *could* do. We sure couldn't climb down. And nobody else knew we were in trouble. Nobody even knew where we were.

I looked around, trying to think. The more I thought, the more I realized just how bad off we were.

The pasture we were in was, as I said, an open-ended valley, bordered by a hill on the south and two wooded ridges to the east and west. To the north—the open end—the valley flattened out and curved away to the right. The road we'd traveled earlier ran along the west fence but was out of sight because of the ridge, and there was little chance anyone would venture close to us if not along the road. There was always the possibility one of the Stallworths would make a routine trip out here, but it wasn't likely. This was the far south end of their farm, and from the look of things, the rest of their stock must be pastured closer to the house. Besides, I thought I remembered hearing something about a cattle auction up near Mount Pleasant today, and if that was true old Leland and his son wouldn't even be home.

The truth was, we were on our own. Barring a miracle, the three of us were alone and would stay alone, in a world neatly encompassed by bobwire and trees on three sides and empty distance on the fourth.

Since we seemed to have nothing but time, I turned to study the bull. He was a giant, probably half a ton, and nine or ten feet long. I'd never seen him before, though I'd been to the Stallworths' a time or two with my dad, to buy peaches. The bull's name, I would find out later, was Midnight—which was a good indication of just how odd Mr. Stallworth was, because the bull wasn't black at all, just a kind of muddy brown. I knew enough about livestock to know he was a Jersey, a breed my dad said was far meaner and more dangerous than the Brahmas so often used in rodeos. And this one looked like he fit the bill.

One thing I knew for certain: If the tree hadn't been here, all three of us would be dead now, trampled and gored to pieces out here in the middle of nowhere.

Davey whimpered and moved a little, and all of us came close to falling. His sister and I grabbed him at the same time, then settled him more firmly on the branch between us, our hands clenched in the faded material of his overalls. After some more adjusting we found that if both she and I braced our backs against the second branch (it was just behind the first and a foot higher) we could drape Davey across our laps so both of us could hold him with one hand and the limb underneath us with the other. How long we could stay that way I didn't know. I was dead tired already. Some of that was due to my hasty ascent of the tree and some to the effort of pulling the others up here with me; but most of it was stress, and that was a condition that might get worse as time progressed.

For I had no false hopes of rescue. Unless the bull grew bored with us and decided to leave on his own, which I doubted, we were in for a long day. If it was true that we could expect no assistance from the owners of the pasture, our only other hope was the road, which was out of sight and a quarter mile away. Even if we screamed and shouted nonstop the rest of the day, a passerby would never hear us over the sound of a car motor. And a road as remote as that one had no foot traffic.

D.J., who'd always had a knack for reading my thoughts, said, "Don't suppose anyone could hear us, do you?"

Her voice sounded so sad I didn't have the heart to say what I believed. "It can't hurt," I said. Some old-timer from town could be up there hunting rabbits on the other side of the fence right now, for all we knew.

So we screamed. And shouted. We even resorted to singing songs at the top of our lungs. All it accomplished was three sore throats and an even more angry bull. He charged about as if he'd had loco-weed for breakfast, swinging his huge yellow-horned head right and left and puffing like a steam engine. It made him look even more terrifying.

There was no doubt in our minds: Midnight the Bull wanted us, and bad.

"I want to go home," little Davey whimpered. D.J. and I looked at each other over the top of his head. He had managed to sum up our feelings pretty well.

The day wore on. After an hour or so Davey started to cry. After all, our perch was uncomfortable, and he was scared.

All of us were scared. I found myself thinking about home, and my mom and dad, and wondering when they would start looking for us. I was afraid it would be too late.

I also thought about the fact that this little adventure had been my idea. It had been D.J.'s, of course, to cut across the pasture, but that didn't help my feelings much.

For the hundredth time I looked down at the bull. He was about twenty yards away, sitting on a little rise and watching us. And he actually was *sitting*, with his back legs tucked underneath him like a puppy. I hadn't even known such a thing was possible. It occurred to me that if I had a camera, a snapshot like that would probably run in every newspaper in the country. "Sitting Bull," I'd call it. I'd make a million bucks.

The fact that I was thinking thoughts like that reminded me just how funky my mental processes had become. I really was scared out of my wits. Deborah Jo had grown fairly calm, considering. At the moment she was just sitting there as still as a painting, watching the bull watch us.

I was suddenly struck by how pretty she was. She truly *was*. Such a fact had never occurred to me before. Her eyes were as blue as the sky itself, and her little nose was turned up just right. Her hair was so yellow it glowed. And it went beyond that, beyond mere looks. She seemed . . . magical. Thinking back on it now, it probably had something to do with the situation, and the possibility I might not live to see the sun set, but at that moment I was aware of none of that. I only knew she was the most fantastic thing ever to happen to me, and I wanted more than anything to reach over and take her in my arms—

She caught me looking at her, and I must have blushed, because she gave me a tired little grin. I looked away, embarrassed.

"Somebody'll come," she said, mistaking the flush on my face. "Somebody'll find us, if we wait. Or maybe he'll go away."

I didn't reply, mainly because I didn't have any idea what to say. My mind was still whirling with the realization of my feelings. I could not imagine a more inappropriate place to be thinking the strange things I found myself thinking, but that was something I couldn't control. I just swallowed and gave her a weak smile.

The hours dragged by. The bull named Midnight paced the pasture as if it were a cage. Every so often he would circle close to the tree and stare up at us. It was during one of these inspections that D.J. made an interesting statement.

"Maybe the Sniper'll come," she said, looking down at the bull. "Maybe he'll shoot him."

I blinked. "What?"

"He shot some pigs, right? Why not a bull?"

I suppose there was some logic to that. If, that is, the guy was in the area, and if he had heard us screaming, and if—once he arrived—he was so inclined to help us out. I doubted all three. It crossed my mind that if he were indeed here, he might shoot us instead. Not that that made a lot of sense either. I sure didn't mention it to D.J.

And then I remembered the slingshot.

"*I* could shoot him," I said, half to myself.

D.J. turned to look at me. "What?"

I already had the Bullseye out, and was digging in my pocket for a pellet. She watched me a moment. "It won't do any good, Jimmy," she said. "Look at him, he's big as a truck. It'd be like trying to kill an elephant with a ping-pong ball."

I kept searching my pocket. I heard her words, but didn't pay them a lot of attention. I knew what the Bullseye could do; she didn't. Besides, I didn't necessarily have to kill him. I just wanted to hurt him. I wanted to hurt him bad enough to run him off.

But my pocket was empty.

My heart sank. I had had at least two dozen pellets in my shirt pocket when I left home—where had they gone? Then I remembered. The mad dash to the tree and the upside-down pull I had given D.J. had done more than just sprain a few muscles. My ammunition was lost somewhere in the grass of the pasture.

Then I found one. It was tucked down into one of the corners of my pocket. Holding my breath, I dug into the other corner and found another. I almost laughed aloud. Inspired, I kept looking . . .

But that was it. Two pellets. I held them in the palm of my hand, looking at them and thinking of what she'd said a moment ago. And I realized, yet again, that she was right. What good were two tiny pieces of metal against a thousand-pound monster?

Then an idea jumped into my mind.

"I could shoot his eyes out," I said.

Deborah Jo blinked. She looked at the pellets in my hand, then up at me, then at the bull, then back at the pellets again. "Could you do that?" she asked.

"Sure I can." And I could, too. "I can hit a bottle cap at forty yards with this thing." I was getting excited now. After all, he couldn't very well catch us if he couldn't see us.

"No, I don't mean that. I mean can you *make* yourself do it. You're talking about putting out his *eyes*?"

"He'll do a lot worse to us if we don't," I said, trying to sound older than my years. Solemnly I turned my attention to Midnight. He was maybe thirty feet away, motionless in a patch of clover, his eyes fixed on our tree.

There would never be a better time.

I slipped one of the pellets back into my pocket and put the other into the leather pouch of the slingshot. With my gaze locked on the bull, I shifted my weight on the tree limb, gripped the oak handle in my left fist, extended my left arm as far as it would go, and with my right hand pulled the sling back beside my right ear. I sighted along it, felt the comforting hardness of the pellet through the thin leather.

I counted to three, held my breath—

And started to shake.

In those days the movie *Deliverance* had not yet been filmed, and I had never heard the term "buck fever." All I knew was that I couldn't get my arm to hold still. Now that I was aiming at a living thing, and not a stick or a rock or a tin can, I had a case of the shakes.

I ground my teeth together and concentrated, aiming at Midnight's huge left eye. But even as I fired, even at the very moment of release, I knew I'd missed. An instant later I heard a dull whine like the ricochet of a bullet, and saw the ragged slice the pellet had taken out of the bull's left horn.

He leaped backward, shook his head, and charged. I barely had time to grab hold before he hit the trunk with his head. The tree actually shook; I felt it move.

Davey screamed, and all three of us held on for dear life. D.J. almost slipped from the branch. Midnight the Bull was hopping mad. He shook his head once more, ran around in more circles, and launched himself at the tree again, hard. The world trembled. I found myself wondering if he could actually uproot a full-grown pecan tree.

Finally he backed off, and gave us a look of pure hatred. I swallowed and watched him, waiting for my stomach to calm down. As if from a great distance, I heard D.J. murmur, "Maybe that wasn't such a great idea." I was in complete agreement. The slingshot went back into my pocket.

Time marched on. And so did the bull, prancing tirelessly back and forth, stopping now and then to graze but mainly just watching the three stranded humans sitting in his pecan tree. The sun climbed toward its midpoint, reached it, started down again. None of us had a watch, but it didn't take a timepiece to tell us we had been sitting here for hours.

It was getting really hot now—nothing unusual for a June afternoon in the Deep South. At least we're in the shade, I thought. At any other time that might have even seemed funny.

By two o'clock or thereabouts, the temperature was probably in the mid-nineties. We were hungry and tired and sweating buckets. At least the perspiration was keeping us from having to use the bathroom. I wasn't sure exactly how we would've solved that problem in mixed company.

Several times during the afternoon I almost nodded off, other times I felt dizzy. Once I thought I saw a flash high up on the hill, in the shadows near the south fence. It had looked like the glint of the sun off a piece of metal, or glass. I squinted, staring until my eyes watered. Was somebody up there, under the trees? Maybe with a gun? Had D.J. been right?

I saw nothing. After awhile I realized my eyes had been playing tricks. No one was there, from either side of the Law, and no one was coming.

By midafternoon the situation was desperate. D.J. was glassy-eyed and pale, her little brother limp in my arms. My head was throbbing. Something would have to be done, and soon. Midnight just stood and watched us, lowering his head every so often to crop a mouthful of grass. As was common this time of year, a storm was brewing in the west; roiling gray thunderheads climbed the sky, and a sudden warm wind pushed my hair back off my forehead. Great, I thought. A cloudburst is all we need, on top of everything else. At least we wouldn't drown.

What would probably happen, I decided glumly, is that lightning would strike our tree, and roast us like weenies.

I ran a hand over my chest. My shirt was soaked through. I glanced down at Davey, dozing fitfully in my lap. D.J. was staring out into space.

What we really needed, I thought, was for lightning to

strike the bull. Or maybe *he* would be the one to drown. Maybe the ditch over there would fill up with rain and he would be so intent on watching us he'd just wander over and fall in—

I opened my eyes wide, staring at the ditch.

At that moment I knew what we had to do. I pondered it for a long time, going over every detail, working it all out in my head before I told D.J. When I finally turned to her I was confident it would work.

"Sit up," I said. "Flex your legs, so you can run." I started massaging my calves and thighs.

She looked at me with eyes that were red and tired. "What do you mean, 'Run'?"

Midnight was still standing there, watching us.

"In just a minute," I said, "I'm gonna jump down from here and run for the east edge of the field. Doofus out there will follow me. When he does, you climb down too, and help Davey down, and run the other way."

"What?!"

"I'll time it so he's as far away as I think he'll get, and then I'll go. I should be able to make it at least a third of the way up the hill before he really gets up to speed."

"What are you *saying*, Jimmy? He'll catch you, you know that. He'll kill you."

"I don't think so." I chewed my lower lip a moment, thinking. "That ditch over there looks really big—five or six feet deep in places, and just as wide. If I can make it there, I can jump it, easy. He probably can't, or won't."

She was frowning at me. "How do you know?"

"Well . . . I don't, really. But I believe that's what'll happen. I don't think he'll try to jump it."

"And you'd risk your *life* on that?"

I sighed. "I think we're risking our lives sitting here, doing nothing. I think sooner or later we're going to doze off and fall, and when that happens we'll be dead."

She didn't say anything for a while.

"If I can make it to that ditch," I said again, "and make it across, I'll be safe. By the time he tries to go around it to get me, I can run all the way to the top of the hill, and the fence. And the beauty of it is, no matter what he decides to do, I can keep his attention—"

"And Davey and I can get away."

"That's right. Back up the hill to the west, the way we came." I paused, and made a real effort to sound better than I actually felt. It wasn't hard to do, since I felt as scared as I'd ever been in my life.

"Remember, I'll be okay as long as I'm on the other side of the ditch. I can stand there and make faces at him if I have to, until I see you're both safe. When you are, I'll keep going up the hill on the other side, and all three of us live to go exploring another day."

She took a while to process all this, her brows knitted in thought. And I knew her well enough to know what she was thinking. She could see that it should work—and that it was the only thing that had a chance—but she could also see that it might not. And if it didn't there wouldn't be enough of Jimmy Hutchinson left to even bother looking for the pieces.

"I dunno, Jimmy," she murmured. She was shaking her head.

"It's our only hope, Deej."

The wind picked up a little. The leaves swished and rattled all around us. It was an odd feeling, being in a tree with a storm coming.

"You know it'll work, don't you," I said, watching the fluttering leaves. "Think about it."

She was quiet a moment. "Yes," she said with a sigh. "I see it might work."

Lightning split the sky to the west. Thunder boomed. Out in the pasture, the bull turned his head, looking into the wind.

"Except for one thing," she said.

"What's that?"

"I'm going to do it. Not you."

Calmly she reached down and started lacing up her sneakers.

"Now wait a minute, D.J.—"

"Shut up, Jimmy. You know it has to be me. No offense, but you can't run as fast as I can. My chances of making it are twice as good as yours. Besides, you're stronger than I am—you need to be the one carrying Davey, not me."

She was faster than I was, that was true. But she was also just as strong. "No," I said.

She finished her other shoe, and leaned closer. "We'll make it, Jimmy. It's a good plan. I'm proud of you."

She grinned then, and at that moment I fell the rest of the way in love. It wasn't just the smile, of course. I'd seen her smile a thousand times. It was partly the tension of the moment, and the knowledge that something of real significance was about to happen down there on the ground in a few minutes, something that none of us—if we survived—would ever forget. But whatever triggered the feeling wasn't important, then or now. The fact is, it was there, and I felt my heart swell until I thought it would burst.

We stared at each other a long time, our clothes riffling in the wind. Finally she leaned even closer and kissed my cheek. I felt something like an electric current go through me. Her hair, even after half a day of sweating and sitting in the limbs of a pecan tree, smelled, to me, like daffodils. I was adrift on the sea of love, as they say, and for the moment the huge ugly bull in the pasture below us was gone from my mind.

Then she bent down to kiss her little brother, who was still sitting in my lap, and I saw the glimmer of a tear in her eye.

"I love you, Peanut," she said to him, and my mind popped back into focus. I was in love, yes, hopelessly and completely, but there were other matters to consider. When she raised up from kissing Davey, I held him out to her. "Give him a hug," I said.

She smiled at that, and held her arms out to take him. As soon as she had him in her grasp, I checked Midnight's position. He was right where I wanted him. He was even looking, for the moment, in the other direction.

Just as she closed her eyes and hugged her brother to her chest, I slipped quietly off the limb and onto the ground below. I landed running, heading for the fence at the top of the ridge on the east side of the pasture, and behind me I heard Midnight whoof in surprise and start out after me.

"Jimmyyyyyy!" D.J. screamed.

"Go!" I shouted over my shoulder. "Go go go go!"

I ran like I had never run before. I tried not to think about things like whether the ditch was a little wider than I'd guessed, or whether it was too far away. I heard the hooves now, pounding the ground behind me. "Come on, catch me," I shouted as I ran. And he was coming on, no doubt about that. I could feel his approach, could feel the pasture itself shaking under my feet, and his hot, stinking breath on the back of my neck. And the fact that the pasture was not actually shaking, or that he was nowhere near close enough to breathe on the back of my neck, didn't seem to matter. He was there, right behind me, and I knew if I didn't run as hard as I could—or if, God forbid, I tripped and fell—I was as dead as one of Leland Stallworth's fenceposts.

The ditch was rushing toward me now. I took a deep lungful of air, picked out the narrowest part I could—and jumped.

As things turned out, it was much deeper than I'd figured, and wider too, and for an instant I thought I wouldn't make it after all—but before I could assess this new information I was already in the air and flying. I landed hard on the other side, and rolled in the grass. A second later I scrambled to my feet, panting hard, and looked back across the ditch. The bull had almost fallen in. He had skidded to a stop inches from the lip of the wash, backpedaled a yard or so, and stood there pawing and blowing, his eyes rolling like marbles. And most important of all, past him and down the hill, I saw D.J. and her brother sprinting up the far side of the pasture. They were about a fourth of the way to the fence.

"How about *that*?" I shouted, giddy with joy. "Try to get me now, why dontcha!" I jumped up and down and turned somersaults in the grass, daring him the way you might dare a vicious dog chained just out of reach. If I could keep his attention for a minute more, they'd be far enough up the slope to be safe. And there was, as I'd hoped, no way Midnight could run all the way around the ditch and get to me before I could reach the fence on my side of the pasture. All I had to do now was keep him from seeing the others.

Thunder crashed again in the distance. Lightning forked the sky. It hit a tree somewhere west of us, in the woods near the road, and before I knew what was happening the bull had turned to look in that direction.

It was the worst thing that could have happened. My heart leaped into my throat.

"Hey!" I yelled. "Look back over here. Hey—"

But it was too late. He had seen them.

For an instant time seemed to stand still. D.J. and Davey had stopped, and were looking back across the field at me and the bull, and Midnight was staring back at them. An expression of pure horror was printed on D.J.'s face. They hadn't made it nearly far enough yet up the hill. If the bull charged them now he would get them for sure, and all three of us—four, counting Midnight— knew it.

The bull gave me one last, triumphant glance, then

wheeled around and charged.

What happened at that point was automatic; I honestly can't remember even thinking about what I was doing. The bull turned away from me, his tail standing straight up like a flag, and with a speed I would never have known I had, I snatched the old Bullseye slingshot from my back pocket with my left hand, plucked my last pellet from my shirt pocket with my right, and loaded it even as I brought the slingshot up to position. In the blink of an eye my left arm was straight and stiff and rock-steady, the pouch tucked in next to my right ear. A cold calmness settled over me.

The bull's huge rump was still less than twenty feet away when I fired. My target was a point about an inch below the base of his tail, and I hit it dead center. I heard a SPLAT like the sound a baseball bat might make hitting wet mud. A split-second after impact both the bull's hind legs jerked, and he seemed to forget how to work his front legs. He sprawled headfirst in the dirt. A hundred yards away, D.J. and Davey stood staring, openmouthed.

"Run!" I shouted, above the thunder. "Run for the fence!"

That seemed to snap them out of their trance, and they tore off up the hill. I looked back at Midnight, making ready to run myself if necessary—but there was no need. The bull was on his feet again, but had lost all interest in his human visitors. He was bucking and kicking and starfishing like a bronc in a rodeo. And behaving, I suppose, like a bull with a pellet up his butt.

As I watched he spun around a few times, fell down again, and then rocketed away toward the lower part of the pasture, where the field wound around and out of sight in the direction of the Stallworths' barn. With a cautious eye on his retreat, I skirted the ditch and made my way through the trees high along the south edge of the pasture, a roundabout route toward D.J. and her brother. Now and then I risked a glance in their direction, silently urging them on. Finally I saw, with vast relief, that they'd made the top of the ridge. They were crawling through the fence at about the same place where we had entered this unlikely battleground earlier in the day.

Seeing them safe gave me new life. I broke into a trot, looking up at the sky as I ran. The storm had drifted north, missing us by half a mile or more. Thunder grumbled in the distance. If it rained at all, it wouldn't be much.

Three minutes later I stepped through the wire and joined D.J. and Davey on the safe side of the fence. Davey grinned at me as I approached. He was sitting, shirtless and crosslegged, on a carpet of pinestraw.

Then I saw the scratches on his forehead and cheek and a gash on the back of his left hand. Apparently he hadn't let the barbed wire slow him down much during his exit from the pasture. Deborah Jo had torn his shirt into strips and was wrapping his hand. She looked grim. I knelt on the other side of him and studied his face. He appeared to be okay, and even a little happy about all the attention.

"What do you think?" I asked her.

She smoothed out his bandage and wiped her bloody hands on her jeans. "He's okay. He might hurt for a while, but he had a tetanus shot just a few weeks ago. He'll be all right."

"Good," I said, getting to my feet. I stole a glance at her as she rose also. I was relieved Davey was okay, but now that he was, my mind turned to other things. I stood there watching her profile while she relaced her shoes and folded what was left of his shirt and stuffed it into her pocket. I decided I could happily watch her all day, doing just about anything at all.

I was still awash in strange feelings, and the girl standing before me now seemed a different person from the one I'd played cowboys with this morning, only a couple of miles away. Or maybe I was different, or maybe both of us were. I didn't know or care. All I knew for sure was that I loved her.

After a moment she finished up and glanced out at the field, and at the big pecan tree at its center, made small now with distance. And then she looked at me—the first time she'd looked at me since we had made it out. And she smiled.

"Bullseye," she said.

I shrugged. "A lucky shot."

"Lucky for me and Davey." Her voice was low, and dead serious.

Our eyes held for a moment. I felt my face reddening, heard my heart thumping away in my chest.

"Hey, you guys," Davey called. He was still sitting on the ground. "We goin' on our 'venture, or what?"

Both of us grinned. D.J. knelt again and took his good hand in both of hers.

"We've already been, Peanut. We need to get you home now, let Mama tend to your battle scars."

He squinted at her. "My what?"

She kissed him on the forehead, then looked up at me. "Can you carry him, Jimmy?"

I nodded dumbly. In my newly-acquired state of mind, the act of staring into her eyes a moment ago had been like a carnival ride. It was taking me a while to return to earth. Still dazed, I squatted with my back to Davey so he could climb onto my shoulders. When he was safely aboard I rose to my feet.

D.J., I noticed, was looking out over the fence again. A misty rain had begun to fall.

"Jimmy?" she said.

"What."

"You don't think you . . . hurt him *bad*, do you?"

I followed her gaze, searching the distant north end of the pasture. No sign of the bull.

"I hope I killed him," I said, and meant it. I shifted Davey's weight to settle him more firmly on my shoulders. His good hand was clamped over my forehead, hanging on. "You okay up there, cowboy?"

"Hokay, horsey," he said.

D.J. was still staring at the empty pasture. I went over to stand beside her. It was eerily quiet for a while, then Davey surprised us both.

"What's his name?" he asked, out of nowhere.

D.J. blinked. "Whose name?"

"The big cow. What's his name?"

She looked at me, amused. I just shrugged. Then I remembered the way the huge animal had sat down in the grass, like a dog, and my thoughts about taking a picture of him.

"Sitting Bull," I answered.

Davey liked that. "Sitting Bull. Really?"

I saw the instant twinkle in his sister's eye, and knew what she was going to say before she said it.

"I don't think he'll be doing much of that," she told him. "At least not for a while." She cut her eyes at me and grinned, and for a brief moment she was my old playmate again. "Ain't that right, Roy?" she said, in her best Gabby Hayes voice.

Then she turned and walked away, still smiling.

Standing there in the mist with her brother on my shoulders, watching her stride down the hill, I was vaguely aware that a part of my childhood had ended here today, and felt a twinge of sadness. Somehow I doubted that D.J. and I would be playing stick-horses any more in her yard.

Then I thought again of her golden hair, and the smooth way she moved, and the twinkle in her eyes, and I didn't much mind.

"Let's go, cowboy," I said to my rider, and followed her down the grassy slope to the road.

***

As I said, I was twelve years old when that happened. I'm past fifty now, and married, with kids and grandkids of my own.

I suppose it would have been logical—or at least appropriate—for me to have married Deborah Jo Hardin, but I didn't. D.J. and her family moved to Michigan four months after our little adventure in Leland Stallworth's back pasture, and I never saw her again. Once, a few years ago, I did notice something odd about a man standing in a crowd in the Memphis airport. I knew his face looked familiar, and as he reached out to pluck his suitcase from the baggage carousel I saw the jagged scar on the back of his left hand. Before I could call to him, the crowd closed up again, and he was gone. I've often wondered, since, if it had really been Davey. I also wonder if he would've remembered me if it was.

There's one more thing I need to mention about our adventure that day. We made a pact, D.J. and I, never to say a word about what had happened, to anyone. No good could ever come of it, we figured, especially since we'd disobeyed just about everybody that morning, and though little Davey wouldn't understand such a vow of secrecy, D.J. somehow kept him from talking about it, and within a couple of days he seemed to have forgotten the whole thing. As to physical evidence, his cuts weren't that unusual, since there were barbed-wire fences everywhere back then, and a few white lies solved that problem.

But a week or so later, just when we thought the incident was dead and buried, I heard my father talking with Joe Pender out in our driveway. Mr. Pender said one of Leland Stallworth's bulls, a giant named Midnight, had been shot. He wasn't hurt bad—the bullet had gone straight through the fleshy part of his neck and out the other side. About a week ago.

They had strolled away then, and I was left sitting there on the porch steps, staring wide-eyed at nothing at all.

Shot?

A week ago?

It was then that I remembered the way Midnight had

acted, just after I popped him with my Bullseye. I had hit him, no doubt about that. I had hit him hard, and right where I was aiming. But it wasn't in the neck, fleshy or otherwise. I found myself thinking about the blasts of thunder while all that was happening. Could they have drowned out a rifle shot? And the bright glint I thought I'd seen earlier, from the trees. Like the sun reflecting off metal. A gunbarrel? A scope?

I still don't know for sure. I went back the next day to that pasture, walked along outside the south fence underneath the hardwoods, looked for tracks, cigarette butts, shell casings, anything. I found nothing, and said nothing. To anybody.

And the police never caught the Sniper. The lumberyard did in fact go union, for better or worse, and there were no more reports of shootings. Which made sense, I guess. His job was done.

The questions remained. Had someone been hidden in the trees that day, when we faced down the bull? Someone with a gun? If so, why did he not do something earlier? Was he waiting for the cover of the storm? And another thing: Was Leland Stallworth against the union? Would his bull have been shot anyway, that day, or that night? Was that why the gunman was there? I have no idea.

But here's what I think. I think the man they called the Sniper was walking or driving along that dirt road that afternoon, beside the fence. I think he stopped for some reason, maybe to have a smoke or relieve himself or spy on the surroundings from the top of the hill, and either saw us in the tree or heard our screams for help. I think he settled in to see what was going to happen, and when it got as bad as it would get—when Midnight turned to charge a defenseless girl and her little brother while another kid stood there aiming a slingshot—he put a bullet through the bull's neck. The storm was an added bonus; no one heard the shot. And the bull, hurting at both ends, left the scene in a hurry.

I think a man no one ever saw, a man feared by everyone in two counties, saved our lives that summer day.

*****

By the way, I still live in Fulton County. I left for a while, after my stint in the Army, but it didn't last long. Home's where the heart is, they say, and I guess mine's in the hills of north Mississippi. My wife and I run a little crafts and frame shop out on Highway 78. It's not much, but it pays the bills, and we sleep good at night. About twice a month my grandsons and I get our fishing gear and hike down the road to Boggs Creek. The beaver dam isn't there any more, but there's a good spot for bass in a pond near the creek.

The way to the pond goes right past the Stallworth place, and the rolling pasture where old Midnight reigned supreme throughout my teenage years. We give it a wide berth. The bull's long dead now, of course, and even though I'm old enough and sane enough to know there's nothing dangerous in that pasture any more, I also know it can't get me if I don't go there.

And down in the bottom of my tackle box, underneath the spinners and stringers and plastic worms, is an old Bullseye slingshot with an oak frame and a leather pouch and a thick rubber sling. Beside it is a matchbox full of Daisy .177-caliber pellets.

Paranoid, you say? Maybe so. But who knows what unseen dangers might be lurking between us and our destination?

After all, I was once a Boy Scout.

A PLACE IN HISTORY

"Dr. Benedict?" Lou Rosewood stepped into the laboratory, closed the door behind him, and locked it. "May I have a moment?"

The woman in the white lab coat looked up from her worktable. She seemed to know what was coming. Rosewood was dressed in a baggy gray business suit, a ridiculously wide necktie, and a snap-brim fedora. In one hand was a brown valise with straps and buckles. He looked as if he should be trying to talk Ingrid Bergman into boarding an aircraft in the fog.

"That matter we discussed earlier?" he said. "It's time to proceed."

"Mr. Rosewood, I—"

"It's time, Patricia. Have you prepared the machine?"

Benedict sighed. "The machine is ready," she said.

Lou Rosewood stood there a moment in his 1930's suit, studying his lead scientist. In his opinion, Dr. Patricia Benedict was the most brilliant physicist in the free world. She was also a tireless and loyal employee of Rosewood Technologies—and the only one Lou Rosewood had trusted with knowledge of his secret plan.

"I don't suppose I can talk you out of this," Benedict said. Her concern was written in every line of her face.

This time it was Rosewood who sighed. "I don't expect you to understand, Patricia. This is just something I have to do."

"But why? You're already a multimillionaire—"

"It's not the money. It's the recognition I want."

"You already have that."

Rosewood shook his head. "You're wrong. A CEO, successful or not, is seldom remembered by the public. It's the celebrities—Tom Hanks, Stephen King, Tiger Woods—they're the ones who'll live forever."

"Immortality," she said. "You think these novels will give you that?"

"They're not just any novels. I'm talking about three of the most popular literary works in the history of the world." Rosewood could actually feel goosebumps on his arms at the very thought. "I've studied them, Patricia, I've read them a hundred times each. I can recreate them, all three of them, almost word-for-word."

"You can steal them, you mean."

"Not if they haven't been written yet."

Benedict's face darkened. "That's the part that bothers me."

"I know." Rosewood stepped closer, laid a hand on her shoulder. "But I have to silence them, you know that. There's no other way."

Benedict swallowed and nodded. They'd been through all this before. The time machine was indeed ready; Benedict herself had taken four test trips, with no apparent ill effects. If Rosewood could go back to a point in time before the great works he had chosen were published, eliminate the three authors, and then write their books under his own name . . .

"Do you have everything you need?" she asked. She looked too tired to argue further.

"Right here." Rosewood patted the heavy valise. "Four cases of gold coins."

"And the location?"

"A city park half a mile from downtown Atlanta. The date and time"—he took a slip of paper from his pocket—"will be a weekday during banking hours. Within an hour of landing there, I'll have converted most of the gold to cash. All I'll need then are a pen and paper and a place to write. I already know what publishers they used."

"What year did you decide on?"

He frowned. "That was difficult. Edgar Rollins's book came out in 1937, Michael Zellweiger's in '39, Margaret Mitchell's in '36. At first '35 sounded like a logical choice, but I got to thinking: what if they kept journals, notebooks, versions of early manuscripts? Mitchell, for example, worked on her novel for ten years."

"So you're going earlier?"

"1932," Rosewood said, stepping back to model his outfit. "It's not far enough back to be foolproof, but it should do. They were all first novels, so I doubt the writers told a lot of people about what they were writing. And all three lived in Atlanta. I should be able to eliminate them right away, and then get to work. Even knowing the stories beforehand, I'll need time to get the books written, typed, submitted, and so forth. No computers or word processors back then, you know."

Dr. Benedict seemed to ponder that. "Edgar Rollins would barely be twenty-five years old then," she said sadly. "Mitchell would be what, thirty-two? And Zellweiger—"

"Twenty-seven."

She nodded. "The prime of their lives."

"Don't dwell on that, Patricia. We're talking about the past, remember? They're already dead. And don't give me that argument about the children and grandchildren they are yet to have. The world will do just fine without three fiction writers and their descendants."

"It's still murder, Mr. Rosewood."

"For God's sake, Patricia, I won't be doing it my*self*. These things can be arranged."

Before Benedict could reply, Rosewood marched over to the machine. "I've left a note in my office," he said, adjusting his cuffs. "As far as anyone knows, I have embarked on a test that somehow went awry. You'll not be blamed—I've taken care of that in my note. I'm leaving you and my wife very well off, by the way." He glanced around. "What do I do? Just get in?"

Benedict pointed. "Get in, stand there, and don't touch the sides of the compartment. And I'll need to dial in your place, date, and time."

Rosewood handed her the slip of paper. While he gingerly stepped inside, she walked across the room to the console and programmed in the information. Minutes later she appeared again, licking the flap of a business envelope.

"Take this," she said. She sealed the envelope and handed it to him. "Put it someplace where you can't lose it."

"What is it?" He tucked it into an inside pocket of his suit coat.

"A remote keypad, and instructions on how to beam yourself back here if you need to."

"I won't need to."

"Keep it anyway," she said. "Just in case."

The two said their goodbyes. Rosewood stood motionless in the glass-enclosed machine as Benedict went back to the computer to press the necessary buttons. A moment later, with a brilliant, sizzling flash of light, Lou Rosewood disappeared.

The machine sat humming and empty in the middle of the laboratory. A metallic smell lingered in the air.

"Bon voyage," Dr. Benedict said, her face solemn.

***

Lou Rosewood was mildly surprised when he arrived not in a grassy park but on some kind of metal platform high in the air. Far below him was a large ship, surrounded by a blue-green inlet dotted with similar vessels.

"Well, damn," he said. They had had a few screwups like this during the early tests; Benedict had come back once with snapshots of a tropical rainforest instead of the Old West.

Grumbling, Rosewood set his valise down on the metal catwalk and took the envelope from his coat pocket. Inside it he found, sure enough, a credit-card-sized keypad and display, along with a handwritten message.

The note said:

DEAR MR. ROSEWOOD,
I REGRET THIS, BUT I HAD NO CHOICE.
DON'T BOTHER TRYING THE KEYPAD—
IT DOESN'T WORK.
THE DISPLAY, HOWEVER, DOES.

With trembling fingers Rosewood took out the card, looked at the display. It said, in tiny green letters:

LOCATION: SPOTTING TOWER, U.S.S. ARIZONA
LAT. 21-21 N, LONG. 157-58 W, OAHU, HAWAII
TIME/DATE: 07:53 A.M., 12/07/41

While he watched, the time changed to 07:54.

Rosewood stared at it in disbelief—and then understood.

The note was signed:

PATRICIA ZELLWEIGER BENEDICT.

As he numbly read the signature a second time, he heard sounds overhead. Distant at first, then growing louder.

Buzzing sounds . . .

THE PONY CREEK GANG

Ed Parrott was cleaning his gun by the campfire, a hundred yards south of the herd, when the stranger stepped from the shadows.

"I understand you need a cook," the man said.

Parrott looked up in surprise. "Where'd *you* come from?"

"Texas." The young stranger moved closer to the fire and held his palms out to warm them.

Ed Parrott studied him a moment. "Good way to get shot, sneaking up on a man at night," he said.

The stranger eyed the disassembled gun. "Looks pretty safe to me."

Parrott opened his mouth to reply, then seemed to think better of it. The stranger was staring off to the east, where another small campfire was burning. Parrott turned to follow his gaze. Some fifty yards away, a lone figure rose from that fire and then sat again, his hands held up to his face. An instant later, the sad whine of a harmonica drifted over on the breeze.

Ed Parrott frowned. "You really looking for work," he said, nodding toward the other campfire, "or did you come to get a look at the famous Ollie Dabbs?"

"I hear you're both famous," the stranger said. He raised a hand to rub the back of his neck, then turned again to stare at the man in the distance. "Why do you sleep so far from the others?" Nearer the herd, half a dozen cowhands lounged around yet a third fire, their voices muted by distance.

"Because we're old men, Ollie and me," Parrott said. "We do pretty much what we please."

"And, you own the outfit," the stranger added.

"Yes. We do." As he worked, Parrott measured the younger man from the corner of his eye. "There's something you should know, my friend—"

"Baker."

"There's something you should know, Baker. The old cook left mad. I'm not an easy man to work for."

"So I've heard." The man named Baker lowered his head and moved it gingerly from side to side, wincing a little. "Must be going to rain soon," he said, as if to himself. Somewhere far away, a coyote howled.

Parrott's eyes narrowed. "What exactly *have* you heard?"

Baker stretched, then stepped back from the fire and sat down on a pine log, facing east. "I've heard you like to be waited on," he said. "You and Dabbs both. They say the cook has to bring you your coffee and meals sometimes, even though you're both perfectly able to go through the chow line like the others."

Parrott felt a twinge of amusement. "Is that so." He took a second to examine the oily rag he was using on his pistol. "What else?"

Baker was still watching Ollie Dabbs's camp. The harmonica music had stopped, and Dabbs was moving around over there, doing something. Baker seemed fascinated by the man. Without looking away, Baker took a tobacco pouch and paper from a vest pocket and began rolling a smoke.

"I've heard you and Dabbs used to ride with Ben Dano and Cactus Jack Curry, down on Pony Creek. I've heard Dabbs knew Jefferson Davis personally, and fought against Cochise, and killed the big grizzly they called Satan's Angel." Baker paused to pour a line of tobacco into the creased slip of paper. "After the gang broke up, years later, I heard he killed Cactus Jack, for the reward money."

Ed Parrott snorted. "Well," he said. "I guess part of that's right, and part of it ain't."

Baker turned to face him, waiting.

"We had a place together on the Pony all right, and Ollie did sure enough kill Satan's Angel, and served with Jeff Davis in Mexico. But he never fought no Indians, far as I know. And he didn't kill Cactus Jack." Parrott leaned forward and spat into the fire. "I did."

Baker blinked. "You killed Jack Curry?"

"Sure did. Him, and that son of his."

"You killed the little boy too?"

Parrott looked up again. "That bother you, does it?"

A silence passed as Baker stuck his newly-rolled cigarette in his mouth, replaced his pouch, and dug a match from the same pocket. "I hear they were shot in the back," Baker said. "While they were sleeping."

"Who told you that?"

"Friend of mine saw the bodies, when they were brought in to San Antone."

"Well, that's a lie," Parrott said. "I only brought Jack's body in. There was no reward on the kid."

"But you did shoot 'em in the back?" Baker struck the match on the seat of his pants, then cupped his hands against the wind to light up.

"Back or front," Parrott said, "the pay's the same."

Baker drew slowly on his cigarette, staring into the

campfire. Parrott was enjoying himself.

"So Ollie Dabbs ain't quite as famous as everybody thinks," Parrott said. "I was the brains of the Pony Creek outfit, just like I'm the brains of this one. And the guts too."

He snapped the cylinder back into his revolver and put away his cleaning gear. As he reloaded the pistol he said, "In a few minutes I'm going over there to Ollie's camp and finish a game of checkers. I'll be back here in an hour or so. You still want the job, I expect you to bring me a cup of coffee before I go to bed tonight. Then, at sunup, take Ollie some breakfast. If all that don't meet with your approval, then get out, and don't spook the cows when you leave."

He turned to look at Baker then, and their gazes held for a long moment.

"Anything else you want to say?" Parrott asked. The gun was loaded now; it twirled once, winking in the firelight, and dropped into its holster. The light wind smelled of woodsmoke and cattle.

To the south, away from the herd, the plains lay flat and empty in the moonlight. For a full minute Baker stared into the distance, his lips pursed around his glowing cigarette. Finally he turned again, and looked Parrott in the eye.

"You take cream or sugar?" Baker said.

***

The next morning was overcast, with a brisk wind rippling the grass. When Baker strolled over to Ed Parrott's campsite, several of the men were already there, standing in a group with their hands stuffed into their pockets. Ollie Dabbs was there too. He walked over to the newcomer and looked him up and down.

"You must be Baker," he said. "I'm Oliver Dabbs."

They shook hands.

"Good name for a cook," Dabbs said, with a smile.

Baker shrugged.

"Ed Parrott told me about you, last night." Dabbs squinted. "Ain't I seen you before? You were in Fort Union, I believe. Santa Fe, too."

"I been following you for a while," Baker admitted.

"Why would you do that?"

"Looking for work."

Dabbs seemed to think that over, then said, "Ed told me you had a long conversation, you and him. That surprised me. Ed tends to run the younger folks off pretty quick."

"I'm glad we talked," Baker said. "He set me straight on a few things."

"I see. And what all did you two talk about?"

"Mutual friends."

Ollie Dabbs rubbed a hand through his beard. "A short list, I imagine. Ed didn't have many."

Baker made no reply. Off to the west, thunder rumbled.

After a pause Dabbs said, "I didn't get my breakfast brought to me this morning, by the way."

"That's because I'm moving on." Baker jerked a thumb toward the chuckwagon, where his horse stood tied and saddled. "I changed my mind about the job."

"You must've changed it last night," Dabbs said.

"What?"

"Looks like Ed didn't get his bedtime coffee brought to him either. At least I don't see a cup around here anywhere."

For a moment both men stared at the body that lay face-up in the blankets beside the burned-out campfire. Its face was drawn into a tight grimace, its eyes bulging. Both forearms were crossed over its midsection, as if the body, even in death, were hugging itself against the early morning chill. The other men were still standing nearby, shoulders hunched and coat collars pulled high. The damp wind had picked up a bit.

"What was it that killed him, you think?" Dabbs asked.

Baker scratched his chin. "Snakebite, I expect. Probably had a rattler in his bedroll. I've heard poison moves fast if the bite's in the head or chest."

Or if you drink it in your coffee, Baker said to himself. The cup he had brought to Ed Parrott last night wasn't at the campsite because Baker had come and pried it from Parrott's cold fingers in the early morning hours. Right now the cup was hidden in Baker's saddlebag, beside the tiny bottle of strychnine he had carried there ever since he'd heard about Dabbs and his cattle drive.

Ollie Dabbs stayed quiet a while longer, adrift in his own thoughts. Finally he said, "Wherever Ed is right now, I imagine he's getting some tough questions from some of those old friends. One, in particular."

"Jack Curry?" Baker said.

Dabbs blinked, then turned and studied him. "That's right. Jack Curry. Not many know the truth, but Ed shot him in his sleep one night, long time ago. Jack's little boy, too." Dabbs paused, the pain obvious in his eyes. "Ed killed 'em both."

"Well, he killed Jack," Baker agreed.

"What?"

"The boy lived," Baker said. He raised a hand to rub the old scar below the back of his neck, then turned and trudged toward his horse as the first raindrops began to fall.

John M. Floyd

A THOUSAND WORDS

Catherine Munsen was less than thrilled about her job. In fact, until the day she met Frank Goodman, she thought it was downright boring.

Catherine was a part-time teller at the Marshlands Bank in Gulf Springs, Mississippi. Her actual position, though not recorded anywhere in her job description sheet, was a combination of teller and secretary and supply-sergeant. The only thing she was not allowed to do was process loans; that was the job of branch manger Doyle Beevers, who was in sole charge of that task because he didn't know how to do much of anything else.

Catherine's responsibilities were threefold: one was to the customer, by handling inquiries and complaints and—when required—routine teller transactions; the second was to Mr. Beevers, by ensuring the timely but politically-incorrect delivery of his morning coffee; and the third was to everyone else in the branch, by ordering and dispensing office supplies, which included everything from paper clips to calendars to printer ribbons.

In the daily course of her job at the bank, however,

Catherine occasionally got a chance to indulge in the one thing she did enjoy. It was done during coffee breaks and lunch hours, and the once-bare walls of the back offices and hallways were a testament to her talent: They were all covered with pictures. Sketches, line drawings, portraits, landscapes, everything imaginable—drawn in pencil and charcoal and ink and even watercolor.

Catherine Munsen, you see, was an artist.

And if her pictures themselves were pleasing to the eye, it was even more pleasing to watch her create them. She worked quietly and smoothly, seemingly without effort. It was not unusual to see her do a detailed sketch of an old car or a bicycle or a delivery truck (or anything that happened to park itself outside the window of the bank) in a matter of seconds, her hand flying over the paper while her eyes remained fixed on the subject. Sometimes she scarcely even looked down at the work until it was finished. The only problem, she often remarked, was that she couldn't draw something from memory. It had to be there and visible to her at the time in order for her to get it down correctly on paper. "If I see a guy jogging past and I decide I want to draw him," she once told one of the tellers, "I have to hope he falls down."

The truth was, Catherine Munsen took her art very seriously. It was both her hobby and her passion. The business of banking, she was fond of saying—especially the business of ordering notepads and rubber bands—was no great stimulant to either her heart-rate or her imagination.

At least that was what she thought until the day Frank Goodman came in. It was a clear, cold morning in February—one she would never forget—when Goodman walked across the street and through the lobby door and into her life.

But, alas, he did not come to claim her heart. He came to claim the deposits of the fine and loyal customers of the

John M. Floyd

Marshlands Bank.

"Everybody freeze!" Frankie Goodman shouted, holding his drawn pistol steady with both hands. He stood there covering the scene while his two accomplices spread out across the lobby. Other weapons were produced, empty canvas sacks were thrust into the faces of the tellers. Customers were ordered to the floor.

Shouted demands and warnings echoed across the large white-tiled room. Mr. Beevers burst out of his office, stern-faced and glaring at the intrusion, and when he took it upon himself to issue his own set of orders he was promptly shot dead by one of Goodman's associates.

Eventually, when the screaming died down a bit, Frank Goodman restated his demands: Fill the bags and fill them fast, make no other sudden moves, and speak to no one. Pressing the alarm buttons, Goodman said with a smile, was perfectly acceptable; they had been disconnected, as had the telephones and security cameras. "Just don't let pushing the buttons interfere with your filling the bags with money, ladies," he added. "Large bills, by the way."

They were almost done when one of the tellers, who was finished with her own bag-filling activities, happened to notice Catherine Munsen. On this particular day Catherine was manning the secretary's desk, and thus was sitting some distance away from the center of the festivities. She did, however, have a clear view of the leader's face, and was quickly and efficiently capturing Frank Goodman's likeness on a plain sheet of stationery.

She would probably have gotten away with it, too, if the curious teller hadn't shot her a glance that lasted a shade too long. As things turned out, Frankie Goodman noticed the teller, followed the direction of her gaze, and saw Catherine putting the finishing touches on an excellent portrait of Bank Robber in Action.

In one swift movement Goodman vaulted the wooden railing between the lobby and the admin area and leveled his gun at Catherine Munsen's extremely attractive nose. "Let's have it," he told her, cutting his eyes down at her paper and back again.

Without hesitation she picked up the sheet and handed it over.

"Commendable," he said, studying the portrait. Amusement flickered in his eyes. "It would've looked great on the ten o'clock news."

That was, of course, the understatement of the century. The rendition he held in his hand was as clear and as sharp as a black-and-white photograph. Frankie Goodman, an average-looking guy with unremarkable hair and facial features, was almost impossible to describe with any degree of accuracy. Words were simply not enough. A picture, on the other hand . . .

A picture like this would have baked his goose, and he knew it.

Smiling, he stuffed the drawing into his coat pocket and waved his gunbarrel. "Move away from the desk," he said as he backed toward the lobby and his two partners. When he had crossed the divider and made his way to the door he nodded a signal to his men, who were waiting impatiently with armloads of moneybags and weaponry. Relieved, they dashed out and into the street.

Just as he was about to follow, Goodman turned and stared Catherine Munsen straight in the eye. He reached down and patted his coat pocket.

"I admire a lady with initiative," he said to her, smiling. "Nice try."

And then he was gone.

For a moment no one moved. Finally one of the senior tellers ran for her cell phone while others rushed to the limp body of Doyle Beevers. He was indeed dead, they found—a fact later verified by what seemed like three dozen police officers.

In the long minutes before the cavalry arrived, however,

while most of the branch staff was standing around wringing their hands and trembling and sobbing into each other's padded shoulders, one of the younger employees happened to notice Catherine Munsen, who was sitting once again in her chair, staring thoughtfully at a sheet of stationery she had picked up off her desktop. There was a satisfied little half-smile on her face as she studied it.

"Catherine?" the girl asked. "What on earth are you thinking about?"

Catherine Munsen looked up at her and said, in a calm but triumphant voice:

"Carbon paper."

NOTHING BUT THE TRUTH

"Mr. McKay," the prosecutor said, "were you involved, in any way, with the May 16th robbery of four million dollars in bearer bonds from the offices of Mr. Broderick Devane?"

The courtroom went dead quiet.

The question was the first of three—each one selected in advance by the prosecution and approved by the defense. There was no judge or jury. Neither was needed: there were no decisions to be made. Arthur McKay's fate lay in his own hands.

McKay took his time answering the question. No one rushed him. Every person in the courtroom knew how serious this was.

For the first time in two years, a man was in the Box.

McKay opened his mouth to speak, and the room froze.

"No," he said.

For several seconds the crowd held its breath, waiting for the flash of light they had all heard about. But nothing happened. Almost as one, the audience exhaled.

Two more questions to go.

In the Box, Arthur McKay swallowed and kept his eyes

straight ahead. Had there been a jury, McKay might have won their sympathy: Though only in his forties, he looked ten years older, and had used a wooden walking-cane to make his way to the special chair. He seemed nervous but confident. The decision to go into the Box had been his and his alone. He was well aware of what three "correct" answers would mean.

Since its invention in 2012, only four defendants had challenged the Box. Three had come out again, as free men. One had not. No one ever knew whether Otto Sampson had been stupid or careless or suicidal. Not that it mattered; the result had been the same.

One wrong answer would do the trick. One untruthful answer.

"And did you," the prosecutor asked, "have any connection or conversation with 'Fancy Dan' Salucci, who was found dead at the scene of that robbery?"

Once again, every eye focused on the transparent cubicle in the back corner of the courtroom. It was, in fact, box-like in appearance, but its nickname came from its location. It occupied the space normally reserved for the jury box. Three of its clear plastic walls were pierced by what looked like giant laser guns, each aimed inward, at Arthur McKay's chair. The chair itself was made of the same plastic as the walls, and was the only non-electronic fixture. Microphones and sensors surrounded it like a minefield.

The sensors were the heart of the system. They were designed to pick up tiny irregularities in a defendant's voice patterns—irregularities which, when analyzed and fed to the monitoring devices in an adjoining room, would trigger the message that signaled a false answer. They would also trigger the guns.

It was the ultimate lie detector.

Arthur McKay drew a deep breath, held it a moment.

"No," he answered.

Another expectant pause. Once again, nothing happened.

Now there was a visible stirring in the crowd. The twenty attendees, handpicked from dozens of reporters and journalists (McKay had no family or friends), were feeling the tension. They were also beginning to feel something else: surprise. While some of them were sympathetic to Arthur McKay, almost all suspected he was guilty.

Carson J. Grubbs, the defendant's attorney, was on the edge of his seat. His carefully styled hair was shiny with perspiration, and his suit had dark patches under the arms. Beneath his moustache, a fat red tongue came out, licked his lips, and disappeared again.

The prosecutor, a meek-looking young man who seemed rather in awe of all this, cleared his throat and announced, "One last question, Mr. McKay. Did you, on the night of May 16th of this year, kill Broderick Devane?"

For a long moment the defendant sat quiet and composed, moving only his eyes. His gaze swept the scene outside his plastic cubicle, stopping for a second on his lawyer, then the prosecutor, then the crowd of spectators, and coming to rest on the rectangular two-way mirror in the south wall of the courtroom, where Clovis Hobson sat hidden from view, watching the proceedings. It was said that Hobson, the man who had designed the Box five years ago, was always present at these Q & A sessions, manning the controls.

McKay's eyes returned to the prosecutor. A hush fell over the crowd.

Everyone was thinking the same thing: one more answer. Strike three. After that, Arthur McKay would either be free of all charges or he would be dead, vaporized into an invisible cloud that left no trace at all. For that was how the system—the Box— worked. The guilty were given no mercy, and no costly jail sentences either. The innocent went free.

McKay raised his chin.

"No," he said. "I did not."

The words seemed very loud in the silent courtroom. Time itself seemed to freeze; no one moved a muscle. Then the room came to life. Some surprised themselves by cheering, some groaned in disgust and disbelief, some closed their eyes and murmured prayers.

Amid the clamor, however, two of the attendees smiled. One was Arthur McKay. The other was his attorney, Carson Grubbs. Their smiles widened into delighted grins that lit their faces. As the crowd dispersed—most of them hurrying to find a space on the courthouse steps for the promised press conference—McKay rose from the defendant's chair, stepped gingerly over the hedgerow of mikes and sensors, and opened the thick plastic door of the Box. Grubbs met him, and they hugged like brothers. Still embracing, they stumbled up the aisle toward the door.

Their footsteps sounded hollow in the vast room. Everyone else was already outside. Even the prosecutor had scurried away.

Halfway up the aisle McKay stopped. He looked alarmed, disoriented.

"My cane," he said.

Grubbs glanced around, then remembered. "I'll get it." He trotted back down the aisle.

McKay turned to watch his attorney. "You know, Carson," he called, "there's something I've been wondering about."

"What's that?" Grubbs asked, over his shoulder.

McKay's voice dropped. "If I'd paid you the whole two million up front, and not just half—would you have let me die just now?"

Grubbs, who had walked in past the sensors and equipment and was lifting the cane from the back of the plastic chair, turned and stared through the transparent wall at his client. Grubbs looked offended. "Of course not."

For just an instant—a split-second—Grubbs seemed to realize his mistake. But it was too late. A sizzling flash lit up the cubicle, then vanished. Carson J. Grubbs vanished with it.

"Wrong answer," McKay said. He stood there a minute, looking at the empty Box. All was quiet again now. Muted voices could be heard outside, in the direction of the front steps.

Then a door opened in the south wall of the courtroom, beside the two-way mirror. A young man with curly hair and thick glasses strolled in. He smiled and nodded a greeting to McKay. The air smelled like fried electrical circuits.

"Sorry about your cane," Clovis Hobson said, glancing at the Box. The cane, of course, had departed with Grubbs.

McKay shrugged. "A cost of doing business."

"Like the million you gave Grubbs to have me switch it off during the questions?"

"Wise investment, don't you think?"

"There's still three million left," Hobson reminded him. Bearer bonds, when issued by companies outside the U.S., as these had been, were not only legal, they were as liquid as cash. "And Grubbs only gave me a quarter mil. You said you'd match that."

McKay nodded. "I will. You did a good job, Clovis. On me and him both." He tipped his head toward the plastic enclosure, and its ring of wicked-looking guns. "It is off again, isn't it?"

"It is now." Clovis Hobson took McKay by the arm. "We better get outside, your fans are waiting. And don't forget to limp."

After only a few steps Hobson stopped. "I just thought of something. You had me do Grubbs so you could keep the extra million. Who says you won't do me too?"

McKay gave him a hard look. "I say so."

The two men stared at each other a moment. Finally Hobson asked, narrowing his eyes, "You really mean that?"

"Clovis, my friend," McKay said. "Would I lie?"

WORD GAMES

When Jenny Polk opened her boss's door, he had his ear to the telephone and his eyes on the gray sky outside the window. She stood in the doorway, waiting.

"No, I *don't* like that offer," he said, into the phone. "That's prime beachfront, and they know it." With that, Cleve Decker swiveled his desk chair around and glared at his assistant. She backed out, closing the door behind her.

Ten minutes later he hung up and took a bottle of Maalox from his top drawer. "Jenny!" he shouted.

The connecting door opened again.

"I've told you not to interrupt me, Jenny." Decker pointed the bottle at the phone. "That was an urgent matter."

She raised her chin. "So was this. Or so she said."

"She?"

"A woman was here to see you. She's gone now, she had to catch a plane."

Decker unscrewed the cap of the Maalox bottle. "Did this person leave her name?"

"No. She left a note." Jenny hesitated. "She was a little . . . spooky."

"What do you mean, spooky?"

"Well, for one thing, she saw your coffee cup sitting on the shelf by the pot. She asked was it yours, I said yes, and she picked it up and looked at it."

"Looked at it?"

"Stared at it. And something about her eyes—"

"Oh God," Decker said. He should have known.

"What is it?"

"Alicia Broussard."

"Alicia who?"

Decker blew out a sigh. "Her husband worked for my father, in New Orleans. Dad loaned them money, years ago. She phoned me yesterday, out of the blue, said she needed to see me."

"And?"

"I told her I'd be tied up all week. I meant to warn you in case she called again, but I forgot. I didn't think she'd come by in person." He took a swig of Maalox and made a face.

"Why'd you lie to her?"

"Why do you think? She probably wants another handout."

Jenny was frowning now. "I still don't get it, Cleve. Why're you so sure she's the woman who came by?"

"Because of the coffee cup thing. Alicia Broussard is a witch doctor."

"A what?"

"Voodoo. Hexes. The evil eye."

Jenny's jaw dropped. "Are you serious? You think she could put a spell on you? Through one of your possessions?"

"I don't believe in spells." He saw the way Jenny was looking at him and added, "And don't worry, I don't feel hexed. I feel relieved she's gone." He recapped the bottle and threw it back into his drawer.

Jenny was hugging her elbows as if cold.

"I'm not paying you to stand around and watch me, Jenny. Bring me some coffee and get back to work."

"Not in *that* cup. I plan to throw it away."

"Great," he muttered. "What about the note? You plan to throw it away too?"

Jenny took a sealed envelope from her pocket, holding it by the corner like a dead mouse, and handed it over.

She waited while Decker, scowling, opened the envelope and unfolded the handwritten letter. He looked first at the signature. Sure enough, Alicia K. Broussard.

Halfway down the page, things became more clear. Alicia's husband Eldred had died two months ago, and her "spiritual nature" demanded that she settle Eldred's long-standing debt to Decker's late father. This repayment was to take the form, apparently, of two simple words.

Stunned, Cleve Decker focused on the end of the last paragraph:

"... and if, at any time henceforth, you are threatened or attacked or otherwise confronted unfavorably, you have only to look the offender in the eye and say, 'Go west.' Once you have spoken, that individual will immediately disappear from your presence. Those two words—GO WEST— and the power they entail, are my gift to you. Use them wisely."

Decker thought a moment. This was even more insane than the evil eye. He silently read the letter once more, then glanced at Jenny. "'Go west,'" he murmured, amused. "For cajuns, that's probably Baton Rouge."

Studying the note, Decker tried to remember what little

he'd heard his father say about the Broussards. All he recalled was how weird the wife was.

Decker looked up again. "Jenny, did she say anyth—"

He blinked in surprise. Jenny was gone. Strange, he thought; I didn't even hear her leave the room. He read the letter a third time, then shrugged and laid it aside. He had no time for games, or voodoo notes written by crazy widows. Go west, indeed.

The idea of the still-unpaid debt, though, annoyed him. Cleve, unlike his generous father, wouldn't have loaned a dime to his own grandmother, much less some gofer who worked for him. Maybe he should sue.

It occurred to him that Jenny still hadn't brought him his coffee. "Damn," he said, under his breath. She had other cups in the cabinet. He stabbed the intercom button and called her name. No reply.

He leaned closer to the intercom. "Jenny?" he said again, louder. Still no answer.

Muttering, he rose and stomped through the door to the outer office. He had only just registered the fact that Jenny's desk was unattended when he noticed he wasn't alone. A darkhaired man of forty or so stood in the doorway near the elevators. Black suit, maroon tie, ice-cold expression. His face reminded Decker of Michael Corleone's, just before he shot the two guys in the restaurant. "Mr. Decker?" the man said.

Decker regarded him blankly. He glanced from the stranger to Jenny's empty desk and then back to the stranger again. "You didn't happen to see a blonde in a short blue skirt when you came in, did you?"

The dark man somehow managed to look even more somber. "Sadly, I did not."

Decker relaxed. "Sorry," he said. "Things are a little hectic around here. Yes, I'm Cleve Decker. May I help you?"

"I don't have an appointment—"

"That's okay, I apparently don't have an appointment secretary. Come on in."

They entered the office together. The stranger introduced himself as Carl Perelli.

"Perelli," Decker said. He walked to the other side of his desk. "The name seems familiar."

The darkhaired man sat down and crossed his legs. "Jake Perelli was my older brother."

Cleve Decker, who was in the process of lowering himself into his swivel chair, stopped halfway down, in midair. He stayed that way a moment, as if sitting on an invisible booster seat. Finally, without taking his eyes off his visitor, he sank the rest of the way into his chair. His stomach felt queasy again.

"I see you remember him," Perelli said.

Decker swallowed. "We, ah, did some business in the old days, I believe. Construction, mostly."

"Actually," Perelli said, "that's not the kind of business I was thinking of." This time a smile appeared, thin and menacing.

Decker didn't reply.

Perelli's statement hung there in the air.

Suddenly the phone rang. Cleve Decker jumped as if poked with a cattle prod. He made no move to answer it. The two men sat and stared at each other.

The ringing continued.

After a while Decker remembered that no one else was around to field phone calls. Dazedly he picked up the receiver. "Decker Realty."

"Cleve!" a woman's voice said. "Thank God."

Decker drew his brows together. "Jenny?"

Another voice cut in. "Collect call for Mr. Cleveland Decker," it chirped. "Will you—"

"Yes, yes, I'll accept charges. Jenny? Is that you?"

John M. Floyd

"Yes it's me!" She sounded terrified. "Cleve, what's happening?"

"Calm down, Jenny. Where are you?"

There was a silence on the other end of the line, followed by what sounded like a sob. "I don't know," she said.

Decker looked across the desk at Carl Perelli, who was staring boredly back at him. "Just a second, Jenny," he said, then covered the mouthpiece with his hand. "Excuse me, Mr. Perelli. I'll be right back." Decker pressed a button, hung up, and hurried into the outer office, leaving the door open. He sat down at Jenny's desk and picked up her phone. From where he was sitting he could see the back of Perelli's head.

"Jenny? Cleve again. What do you mean, you don't know where you are?"

"I *don't*," she said. "One minute I'm in your office, and the next—" Decker heard her draw a jerky, ragged breath. "The next, I'm somewhere in the desert."

"The desert?! What do you mean, the desert?"

"Stop asking me what I mean!" she almost screamed. "I'm at a pay phone inside some kind of . . . abandoned gas station in the middle of the desert. In the middle of nowhere!"

Decker let out a lungful of air. My God, he thought, how many crises could a person face in a single day? Carl Perelli's words came back to him—ominous, gut-tightening words: *That's not the kind of business I was thinking of.* Decker had a pretty good idea what kind of business he *was* thinking of, though, yes indeed. And now this, with Jenny. The stupid woman had obviously lost all her marbles, not that she'd had many to begin with.

"Just slow down," he said. "Tell me exactly what happened."

She was quiet a moment. Decker could hear what sounded like sniffling. "I just . . . landed here," she said. "It was like I just woke up and here I was, sitting on my butt in a pile of rocks and sand. I looked around and all I could see was desert.

Desert, and a dirt road, and this ratty little filling station."

She stopped and blew her nose. Decker waited.

"The door was unlocked," she went on. "The phone's the only thing in here that works. I had some change in the pocket of my skirt."

Decker had a thought, and looked down at the floor beside Jenny's chair. Sure enough, there was her purse, propped against the file cabinet where it always was. And her cell phone was sitting on her desk. Jenny never, ever, went anywhere without her purse and cell phone.

He hesitated, thinking hard. She was hallucinating, that was obvious; Jenny Polk had been standing right here in the office less than twenty minutes ago, talking to him. She had given him the note from that woman, and he had read it—

Decker's mouth fell open. He almost dropped the phone.

He had read it . . . and he had said the words.

He had repeated them only because they were so absurd— but he had done it aloud, and had glanced up at her. He was sure of it.

He had spoken the two words . . .

And Jenny Polk had disappeared.

"Good God," he whispered.

"What?" Jenny asked, from somewhere in the desert.

Decker fell silent, gathering his thoughts. He could feel his stomach churning. Was this really *happening*?

"Listen to me, Jenny," he said. "Give me the number on that phone." As she read out the number, he wrote it on one of her desk pads. "Okay. That helps in a couple ways. One, I can reach you in case we're cut off somehow, and two, we know your area code, so we know where you are. Let's see . . . it's 602, so you're in—" He had pulled out a phonebook and flipped to the map in the front. His fingers were trembling. "You're in . . . Arizona."

"*Arizona?*"

"Just listen. We're not going to worry right now about how you got there, we're just going to get you back. Okay?" His mind was spinning. "Are there any windows around?"

Dead silence.

"Jenny? Answer me. Any windows in the building?"

He heard her clear her throat. "Just one," she said.

"Well, look through it, and tell me what you see. Anything. Landmarks, buildings, signs—"

"I see a sign beside the road, a long way off. I can't read it from here. But that's all. No buildings, no landmarks."

"Think it could be a highway sign?" he asked. "A numbered highway sign?"

"For God's sake, Cleve, it's a *dirt road*."

"Go see what it says, Jenny. I'll leave the line open, if it disconnects I'll call you back. All right?"

"Okay." Her voice sounded stronger, more hopeful. "Five minutes should do it."

"Right."

When she had gone, he put the phone down, set the timer on his digital wristwatch, and took another long breath. What a way to start the week, he thought. A note from a sorceress, a visit from someone straight out of *Goodfellas*, and a phone call from a secretary who's been beamed into the Arizona desert.

He rose from the chair and trudged, on legs as heavy as blocks of stovewood, back into his office.

"You look like you just saw a ghost," Carl Perelli said.

Decker raised his hands, then let them fall. "Long story. I have something of an emergency here, Mr. Perelli. Think we could postpone this?"

"Afraid not," Perelli said. His voice was sympathetic, but his eyes reminded Decker of the residents of the reptile house at Heritage Park Zoo, just down the street.

Decker watched him, waiting.

"I know about the fire, Mr. Decker." Perelli's gaze wandered over the room as he spoke. "I know you hired my brother, in '95, to torch one of your houses. So you could collect the insurance. I know because my brother told me, three days ago."

"You're lying," Decker said. "Even if that were true, Jake would never tell you. He'd be as guilty as I—"

"He's past that, I'm afraid. He told me this on his deathbed." Perelli reached into his coat and took out a small audio cassette. "I taped the whole thing."

Cleve Decker was sweating now, and for good reason. Two innocent people had died in that house fire. A house that Decker had thought was empty. A simple little gamble that took a bad turn.

"I was alone with him when he told me," Perelli added, with a sneer. "No one else knows."

Decker heaved a sigh. Every muscle in his body seemed to ache. "What do you want from me?"

Carl Perelli leaned forward and looked Decker in the eye. "I want your agency. And a hundred thousand cash, to get me started." He broke out a grin. "Perelli Realty," he said, as if testing the name on his tongue. "Has a nice ring, don't you think?"

At that instant Decker's wristwatch alarm went off. He stared down at the watch, his mind blank. Then he remembered. He raised his head and met Perelli's gaze.

"Excuse me again," he said.

With an effort he stood, straightened his cuffs, and marched to the outer office. His hand was shaking when he picked up the receiver. He hesitated for a beat before speaking, trying to sort out his thoughts.

"Jenny? Are you there?"

"Gunnison, Arizona," she blurted. She sounded out of breath.

It took a moment for him to process this new information.

"So it *was* a highway sign?" he asked.

"No, no, the sign said PRAISE GOD, which I'll do as soon as I get out of here. I just found an old business card for the gas station, in one of the trashcans."

"Sure it's the same place?"

"Lomax Garage, Old Burnham Road, Gunnison, Arizona," she said. "The name's even painted on the side of the building, what's left of it. You can find it now, right?"

"Right. No problem." Decker's head had cleared; he was jotting everything down on the pad. "The phone company could've tracked down the number, but this is better." He finished writing and sat back, watching Perelli in the other room. "You holding up okay?"

Jenny sighed. "Better, now. It's hot, but not too bad. I think . . . I think I'll be all right, till you get somebody out here."

"Good," he said. "I better get moving." Decker realized, with no guilt whatsoever, that he was concerned about Jenny only because he needed her for his business. He couldn't run this place without her. Besides, how many secretaries fetched coffee for their boss anymore?

Then again, he might soon no longer have a business to run.

"Cleve?" she asked.

"What."

"Tell me what happened."

Decker stayed quiet for several seconds. He'd swiveled a bit to keep an eye on his visitor in the other room. The man was paging idly through a magazine. Watching him and thinking about what to tell Jenny, Decker had a flash of inspiration.

Of *course*. His heartbeat quickened; his mouth went dry. Maybe this whole crazy deal could work to his advantage!

But he would have to handle it—and Jenny—very carefully.

Before he could speak, she said, "I've been thinking, Cleve. Could that Broussard woman have caused this? Could she have put a curse on me!?"

The question startled him. He waited a moment more, working out the details of the plan in his head.

"No," he said. "I think it has to do with that Larrimore business last year. The Blue Lake development, remember?"

"I remember. I typed up the contracts."

"Well, they think we screwed 'em. They think I knew ahead of time that the shopping center would fall through. Ralph Larrimore lost three million on it, and he blames the agency. You and me."

"That's ridiculous," she said. "You didn't know about—"

"But that's what they think."

Decker heard her swallow. "And?"

"And it turns out Larrimore's tight with the mob. Really tight. I think they're out to get us, Jenny." He paused. "Both of us."

It had gone very quiet on the other end of the phone. Finally she said, in a tiny voice, "You mean those people . . . *sent* me here? How? WHY?"

"The how I haven't been able to figure yet, except that one of their connections is big in the scientific community. Biological research projects, genetic experiments—"

"My God," she said.

"The why is simpler, when you stop and think about it. I think they wanted you isolated, away from everything and everyone."

"So they can kill me," she whispered.

Decker didn't reply. He just sat and watched the black-suited man in the other office and visualized the next few steps of the plan. He needed to let her stew for a minute.

Despite the tension, Decker couldn't help smiling. Anyone but Jenny would've seen through a story like that in two seconds—or at least questioned it. After all, why would an irate client be after *her*? She was just a secretary. Dear, sweet Jenny,

Decker thought. I'm glad I let you watch those soaps on your desk TV all these years. They've deadened your brain cells.

He looked again at Carl Perelli, sitting in his chair in the next room, as cool and deadly as a cobra. Nothing wrong with *those* brain cells. And he had to be getting impatient. It was time to wrap this up.

"You'll be okay, Jenny," Decker said, keeping his eyes on Perelli. "You have a working phone there, which is a miracle in itself. But you gotta stay put. Above all, don't leave that building again, for any reason." He checked his notes. "You said the door was unlocked. Can you lock it, from the inside?"

"I think so."

"Lock it, then. And push a piece of furniture against it. You said there was a window?"

"Only one. It faces the spot across the road, where I . . . landed."

"Any way you can cover it over? Block it, like the door?"

"Won't have to. It has burglar bars."

"Good. Okay. I want you to just stay right where you are, Jenny. I'm going to leave for a minute and arrange some things, then I'll get back on the line. All right?"

"Okay, Cleve." The fear was back in her voice again, but she at least sounded controlled.

"Be right back," he said again.

Decker set down the receiver and reentered his office. Carl Perelli gave him a grave look as he rounded the desk and dropped into his chair. The two men studied each other a moment.

"You're convinced you want to go through with this?" Decker asked.

Perelli tossed his magazine aside. "Why shouldn't I?"

"And you say you're the only one who knows about your brother and me?"

"This is the only record," Perelli said, holding up the

cassette.

Decker stared at him. "So what's next?"

Perelli shrugged. "An answer," he said. "Two words: 'I agree,' or 'I refuse.' If you agree, you pay me and sign over your agency. And I give you the tape." He placed the cassette on the edge of the desk and sat back. "If you refuse, I take it to the cops." He raised his lizard eyes to look at Decker. "After all, I had nothing to do with the crime, and I'm not concerned about my dear brother's good name. And I'll deny there was ever any mention of blackmail."

A silence passed. Decker turned and gazed out the window, then faced his visitor again.

"You want two words? Decker asked. "Well, I'll give you two words."

Perelli folded his hands and smiled, waiting.

"Go west," Decker said.

The result was almost anticlimactic. There was no puff of smoke, no flash of white light, no sound at all. Carl Perelli simply vanished. The cushion in his chair, freed of his weight, rose slowly to its original height.

Decker was alone in his office.

For a moment he sat frozen, gaping at the empty chair, then blinked and recovered his wits. He jumped to his feet, pocketed the cassette, dashed through the door to Jenny's office, and snatched up the receiver.

"You there?" he asked.

"Of course I'm here." Her voice sounded scared and weary at the same time. "What is it?"

He swallowed and said, "Look out the window."

"What?"

"The window. Tell me what you see."

Several seconds passed. "I don't see anythi—" She gasped. "Good Lord."

Decker held his breath.

"There's a man out there in the desert," she murmured.

Decker could hear the disbelief in her voice.

"On the other side of the road, where I landed."

Decker closed his eyes. He could hear his heart pounding in his chest. It had actually *worked*.

"What's he doing?" he asked.

"He's just sitting there in the sand. Like I was."

"And his clothes," Decker said. "What's he wearing?" He had to be certain. He couldn't risk a mistake, here.

"Black suit, looks like. And a tie. He looks Hispanic— or maybe Italian." She paused. "Who is he, Cleve? What's going on?"

Decker hesitated, selecting his words with care.

"He's a killer, Jenny. A hit man."

Decker heard her suck in some air.

"The mob must've sent him," he said. "Do you under- stand me?"

She said nothing.

"Jenny, I want you to make absolutely sure the door's locked, and barricaded. If he approaches the station, you stay out of sight. You stay inside and make sure he stays *out*side. Whatever happens. Understand?"

Still no reply.

"Do you *understand*?"

"Yes," she said, her voice faint. "Yes. I understand."

"What's he doing now?"

"He's still sitting there. He looks confused. It'll . . . take him a while to get oriented, I think."

Decker nodded, as if she were here in the office with him. "Okay," he said. "Stay hidden. Help's on the way."

He hung up the phone, wiped a trembling hand across his face, and strode out of the office toward the elevator.

***

Eight minutes later, Cleve Decker sprinted along a winding concrete path bordered on both sides by landscaped gardens. He finally stopped, puffing hard, beside a waist-high chain-link fence. On the fence was a sign that said KEEP A SAFE DISTANCE, and four feet beyond the sign was a wall of closely spaced iron bars. Decker was reminded, just for an instant, of the window Jenny Polk had described to him a while ago.

He thought about Jenny now, as he stood there beside the fence with his eyes closed, waiting for his heart to slow down. He felt no remorse for not having yet placed the call to have her rescued. She'd be okay, if she stayed put. According to his plan, he would phone the Arizona Highway Patrol in half an hour or so. That should be plenty of time.

There was one thing that had to be done first.

Decker opened his eyes.

On the other side of the bars, less than five feet from the spot where Decker's hands gripped the guardrail, staring back at him with heavy-lidded yellow eyes, was an 800-pound Bengal tiger. It opened its mouth and growled lustily, baring its fangs. It looked hungry.

Decker smiled as he pictured what would be left of Carl Perelli by the time the rescuers arrived on the scene. They might, if they were lucky, find his shoes. Jenny, safe inside the locked station, probably wouldn't even know what had happened until it was all over.

Somewhere in the zoo a jungle bird screamed, and Decker jumped. Still breathing heavily, he took a moment to check his surroundings. The only people in sight were a woman and her young son, sitting together on a bench thirty yards away. She seemed to be watching a group of ducks on the sidewalk. The boy was licking a pink ice-cream cone. The coast was clear.

Decker turned again to face the tiger, and looked at it

closely this time. When he did he found, to his surprise, that he could see his own reflection in the animal's glassy eyes. That was appropriate, Decker thought. He would be able to look at his own smile even as he dispatched the ultimate weapon against his enemy.

Holding the tiger's gaze, Cleve Decker leaned forward over the guardrail until their faces were three feet apart. The big cat bared its teeth again.

Decker smiled, staring straight at the image of his face in the fierce yellow eyes.

Alicia Broussard, he thought, you are a fine lady indeed.

"Go west," he said.

***

"Momma," the little boy whispered.

The woman looked at him and smiled. Absently she wiped a napkin across his chin, which was covered with strawberry ice cream. "What is it, honey?"

"Look," the boy said, pointing with a chubby finger. "The tiger's gone."

She raised her head and looked out across the open area between them and the cage marked "BENGAL TIGER—Leo tigris." The wind moaned in the trees overhead; fallen leaves rattled across the pavement. "No, the tiger's there, baby. See?" She pointed also.

"Not that one," the child said. "The one in front, by the bars." He looked up at her. "A man was there, too."

"So?" She raised the napkin again, but he backed away in time to avoid it. Most of his ice cream had leaked unnoticed out of its cone by now.

His mother sighed. She looked again at the cage. Sure enough, she did remember noticing someone there a moment ago. A rather nice-looking man. And it seemed there *had* been another tiger, a really big one, lying just inside the bars.

"Oh, well," she said, and began to gather their belongings. "They're gone now."

"I know they are," the little boy said, frowning.

Something in the child's voice made her look at him. Carefully she asked, "What is it, Tommy? Did the man scare you?"

The boy had turned again to stare at the cage. "He talked to the tiger," he murmured. "The man leaned over and *said* something to the tiger."

The woman watched him, waiting.

"And then they both disappeared," he said.

John M. Floyd

LADIES OF THE NORTH

Hank Stegall saw her as soon as he stepped outside the building.

She was standing alone on the walkway that encircled Resolution Park, near the corner of Third Avenue and L, her arms folded on the wooden railing and her gaze fixed on the blue mountains on the other side of the inlet. Those mountains, Stegall had heard, were forty miles away, but on this spring day they looked close enough to touch. Far beyond, the always-white peaks of the Alaska Range marched across a cloudless horizon.

Stegall focused again on the woman. It bothered him that he couldn't place her. The park was a favorite lunchtime spot for the employees of the magazine where he worked, but he knew most of those people. Was she a tourist? Probably not; he saw no camera.

He approached to within ten feet or so, then stopped and leaned against the railing, studying her profile from the corner of his eye.

She was between thirty-five and forty, he guessed, and pretty in a kind of tomboyish way. Rosy cheeks, strong chin, short blond hair that rippled in the breeze like a field of yellow wheat. She wasn't warmly dressed—a light blouse and skirt—but the coolness of the wind seemed not to bother her. A practical-looking leather purse hung from one shoulder. Beneath the purse, and clipped to a pocket of her skirt, was a plastic ID badge with the magazine's blue-and-red logo. Good, he thought. They were colleagues after all.

He inched closer, and she gave him a sidelong glance. Her expression was neutral—neither friendly nor unfriendly. Hank Stegall, a man accustomed to being frowned at, took that as a positive sign.

Suddenly she turned and looked him straight in the eye.

He retreated a step, cleared his throat. "Good morning," he said. "Ah . . . nice weather, for April."

Her face softened a bit. "It's afternoon. But yes, it is nice." With the hint of a smile, she went back to her view.

Stegall glanced again at her badge. "You're fairly new, aren't you?"

"Actually, I'm fairly old," she said, without turning. "But yes, I'm new to town."

Stegall didn't know how to reply to that. He wasn't sure whether she was teasing him or snubbing him.

"Do you always correct a person," he asked, "and then agree with them?"

When she looked at him this time, he saw an amused twinkle in her eye. "It's 'him,' not 'them.' And yes, I suppose I do."

Her tiny grin took the sting out of the grammar lesson. He grinned too, a little lamely, but she had already turned away again.

Stegall hesitated. She had smiled at him—twice—but he wasn't at all sure what that meant, if anything.

"Do you, ah, mind if I join you, here?" he asked.

"It's a free park."

And free parking's hard to find, he started to point out, but didn't. This playful banter was okay if you were a quick thinker. He wasn't, and he knew it, and if he wasn't careful she'd know it too.

Instead he just leaned over the railing six feet from her elbow and stared out over the water for a while.

"She really does look like she's asleep, doesn't she?" the woman asked.

Hank Stegall blinked. He followed her gaze, saw only mountains and sky and water, and looked at her again. He had no idea what she was talking about.

She turned to face him. "Susitna," she said. "It lives up to its nickname, if you study it awhile."

Stegall looked again at the blue mountain across Cook Inlet. Then he remembered. Mount Susitna was called The Sleeping Lady, not that he had ever given it much thought. He was, after all, a writer, not a tour guide. Staring at the mountain now, though, he could see the reason for the name. Its shape looked like that of a woman lying on her back, her head aimed south and her feet north. He had probably seen the view a thousand times, but had never taken the trouble to make the connection.

A silence passed. Out on the tidal flats between the park and the water, something moved. Stegall squinted at it a moment, then realized it was only a brown paper bag, tumbling end over end in the wind.

"Do you work at *The North Woods*?" she asked, tipping her head toward the building behind them.

"That's right," he said, glad to get back to more comfortable topics. He started to ask her if she worked there also, then remembered that he already knew she did, from her badge. That threw a snag into his train of thought, and before he was able to formulate another question she solved the problem.

"Me too," she said. "This is my first week."

He had a flash of inspiration. "Third floor?"

"Yes." She cocked her head, studied him more closely. "Have we met before?"

"I'm afraid not. I'm just . . ."

"Perceptive?" she said.

Hank Stegall put on a smug look. If there was one thing he was not, it was perceptive. But he had heard that two new secretaries—assistants, they called themselves now—were about to be hired. And he had enough sense to know that the best and brightest were always assigned to the third floor. The rest went to the less prestigious offices downstairs, like circulation and accounting and advertising—

"I didn't catch your name, Mr.—"

"Advertising," he said, and blushed a deep scarlet. "I mean Stegall. Henry Stegall. You can call me Hank."

"I'm Alice Findlayson. You can call me Alice." She smiled again, not terribly friendly even yet, but certainly not the get-lost look he normally received from people who knew him well.

She turned again to the view.

So did he. Miles away, across the blue inlet, Mt. Susitna slept on.

After a moment, afraid that she might bring up some other local geographical fact of which he was unaware, he asked, "Where were you before?"

"Before Anchorage?"

"Before . . ." He thought for a second. "Journalism."

"The Park Service," she said.

"Municipal?"

"National."

He nodded. That made sense. She was too classy to sit at a desk in some city hall.

John M. Floyd

"I write a piece, myself, on area wildlife," he said. "Moose, bear, wolves, eagles, you name it."

Her smile returned. "Sounds interesting. I suppose you're outdoors a lot, then?"

"Almost all the time." He nodded toward the building. "This is my first day in the office in a week. They give me pretty free rein here."

"I understand. Field experience is a big plus." She glanced at her watch.

"Well, I've had more than my share of it," he said, drawing himself up to his full height. "I've been all the way to Valdez in a kayak, and once spent a whole winter trapping on the Yukon."

She was still smiling politely, but seemed distracted. Suddenly he wanted very much to impress her.

"I was the one," he said, "who shot old Three-Toes, a few years back."

She looked up. "Excuse me?"

He smiled to himself. Everyone in Alaska had heard of Three-Toes. The giant grizzly had killed seven people in the mountains near Willow before he was finally tracked down and shot in the late nineties.

"I don't like to talk about it," he said. "It was touch and go. I'm lucky to be alive."

She studied him a moment. "You're an interesting man, Mr. Stegall."

"Hank," he said, basking in her gaze.

She was still staring at him when Zack Benning appeared. Benning was Ad Services Coordinator, on the second floor. As usual, he had his shirttail out and his pipe clamped between his teeth. He might have been smiling, but no one was ever sure: A thick beard covered his face from the nose down. "Afternoon, comrades," he said, around the pipestem.

Alice turned and smiled. "Hello, Mr. Benning. We were just enjoying the warmer weather."

Hank Stegall, annoyed at the intrusion, said nothing. After a moment Alice Findlayson hitched her purse strap a bit higher on her shoulder and pushed away from the railing. "Well," she said, "duty calls." She nodded to Stegall. "A pleasure meeting you, Mr.—"

"Hank."

"Yes. Hank Stegall. I'll remember the name." With that, she nodded to Benning and left.

"Nice lady," Zack Benning said. He had produced a pipe tool from somewhere and was tamping down his tobacco.

Stegall shrugged as he watched her enter the building. "Like all the rest." He wiggled his eyebrows. "In a month or so she'll just be another check mark on my scorecard."

Benning placed his pipe between his teeth again and lit it with a wooden match. "I'd be careful there," he said, puffing.

"Would you now. And what would you know about her that I don't?"

"Well, I know she's the new managing editor. Took old man Boggs's place, two days ago."

Stegall blinked. "But she said . . . I thought she was a secretary. On the third floor."

"You're half right: She's on the third floor. But she has a secretary of her own. Not to mention an army of peons like you and me." Benning paused. "Tell me you didn't try to snow her."

Hank Stegall frowned, remembering. He had stretched the truth a little, sure. He always did. But what business was it of hers that he'd never been inside a kayak in his life, or that the winter he'd spent on the Yukon consisted of an hour inside the terminal at the Dawson airstrip?

In fact, he began to feel a little annoyed that she hadn't told him about her position. There had been plenty of chances for her to do it. The more he thought about it the more annoyed he became.

"Why the hell do we need a woman running a sportsman's magazine anyway?" he said. "She wouldn't know a rifle from a damn shotgun."

"Don't bet on it." Benning turned his head and blew a smoke ring. "I hear she comes highly qualified."

"At what?"

"At rangering, for one thing."

"The Park Service?" Stegall barked a laugh. "I got news for you, Zack. Pushing paper and tracking litterbugs ain't rangering."

"That's not the kind of tracking I'm talking about."

Stegall's eyes narrowed. "What?"

"She's the one killed old Three-Toes," Benning said. "Ten years ago."

SILENT PARTNER

"So if he dies," Niles said, "I get everything. Right?"

C. Spencer Booth, Attorney at Law, studied him over the top of his glasses, then closed the file folder. "You'd get the company and all its assets. Vice versa if you die first. If both partners go at the same time, since you're single, his wife gets it all." Booth handed the folder back. "What's going on here, Niles?"

"Money trouble. I'm examining my options."

"I thought you were an investigator."

"So?"

"So find out what the problem is."

"The problem," Niles said, "is me. I owe twice what I make."

Booth leaned back and folded his hands across his chest. Looking lawyerly. "I thought T & P was doing well."

"That's the company's money. Not mine."

Booth shrugged. "You could sell your partner your half."

Niles looked amused. "You really think that's an option?"

"You think murder is?"

"It was for *you*, last year. You'd be broke by now, if not for me."

Booth shifted in his seat. "That was blackmail," he said, looking away. "The guy had it coming."

"Well, he got it, didn't he."

"If I recall, I hired you to watch him, not kill him."

"But you sure didn't complain." Niles smiled, his gaze steady. "You owe me, Spencer. You know it, and so do I."

A silence passed. Finally Booth cleared his throat and asked, "What exactly do you want?"

"I want to go fishing," Niles said.

***

Clarence Spencer Booth owned a restaurant on Appaloosa Lake, forty miles north of the city. Niles Turner had never seen the place, or the lake either, but his partner in their PI firm, Jack Perriman, was an avid sportsman. Jack had been pestering Niles to go fishing with him on Appaloosa ever since they joined forces, two years ago. "Call it a victory celebration," Jack had said, more than once.

And he had a point, there. T & P Investigations had been extremely successful, partly because of Niles's knowhow—he'd been a homicide detective before leaving the force—and partly because of Jack Perriman's business sense. They made a good team.

But Jack controlled the funds, and was as single-minded as a hen guarding her eggs. He could afford to be; a former security consultant, he had no vices, at least none Niles knew about.

Niles had many. And one of them—gambling—had him over a barrel.

And then, last week, Jack had again mentioned a fishing trip. It'd do them both good, he said.

Later that day, on the way back from the appointment

with Spencer Booth, Niles smiled to himself. Jack's prediction, he figured, was half right . . .

***

They drove up the following Friday night, pulling a motorboat behind Jack's Jeep Cherokee. The motel they had booked was a mile from Booth's restaurant, which in the dawn chill turned out to be no more than a cafe with a souvenir shop attached. Jack and Niles had breakfast there, and a man who looked strangely out of place behind the counter fixed them each a thermos of coffee to take on their outing. He gave Niles a dark look—and a tiny nod—as they left. Niles nodded back. Booth's friends had always made him nervous. Niles doubted any of them had much backbone; if they did, Booth would have used them for that extortion trouble last year. But they made up for it with stealth and meanness, like a dog that wouldn't bite you unless you weren't looking. Niles realized he was sweating.

Within twenty minutes Niles and Jack were alone in the boat with their fishing gear and their lunch sacks, puttering their way to the middle of the lake.

An hour and two catfish later, Niles watched with interest as Jack put down his fishing rod, unscrewed his thermos, and poured a cup of coffee. The thermos was red, with yellow trim. Niles' was blue. The red one, Booth had promised, would contain the poison.

When Jack had finished his second cup, Niles poured one from his own thermos and drank it down, keeping one eye on his partner. The coffee was hot and strong, and good.

Booth had said it would take about ten minutes for the poison to work.

Jack heaved a long sigh. "I love this place," he said, staring out over the lake. Somewhere far away, a fish splashed. The morning sun glinted off the water. "I grew up near here, you know."

Niles frowned. "I thought you were from Atlanta."

"We lived here till I was sixteen." Jack grinned, as if remembering happier days. "I met Samantha here."

Ah yes, Niles thought. Samantha. Though he hadn't mentioned it to Booth, Samantha Perriman was an added bonus of today's little operation. With Jack gone, Niles and Samantha would finally be together for good, with no more sneaking around. She had actually smiled at him when they pulled out of the Perrimans' driveway last night. Niles was surprised. Samantha rarely smiled, about anything. Maybe she felt it somehow, sensed that something big was about to happen.

Niles had a sudden thought. "You don't know C. Spencer Booth, do you?" Booth had once told Niles he was born here.

Jack took another sip of coffee. "You did some work for him last year, right? I saw it on the books."

"Yeah. Surveillance."

"We went to high school together," Jack said.

Niles' jaw dropped. Jack and Booth knew each other? How well? he wondered. What if they were friends? Niles hadn't known either of them for more than a few years.

What if Booth had told Jack about the *plan*?

Niles found himself staring into his coffee cup, his imagination running wild.

"You okay?" Jack said, looking at him.

Calm down, Niles told himself. I'm a private eye, I can tell if somebody's lying to me. There's nothing wrong with my coffee, and the poison in Jack's should take effect any minute now. Jack and Booth probably haven't spoken for years, probably wouldn't recognize each other if they passed on the street.

Still . . .

"How well do you know him?" Niles asked.

"Clark? We go way back. Once, in the tenth grade, we—"

Jack paused, looking puzzled. His face had gone pale.

It's happening, Niles thought. He could see the sudden pain in Jack's eyes. According to Booth, chills would come next.

"In the tenth grade, he and I went . . ."

Jack stopped again, put a hand to his chest.

And then Niles had another thought. One that, for an instant, made him forget about his partner's approaching death.

"Who's Clark?" Niles said.

Jack gave him a vacant look, still holding his chest. "What?"

"You said 'Clark.' I thought Booth's first name was Clarence."

"Clark's what she calls him." Jack swallowed, trembling now. "She . . . used to think he looked like Clark Gable."

"She?" Niles said.

"Samantha."

Niles blinked. "Samantha knew Booth too?"

"He's her cousin," Jack said, and collapsed.

And it was then, at that moment, that two things happened to Niles Turner. One was a searing pain in his chest, and the first wave of chills. The other was the thought of Samantha—dear, devious Samantha, whose love for money, he knew, had always been stronger than her love for him *or* Jack—and of her radiant, almost *knowing*, smile when she waved goodbye to them both last night.

Because Samantha rarely smiled . . .

John M. Floyd

THE GARDEN CLUB

Rudy Tullos was in love with his neighbor. Her name was Karen Pennington, she was staying the summer with her aunt and uncle next door, and she was eleven years old. To be exact, she was eleven and a half—two months younger than Rudy. Which was a good thing: it meant he wasn't dating An Older Woman.

Then again, they weren't actually dating, he reminded himself. What they were doing, and had been doing since her arrival on Farrell Street three weeks ago, was just sort of hanging around together. Going fishing, playing checkers, riding bikes. Or at least that's what Karen was doing. Rudy was more or less tagging along and going through the motions. And looking at her. He felt certain he could spend hours on end doing nothing but looking at her—and the more he did, the more hopelessly lovesick he became.

On this particular day, as Karen Pennington sat beside him in the wooden swing on his front porch, Rudy decided he'd like to try something a little different. Specifically, he'd like to convince her to walk with him along the path beside the creek, and even more specifically, he'd like to steer her to a spot under the big oak tree halfway down the path. The oak tree with all the mistletoe in the top branches.

As he sat and tried to formulate the right way to phrase such a suggestion, she came up with one of her own.

"Want to play Monopoly?"

Rudy sighed. *He who hesitates,* he thought.

"Why not?" he said, with a shrug. At least with Monopoly he was sure what he was doing. And he could still look at her.

Rudy went upstairs to fetch the game box while Karen wandered to the living room and dropped into a chair to wait. When he came back he found her staring at a point on the floor near the doorway to the dining room. Puzzled, he followed her gaze, then understood. On the carpet between the coffeetable and the open door was a big, ugly stain. Even though it was close to two feet in diameter, it wasn't terribly noticeable—it was just a dark gray spot on a lighter gray floor—but Karen had noticed it anyway. It was in the shape of a circle with a couple of splashes on each side, making it look like the planet Saturn. "What's that?" she asked, pointing, as Rudy plopped down crosslegged on the floor and spread out the game board.

He glanced at the strange-looking spot on the carpet, then started counting out the play money. "It's a long story," he said.

Karen waited a moment, watching him. When he didn't elaborate, she said, "Did your mom spill something there?"

"Not exactly. What kind of man do you want?"

She frowned at him until she saw he was holding out a handful of little metal tokens. "Oh. The top hat, I guess."

Rudy placed it on the board and selected the race car for himself. His man was always the race car. "You can go first," he said, handing her the dice.

Her eyes were still on his face. "Aren't you going to tell me what happened?"

"I suppose. If you really want to know."

John M. Floyd

She stared at him, waiting.

"It was a Garden Party," he said.

***

He began the story with an observation: He had never really understood why they were called Garden Parties. Nobody in Morgan's Hollow even had a garden, at least not the kind you see on TV, or in the fancy magazines. The gardens this far south of the Mason-Dixon were several long rows of peas and okra and butterbeans. Still, the ladies of the town called their organization the Garden Club, and their little gossipy gatherings were named accordingly. They were dull affairs, these parties, Rudy thought that day as he looked down at the proceedings from his hiding place at the top of the stairs. A dozen stiff and proper ladies, all gussied up and staring down their powdered noses at everyone else, were milling about the living room and dining room like corralled cattle and murmuring to each other while they munched odd-looking little goodies laid out in bowls and platters on every flat surface in sight. Rudy found it hard to believe that his mother had invited them here in the first place.

Well, that wasn't quite right. What he found hard to believe was that they had accepted the invitation. His mom had wanted to join the exclusive group—or at least to be in some way acknowledged by them—for most of her adult life. The truth of the matter was, he and his mother and little sister were from the Other Side of the Tracks, so to speak, and until now had been consistently and pointedly ignored by the "finer" citizens of Morgan's Hollow. That bothered Rudy not one bit, of course— the children of these particular folks were no fun anyway. But his mother wanted their acceptance, and always had. Ever since his father had run away three years ago and left them with next to nothing, his mother's irrational desire to be a part of the Garden Club had grown into an obsession. Hardly a day went by that she didn't go all dreamy-eyed and mumble something about "that fine and dignified group of ladies." Rudy snorted under his breath. His mother, so smart and level-headed about most everything else, was horribly mistaken about that, he thought. The only thing these women wanted today, the only reason they were here at all, was to snoop around and peer into corners and eat the tiny cookies and sandwiches and make fun of Dorothy Tullos and her simple lower-class existence.

The one exception was a woman named Edith Garland. Mrs. Garland had recently moved down here from Memphis. In fact she was the new doctor's wife, and had defied the rules this afternoon by bringing along some goodies she and a friend of hers had made, to help out. Rudy didn't know her personally, but he was a pretty good judge of character, and from what little he'd seen so far he figured she was the only one in the gathering today, besides his mom of course, who was worth a damn.

Once, a few minutes ago, Mrs. Garland had caught him peeping at them from the top of the stairs and had winked at him slyly.

As Rudy sat there thinking these thoughts, a prunefaced old woman named Maude Ogletree rose from her chair beside the window, marched over to his mother, and stood there looking at her from three feet away. Dorothy Tullos, who was busy gathering up some of the used plates and glasses, turned to find the old woman blocking her way to the kitchen.

"Excuse me," Rudy's mother said, with a smile, and started to go around her. Maude Ogletree simply moved to the left a step, just far enough to again block the way. The two women stared into each other's eyes for a moment. "Is something wrong, Mrs. Ogletree?" his mother asked, her hands full of dishes.

"I'm afraid so," the old lady said, in a cold voice. "You seem to have missed the mark a bit, on those balls."

Dorothy Tullos frowned. "I beg your pardon?"

"Those things over there on the cabinet, in the little blue bowl. They taste a bit like sausage balls, but not quite." Mrs. Ogletree raised her head and thrust out her chin like the Wicked Witch of the West. "Personally, I wouldn't feed them to my dog."

Surprised and blushing, Rudy's mother pressed her lips together and took a slow breath. This kind of thing had been going on all afternoon. "I'm afraid you'll have to speak to some-one else about that, Mrs. Ogletree. They aren't mine."

The old woman gave her a stony look. "Indeed," she said. "And who else would have brought food here, may I ask?"

"I believe Mrs. Garland brought them." Dorothy Tullos paused, then added, "Maybe she feeds them to *her* dog." After another smile, she tightened her grip on the dishes and trudged past Mrs. Ogletree to the kitchen door.

The old lady's eyebrows, which had shot up at the men-tion of her distinguished neighbor, swooped down again. Her gray head swiveled in a slow arc, searching the room for Edith Garland. Even from his distant vantage point, Rudy Tullos could see the sudden gleam in Mrs. Ogletree's eye. And he knew what she was thinking. Mrs. Garland, as the new doctor's wife and the most recent member of the Club, might at last be a lady deserving of Maude Ogletree's valuable time and attention.

After a moment the old woman spotted her, and on the way across the room detoured to the cabinet to pick up the bowl of sausage balls. With the container in hand, Mrs. Ogletree strode over to stand beside Dr. Garland's wife. As Rudy watched, the old woman interrupted with an upraised finger the conversation Edith Garland was having with several of the other ladies, and during the awkward silence started ranting about how wonderful Mrs. Garland's little sausage balls were. Every few seconds Mrs. Ogletree would pause and pop another one into her mouth. Yum, yum. Rudy's mother had noticed also, he saw, and she sighed tiredly before turning back to the dining-room table to set out another plate of cookies.

To Rudy's pleasure, however, the good doctor's wife seemed unimpressed with the old woman's performance. After a long, lip-smacking dissertation by Maude Ogletree about everything from her Confederate ancestry to her bank account, Edith Garland excused herself and glided away, leaving the old biddy standing there alone, chewing on the last of the balls. And though Rudy didn't hear all of Mrs. Garland's parting remark, he caught enough to hear her say the sausage balls were, regretfully, none of her doing—but she was glad Mrs. Ogletree had enjoyed them.

The old woman stood there a minute, stunned and blinking. The little blue bowl, empty now, was replaced on its cabinet so loudly it almost broke. Fuming, Mrs. Ogletree stomped back across the room, mumbling to herself and rubbing her mouth with a napkin.

At about that same time, Rudy was struck with an idea. An idea so simple and so brilliant it made his insides tingle just thinking about it.

Slowly he rose to his feet and crept down the stairs. After a moment he caught his mother's eye and weaved his way over to where she stood, between the living-room coffeetable and the doorway to the dining room. As he approached his mom, Mrs. Ogletree apparently noticed him, and came over also.

"Mrs. Tullos," she announced, "I'm afraid we don't allow children at our gatherings."

Both Rudy and his mother turned to stare at her. "Mrs. Ogletree," Dorothy Tullos said, when she had regained her composure, "this is not just a child. This is my son, and this is my house." To Rudy she said, in a quiet and unsteady voice, "Rudy, honey, this is Mrs. J. L. Ogletr—"

"I repeat," the old woman said, louder this time, "children are not welcome. He must leave at once." She stamped her foot hard on the carpet to underline this last word.

Everyone there had overheard them by now, and most were gathering around. Several of the women's expressions were cold and aloof, but a few showed open concern.

One lady said, "But, Maude—"

"Shut up, Nell," Mrs. Ogletree snapped, without turning. "Leave now, young man," she said to Rudy. "And do not return until our meeting is finished. Do you understand?"

Dorothy Tullos, her pretty face reddening, opened her mouth to reply, but Rudy cut her off. "I'm leaving, ma'am," he said politely. "I just came for my eggs."

Everyone looked at him. "What, honey?" his mother said. For the moment her anger was sidetracked.

"My eggs," he repeated. "Tommy wants 'em back."

There was a puzzled silence. "Rudy, what do you mean?"

Rudy smiled his most innocent smile. "I mean the eggs Tommy and I cut out of his dead turtle yesterday, Mom. They were in a little blue bowl on the cabinet . . ."

***

Karen Pennington sat and stared at him for a long time.

Finally Rudy blinked and focused on her. "Sorry," he said. "I told you it was a long story."

"I think it's fantastic," she said, in a hushed voice. The look on her face made it clear that she was seeing Rudy Tullos in an entirely new light. "It's the absolutely coolest thing I ever heard."

He just shrugged.

She turned to look at the big gray stain on the carpet. "So she did that? Mrs. Ogletree?" Her voice was faint, almost a whisper. She seemed awestruck.

"That's just some of it," he said. "Mom scrubbed most of it out, the next day." He thought for several seconds, remembering. "But it was something to see, all right. Soon as I said the words 'the little blue bowl,' the old lady just pulled the plug. Mom and I ducked and missed the worst of it, but poor Mrs. Polk got covered head to toe, and Miss Russell and Mrs. Bennett and Mrs. Watkins got a pretty good soaking, and they were five or six feet away. A couple of ladies tried to run and slipped down in it. Pretty gross." He shook his head, smiling at the memory. "I never saw anybody throw up like that except the little girl in that exorcist movie."

Karen didn't seem to know what to say. She was still looking at him as if he had just waved his cape and pulled a white rabbit out of the Monopoly box.

"Well," he said, with a glance at the board. "You want to roll first?"

She stayed quiet. Rudy could hear the growl of old Mr. Burnley's lawnmower two doors down, and the crunch of gravel as a car rumbled by on the dirt road. The smell of honeysuckle floated in through the open window.

"Karen?" he said.

She had tilted her head a bit, watching him. "Why don't we go outside?" she asked, in that low, strange tone.

"Outside?"

"Yeah." A tiny smile played at the corners of her mouth. "We could maybe take a walk down the path. You know, the one beside the creek?"

Their eyes held, then he shrugged again. "Okay. If you want to."

Rudy closed up the game box and walked with her across the living room. Before following her through the doorway, he paused a moment, smiling, and turned to study the big gray Saturn-shaped spot where his little sister's dog had wet the carpet last month.

Imagination, he said to himself, *is a terrible thing to waste . . .*

John M. Floyd

BUTTON'S AND BO'S

"He got another one last night," Button said.

Ray Woodson turned to look at her as he zipped his coat. His eyes were dark, his jaw set. "I heard."

Button just nodded. Everyone in town had heard by now about the killings—one every Sunday night for the past four weeks. Whoever it was, he was stealthy and quick and always left behind messages scrawled in pink lipstick, messages that were four different versions of the fourth commandment: OBSERVE THE SABBATH; SIX DAYS SHALL YE LABOR; HONOR GOD'S DAY OF REST; ONLY SINNERS WORK ON SUNDAY. The press was calling him the Holy Ghost.

And every single victim—three women and one man, so far—had been a convenience-store clerk.

Like Button McKenna.

Ray's face softened a bit. "You'll be okay," he said.

And she believed him. Never mind that today was a Sunday, and that she would go on duty at eight p.m., and that all the murders had been between eight and nine, and that she always worked alone. That didn't matter. Button believed him.

She thought she *would* be okay.

Because Ray was the killer.

She wasn't positive; there was no hard evidence. But she was pretty sure. Every Sunday night for the past month—almost as long as they'd been dating—Ray had told her he had to go somewhere. On the one hand, that seemed reasonable: Button was on duty every weekend night, and had made it clear to Ray that she didn't need him babysitting her at the store during work hours.

But last night she had phoned Eddie's Bar and Grill, where Ray had told her he was going, to finish writing his newspaper column. He wasn't there.

And there were other factors. Like the pistol he'd kept hidden in his waistband lately, and the scratches she'd noticed on the shoulder of his old leather jacket. A whole row of scratches—like the kind fingernails might make.

And this morning she'd found an old tube of her lipstick—like her late mother, Button had always favored pink—that she'd left in her glove compartment weeks ago. Ray could easily have been using it, then putting it back.

Button sighed. Was Ray actually a religious fanatic? Had he kept it hidden, like his gun? More important, did she have enough evidence to call the police? She didn't know. *Would* she call the police, even if she did? She didn't know that either.

What she did know was that she loved Ray Woodson. She loved him completely and desperately, in a way that she could never have imagined before she met him. And she knew he loved her too.

They'd both had hard lives—he was a smalltime writer, she a struggling divorcee—but their unlikely meeting and growing relationship seemed, to Button, a beacon of hope. A promising future.

And then the killings had started.

John M. Floyd

Maybe she was wrong. Maybe he was innocent, and the only fault was her overactive imagination. She hoped so. With all her heart she hoped so.

And at that instant, as she stood there in the hallway of her apartment watching him leave, Button had an idea. She knew how she could find out, once and for all. And it involved a *real* religious fanatic. At least a former one.

"I need a favor, Ray," she blurted.

He stopped and turned, his hand on the doorknob.

"My dad called a few minutes ago," she said, "while you were in the bathroom." The call had actually been one of those telemarketing surveys, but Ray wouldn't know that—he would only remember hearing the phone ring. "He's sick, and needs me to drive over. Could you fill in for me tonight, at the store?"

Ray hesitated. Button held her breath.

Her reasoning, she thought, was sound. If Ray was tending the store, he couldn't very well go wherever it was that he was going. And if nine o'clock came and went, and no one was murdered . . .

Button swallowed. At least she would *know*.

But Ray was no fool. He'd never met her father, but she knew Ray was aware of their problems. Button's dad, even though he lived near here, had never known her ex-husband Bo either, and didn't even know where she worked. Button hadn't spoken to him in months. A week ago, when she'd taken him a package of clothes for his birthday—mostly things Bo had left behind—her dad hadn't even answered the door. She left the box on his porch.

Button's father, a onetime Baptist minister, was a Lost Cause. Alcoholic, abusive, violent—none of the adjectives were pretty. He'd always told her he would become famous someday. Rich and famous, like Billy Graham. But all he ever became was a failure, at just about everything he tried.

Button knew she would be the last person her dad would call if he were sick. Ray probably knew that too.

Even so, after a long pause, he smiled. "Sure. The poker game can make it without me, I guess." He pushed the door shut, held out his arms, and Button (barely five feet tall, which was the reason for her nickname) stepped into them, pressing the side of her head against his broad chest as he hugged her.

But she could feel, through his coat, the handle of the gun in his belt.

***

An hour later Button was kneeling at the edge of the woods, fifty yards from the parking lot of the convenience store where she worked. Mosquitoes buzzed around her face, and needle-sharp blackberry vines pricked her hands when she pushed aside the undergrowth so she could see.

The Button's and Bo's Mini-Mart, a cinderblock building containing everything from pocketknives to Hostess Cupcakes, was the last in a row of small businesses lining the frontage road of I-55, on the south edge of the city. She had received the store as her part of the settlement when Bo McKenna divorced her six months ago, and despite its seedy location she'd decided to keep it, along with its name. Now, from her vantage point here on the hill, Button could see only one side of the building and some of the front, but the parking lot was brightly lit. She would have a clear view of anyone coming or going.

At the moment, Ray Woodson was inside, and Button wanted to make sure he stayed there.

She glanced down at her luminous wristwatch. 8:07. She decided to wait until nine, then trudge back through the woods to her car and drive over to relieve him. And if tonight's ten o'clock news reported no further victims, she would know.

She'd also know if they *did* report another victim.

God forgive me, Button thought, that would be even better.

She sat down crosslegged in the damp leaves of the hillside and watched.

***

At 8:45 she jerked awake. She rubbed her eyes with her knuckles, furious with herself, then focused on the scene below. Nothing seemed to have changed, except for the cars outside Button's and Bo's. There were two of them there now, a late-model Lexus and Ray's white Toyota.

Then, so suddenly it made her yelp, she heard a gunshot.

She sat up, wide-eyed, and saw a longhaired young man burst through the front door and out into the parking lot. He stood there a moment, as if dazed, then broke into a run, heading north up the now-deserted frontage road.

Oh my God, Button thought. What have I done?

For a full ten seconds she watched the building, hands over her mouth and tears stinging her eyes. No one else came out.

Finally she snapped out of it. *Maybe he's not dead . . .*

Button rose, trembling, and tried to run—but one of her legs was asleep. She fell heavily, slid sideways, and tumbled down a muddy embankment onto a pile of rocks. Her left leg and hip took the brunt of the fall, sending a blinding jolt of pain through her body.

For a long time she lay stunned at the bottom of the ravine, out of sight from the rest of the world. She was vaguely aware of the sound of approaching sirens. At some point she spotted a broken tree limb several yards away, and crawled toward it.

***

Ten minutes later, using the branch as a crutch, little Button McKenna limped into the parking lot of the mini-mart. Police cars were everywhere, lights blinking and flashing. Off to one side, an attractive middle-aged blonde was shouting at a policeman about something.

For a moment Button just stood there, tears shining through the dirt on her face. She had already glimpsed the body being loaded into an ambulance—at least the bottom fourth of a body, wearing jeans and hiking boots.

Ray's hiking boots.

She drew a rasping breath.

The man on the stretcher was Ray Woodson. She knew it was. It was Ray, and he was dead, and she was the reason he was dead.

And then she heard someone behind her. She flinched, turned, stared—and threw herself into his arms.

"You're alive," she whispered, her voice muffled by his soft leather jacket. "I can't believe it. I thought—"

Ray hugged her, then held her away long enough to see that she was hurt. But before he could speak, she saw again the scratches on his jacket, and this time she knew what had made them.

"Blackberry bushes," she murmured. Their eyes locked. "That's where you were, those nights. Up there in the woods, watching out for me."

He shrugged. "Good thing I wasn't up there tonight, and you down here. I'd've probably got us both killed."

"What do you mean?" Through a haze of tears she looked at the ambulance. "Didn't you shoot the guy?"

"I was too slow. He pulled his gun and made me hand mine over."

"Then how—"

"A lady customer was about to check out. He pushed her away from the counter, and when he did I hit him over the head with an orange juice bottle. He's not dead, he's just unconscious."

Button gaped at him. "But I heard a shot—"

"He did that, when he fell. Your Coke machine was mortally wounded."

She felt her head whirling. This was too much to take in, all at once. "Is he . . . is he the one, Ray?"

"Yeah. Positive ID, according to the cops—video and audio. Last week's victim had a security camera."

"Audio?"

"He repeated himself," Ray said. "He told me, before I beaned him, that he'd been sent by God."

"Did he say why?"

"To teach sinners to respect the Sabbath."

Button swallowed, still half sick with relief. "Caught on camera," she said. "I guess he wasn't a ghost after all."

"Holy, either." Ray paused, then added, "But I have some bad news too—"

"Mr. Woodson?" a voice said. Button turned to see a blond woman standing there, with a teenaged girl in tow. The woman was the one Button had noticed earlier, arguing with the cop. The girl looked as if she'd been crying.

"Button, this is Ms. Farrell," Ray said. "She and her kids were here when it happened."

And suddenly Button understood. The Lexus parked beside Ray's car belonged to this woman; the killer must've come on foot, planning to escape into the woods afterward. And the young man Button had seen dash out of the store—

"Her son ran to a pay phone down the street to call 911," Ray said. "Our line had been cut."

"And for once I'd left my cell phone at home," Ms. Farrell said.

"My God," Button murmured. "You must be the lady he pushed, just before Ray hit him."

Ms. Farrell grinned. "It was my orange juice bottle."

"No charge," Ray said.

Then Button remembered his earlier comment. "What did you mean, about bad news?"

Ray sighed. "My gun. It's not licensed. It's not even mine—I borrowed it from a friend when all this started, a few weeks ago."

"And?"

"And the city cops and I go way back."

Button's eyes widened. "You have a record?"

"Not that kind. But I used to be a reporter. The police brutality cases got a lot of coverage."

"Don't worry," Farrell said. "That's been taken care of."

Ray looked at her. "It's what?"

"I had a little talk with our boys in blue." To Button, Ms. Farrell said, "This man"—she nodded to Ray—"saved our lives. That's what I explained to the cops. In about an hour I'll explain it to the rest of the city. By tomorrow, he can run for mayor if he wants."

Button's mouth dropped open. "Of course. Melissa Farrell . . . You're Channel 5 News."

"I'm the anchor," Farrell agreed, smiling, "but believe me, your husband is the news."

She left with one arm around her daughter. On the other side of the lot, past the milling crowd and the policemen and the flashing lights, the TV crews were beginning to arrive.

"Come on," Ray said. "Let's get you to a doc."

Only then did the Farrell woman's last words register. *Your husband?* "My God, Ray," Button said. "She thinks I'm your wife! What if she says that on TV?"

With his fingertip he brushed a muddy lock of hair from her forehead. "Then I guess I'd have to correct the situation."

"Tell her the truth, you mean?"

"No," he said, and grinned. "That's not what I mean."

And for the first time in days, Button smiled too. Only hours ago, she'd been convinced that Ray was a killer, that he was the religious zealot who punished Sunday workers. Now he was a hero. And, apparently, her fiance.

Then she thought of something. "Ray," she said, solemn again, "I lied to you. I didn't go to my father's tonight."

"I know."

"You know?"

"I called his house," Ray said. "His number was on your bulletin board, beside the counter. No one was home."

She nodded. "He's probably dead drunk. Or in jail." She drew a shaky breath and let it out. "I can't believe I didn't trust you. A few minutes ago, when I saw that guy's hiking boots—I thought it was you, that you'd been shot."

"His boots?"

"They looked like the ones you bought a few weeks ago."

"But I didn't keep them, remember?" he said. "They didn't fit."

She blinked. "What?"

"I put them in the box you took to your dad's. I thought maybe he could use—"

He never finished the sentence. Button had turned away, to look at the retreating ambulance. And just as the truth hit her, as she remembered her fundamentalist upbringing, as she remembered leaving her mother's cosmetics packed in boxes at her parents' house, as she gasped and clapped her hands over her mouth, she had another thought. A crazy but somehow logical thought:

Her father had become famous after all.

DOOLEY'S CODE

Honest John Dooley.

It was the name he'd always used, the name that had gotten him elected to the City Council for eight straight years. It was also ironic, since John Dooley had not an honest bone in his body. He was as crooked as a trial lawyer's smile.

Did that matter? Certainly not to John. Did it matter to the voting public? Well, it would—if they knew about it. Therein lay the beauty of the system. Success in politics, like success in the business world, is based more on perception than reality. If the lobby looks respectable enough, the seldom-seen back rooms (in either a bank building or a candidate's character) can be downright seedy.

John Dooley's disguise—his thousand-watt grin—was at its brightest today, as he stepped onto the porch of a small suburban home near the city limits. Behind him, on the front lawn, a man in a power-company uniform was talking on a cell phone beside a recently dug hole. Dooley straightened his back, cleared his throat, tightened his grip on the stack of campaign flyers, and rapped on the door.

Within seconds, a young woman answered his knock. She was holding a children's book. *The Cat in the Hat.*

"Morning, ma'am. I'm Honest John Dooley." He handed her a flyer and widened his smile another notch.

"Suzanne Crowson," the lady said.

"Hope you don't mind my parking in your driveway. I'm asking all your neighbors to re-elect me next week."

Before the woman could reply, a blond girl of four or five appeared beside her in the doorway. The child studied Dooley a moment, then announced, "I'm Melissa. I have a pet rabbit."

"I had one too, growing up," he lied. He reached down and shook her small hand.

"His name's Harvey," Melissa said.

Footsteps approached from inside, and Ms. Crowson stepped aside to allow a second electric-company worker to shoulder past them and out the door. In his hand was a square metal toolkit, scratched and worn; on his face was an arrogant scowl. Without turning he muttered, "Your breaker box looks okay."

This was, in Dooley's view, rude behavior. His personal and admittedly lax Code of Conduct did at least demand courtesy to the general public. Lie and cheat if you must, but be friendly about it.

Dooley turned to watch the man join his colleague, who was now knee-deep in the hole. "Electrical problems?" Dooley asked Ms. Crowson.

"We're used to it," she said. "If it's not the power company it's the TV people. We have underground power lines here—the electricians come to make repairs in somebody's yard, then the cable company shows up later and says the other guys have nicked their cable and customers are complaining about reception, so they re-dig the holes to fix it. But they somehow manage to mess up the electricity again, and the power people come back the next day, and so on. These guys'll undoubtedly cut the cable again. I guess our water line'll be next."

She heaved a sigh, and Dooley shook his head in sympathy.

"On top of all that, we've had a lot of burglaries lately. And this is supposed to be a low-crime area."

"Well," Dooley said, lifting his chin, "I can remedy both problems. On the one matter, I'm already working closely with the police chief to increase patrols in suburban neighborhoods, and on the other, I plan to introduce measures which will force both private and public service companies to promptly reimburse customers for any inconvenience caused by—"

He stopped in midsentence. The look Ms. Crowson was giving him implied that she thought he might be making that up as he went along. Which he was.

"Well," he said, backing away and rekindling his smile. "I better move on. I'd appreciate your vote. Remember the name—Honest John."

"G'bye, mister," the child called.

"Goodbye, Melinda."

"Melissa," she said.

On the way to the Cadillac that he'd left in the Crowsons' driveway, Dooley glanced over at the hole in the yard. The two-man workcrew had disappeared, probably on their lunch break, leaving the hole open and the job unfinished. Dooley was glad they were gone. Otherwise he'd have had to stop and shake their hands and ask for their votes, and he didn't want dirt on his new suit.

And then he saw the rabbit.

It lay squashed on the concrete, just behind his left front tire. He must've run over it pulling into the drive. Right now it was out of sight of the house, but if he moved the car . . .

He opened the door and tossed his flyers in, then took a step back and thought a moment. The lady and her daughter had of course seen his Caddy parked there, and as soon as they saw the rabbit's flattened remains they would know what he'd done. Worse, they would know *he* knew, since he would certainly have noticed the poor thing's body when approaching the driver's-side door.

What a screwup. Should he go back to the house and confess to the accident? No. People didn't vote for candidates who ran over their pets, intentionally or not. Besides, confessing was a blatant violation of the Dooley Code. He rarely confessed to anything. It might be good for the soul, but not for one's political aspirations.

He checked out the street, right and left. Nobody in sight. It was noontime, and hot as a nickel pistol. Folks who weren't at work were inside their air-conditioned homes, eating lunch.

Again he looked at the open hole twenty feet away, and at the tools the crew had left in the grass beside it.

Why not?

His jaw set, Dooley strode to the work site, grabbed a shovel, and stepped down into the muddy hole. So much for keeping his suit clean. The crew had apparently finished their digging; black conduits and cables lay exposed at the bottom of the hole, along with an inch or so of grimy water. Dooley probed in the mud beside the cables, and felt the shovel blade clank against something flat and hard. To one side of the obstruction, he dug a little deeper, then he returned to the driveway and scooped up the dead rabbit with the shovel. He dropped the little carcass into the bottom of the hole and packed soggy dirt over it to keep the crew from finding it when they resumed their repairs. It took no more than five minutes.

Puffing and redfaced, he crawled out onto the lawn, replaced the shovel, and looked around. No witnesses. He wiped sweat from his forehead and hurried to his car. Moments later he was a mile away.

He couldn't help grinning. His clothes were dirty, sure,

and the day was shot, but things had turned out rather well. He was of course lucky not to have been seen—but that was nothing unusual. He had always been lucky.

And then he remembered the water at the bottom of the hole.

That was odd. If the hole was dug to repair TV cable and power lines, why was there water inside?

He frowned, thinking hard. Maybe there was a leak some-place, or just a high water table at that particular spot. That could happen, right?

He didn't know. What he did know was that the woman— Ms. Crowson—had said something about it too. He couldn't recall exactly what, but she'd mentioned water lines.

And that triggered another thought. He remembered Kevin Costner, in *Dances With Wolves*, about to dip a bucket into a creek for drinking water and seeing a dead deer submerged a few feet upstream. If he hadn't spotted the deer carcass in time, he'd have drunk poisoned water.

What if the dead rabbit caused the same thing?

John Dooley began to sweat again. What if the water lines *had* been damaged? If there was a leak at that point, could the dead rabbit contaminate the drinking water of the household? Or of the whole street?

Dooley could see the headline now: 200 RESIDENTS OF SUBDIVISION DIE FROM TAINTED WATER. WHO IS TO BLAME?

What if there was an investigation? Would the rabbit's remains be found? Had anyone seen Dooley with the shovel? He could certainly be placed at the scene—he'd given a flyer with his photo on it to the owner of the house, not to mention most of her neighbors.

John Dooley's head was spinning, his heart jackhammer-ing in his chest. However remote, the possibility was there. Death, accusations, disgrace. His reputation, his whole future, was at stake here.

He couldn't allow that to happen.

He U-turned and roared back toward the Crowsons' house. It wasn't yet one o'clock. Maybe there was still time . . .

As he approached he saw the hole still open and unattended, the streets and sidewalks deserted except for a lone woman who looked to be at least a hundred years old, walking a woolly black dog. This time he parked at the curb, poised for a fast getaway.

He rolled down all the windows and sat there a minute or so, watching and listening. Now or never, he thought.

Head down and coat off, he marched across the yard, grabbed the shovel, and stepped into the hole. Within seconds he had uncovered the carcass, which he scooped up and carried to his car. The woman with the dog, not far away now, was paying him no attention whatsoever. Even so, there was no time to pop the trunk. He threw the dead rabbit, mud and all, through the open window onto his back seat.

Sweating and filthy, Dooley jogged back to the hole, replaced the shovel, and almost laughed aloud. He had done it. What could have been a disaster had been averted.

He turned to go back to the car—

And stood facing Suzanne Crowson and her little daughter. Ms. Crowson was standing on her front walk, her purse and car keys in her hand.

"What are you doing?" she said to him.

Dooley swallowed. "I just . . ." He waved weakly toward the hole at his feet. "I used to work for the power company. I thought I might be able to spot the trouble—"

"I read your flyer," she said. "It says you've always been an attorney."

"I, ah, represented the utilities for a time."

"And that qualifies you to fix a power outage?"

Whatever he was going to say next, he never said. The work crew had finally returned, and were climbing out of their truck. Also, the dog the old lady was walking had taken a keen interest in something inside Dooley's Cadillac. It had dragged her by the leash to the car and was trying to scramble through the open back window.

"Look, Mommy," little Melissa said, pointing.

The old woman's screams and protests had attracted not only the workers but the occupants of several nearby houses. A large crowd was now gathering around Dooley's car. On the cross-street a hundred yards south, a passing police cruiser had slowed, hung a left, and was headed this way.

Good God. Dooley felt his stomach turn over.

Ms. Crowson, who knew the car belonged to Dooley, turned and—without taking her eyes off him—waved to the approaching cops. They wheeled their cruiser into her driveway and got out. By this time Rover, to the horror of its owner, had retrieved the brown carcass from Dooley's back seat (leaving a streak of mud and entrails along the side of the car) and was having a happy and noisy noontime snack. The two cops, one of them very young, studied all this from a distance, then turned to look at Dooley with their thumbs hooked casually in their gunbelts. Neither appeared particularly bright, but they were bright enough to connect the muddy man with the muddy car.

The crowd, realizing the excitement had now shifted to the Crowsons' front yard, trooped over to watch.

"Want to tell us what's going on?" the older cop asked him.

For perhaps the first time in his life, John Dooley was at a loss for words. After all, what could he say? It didn't much matter that he hadn't broken any laws—the truth would be just as damaging. A coverup was a coverup. And even a lie wouldn't help, now: Everyone had seen the dead rabbit. The fact was, a well-known City Councilman was exhibiting unstable behavior in public. Whatever he said, this little debacle could easily end his political career. He might just as well have climbed naked onto the roof of City Hall in an Easter bonnet during rush hour.

So he said nothing. He stood there in the hot sun, surrounded by several dozen citizens he had sworn to represent in the hallowed halls of municipal government, and said not a word. He was sure something would come to him in time; it always did. But right now his mind was as blank as the cops' faces.

Until he saw the toolkit in the hand of one of the power-company men.

He had seen a similar box in the hand of the other worker earlier, after Ms. Crowson answered the door. The rude worker who had pushed past them on the way out of the house.

Suddenly Dooley forgot all about his dilemma. His mind, though devious, had always been quick, and right now it was running at top speed. What he saw, in his mind's eye, was a series of images: (1) the square metal toolkit, (2) the muddy hole, (3) last night's news coverage of a local crime spree, and (4) Ms. Crowson telling him about how the cable company and the power company had been playing musical chairs up and down their street lately. And what he heard in his head, during this semi-trance, was the dull CLANG his shovel blade had made earlier, against something underneath the brown water.

Slowly he turned to look at the hole, then at the work crew, then at the house. Was it possible?

"What's the matter?" Ms. Crowson said. Even in her suspicious state, she had apparently noticed the change in Dooley's face.

"I need a moment in private," he told the two cops. Before they could respond, he turned his back to them and whispered a hurried request to Ms. Crowson. She listened, clearly wary, then frowned.

"Do *what?*" she said.

"Please. I'll explain everything then." To the cops he said, "Give us just a moment, gentlemen."

For the next few minutes, after Ms. Crowson and her daughter disappeared into the house, Dooley and the two policemen and his new audience stood and waited. In the pockets of his grimy trousers he crossed the fingers of both hands, and silently mumbled his first prayer in twenty years.

When Suzanne Crowson returned, she gave him a long and curious look. Then she handed him a notepad. On the top sheet were several words written in pencil.

Dooley looked at it and nodded with relief. Maybe he was right after all.

"Okay, buddy," the younger policeman said, "enough of this. We got a few questions—"

"So do I," Dooley said. "For these guys right here." He turned to face the two men in power-company uniforms. Their eyes went wide.

"Us? Whaddaya mean, us?"

"Where's the toolkit I saw you with, earlier?"

"You mean this?" One of them held up his toolbox.

"The other one. With all the scratches on it."

The two guys exchanged a worried glance. That was enough for Dooley.

He turned, picked up the shovel, and stepped into the hole. Within seconds he had unearthed the flat metal box he'd bumped into earlier. Wiping it off with his shirttail, he set it on the grass, looked up to make sure the policemen were watching, and pried open the lid. Inside the toolkit, in a clear watertight baggie, was a crystal dolphin, a pocketwatch, and a gold paperweight. He heard Ms. Crowson gasp.

"Are these yours?" he asked her.

She swallowed and met his gaze. "They're from my

husband's study."

"Which is where the electric switchbox is located," he said. "Right?"

She nodded, still stunned.

The power-company men, pale now, were both pointing at Dooley. "He did it," one of them blurted. "We saw him climbing out of the hole when we got here—"

"I wasn't the one who went inside," Dooley said. He turned to the gaping policemen and handed them the notepad. "I asked this lady to write down anything she might find missing from the room that contained the breaker box."

In Ms. Crowson's flowing script were the words PAPERWEIGHT and DOLPHIN FIGURINE.

"I didn't notice that the watch was gone too," Ms. Crowson added. "It was all there early this morning." She couldn't seem to take her eyes off Dooley's face.

Both cops examined the note, the stolen items, and the electric company workers for a long moment. "I don't get it," the younger cop said. "Why'd they bury it at all?"

Dooley turned to Ms. Crowson. "I was telling the truth about working with the utility company awhile back," he said to her. "I knew they had set up random searches of power-company vehicles, after that terrorist threat, when bombs were found in two of the trucks. The spot-checks are still going on."

"So what are you saying?" the cop asked.

"I'm saying they'd be afraid to transport stolen goods in their truck, even hidden in a toolbox. The searches are very thorough."

"But why bury it?"

"I think they were hiding it for the cable folks."

Both officers stared at him. "You mean like, cable TV?"

"According to this lady, a cable crew always comes around shortly after the electric company does repairs, to work in the same location. I figure they've been digging up the stolen goods." He turned to look at the two electricians. "Far as I know, there are no spot searches of cable vehicles. They could safely carry the loot away, meet these guys later, and divide the take."

"So the thefts were always by the power company's people?" the young officer asked.

"It would make sense. Electricians have easier access to the houses, because of the inside switchboxes. Nowadays most TV cable work is done outside."

A silence fell as everyone thought about that. Everyone, that is, except the repairmen. They seemed to be thinking about escape routes. As if reading their minds, the older cop pointed to them and said, "You two come with us. Charlie, call another unit and tell 'em to wait here for the cable guys." After a pause he added, "You come along too, Mr. Dooley. Follow us in your car."

"You recognize me?" Dooley asked, surprised.

"Honest John, right?" The cop studied him. "You look taller on TV." The little girl grinned at that, and the cop smiled back at her.

Dooley wiped his muddy hands on his pants and climbed out of the hole. Everyone was still looking at him, except the policemen and the handcuffed repairmen, who were being escorted to the squad car. A few people applauded, others came by to shake his hand. Strangely, he felt no pleasure over what had happened. One of the key points in his tried-and-true code was ALWAYS TAKE CREDIT WHETHER YOU'VE EARNED IT OR NOT. But this time, even though he did deserve it, he felt empty rather than pleased.

And he thought he knew why.

When the crowd finally dispersed, he hesitated, then turned to face Suzanne Crowson and her daughter.

"There's something I need to tell you," he said. "Both of you."

And he did. In a low, shaky voice he told them about running over Melissa's pet rabbit, finding it on the pavement, burying it in the yard, sneaking away, and then returning to dig it up again. The unflattering story of a spineless coward. And, incredibly, he lied not once.

When he was done, when the ugly truth was out, he looked at Melissa and said, "I'm sorry about your rabbit. I truly am."

"I am too," she said. "But he wasn't mine."

Dooley blinked. "What?"

"Harvey's white. And he's out back, I just fed him." She pointed a chubby finger at the driveway. "That one was wild— Daddy ran over it when he left for work. Mommy didn't think I saw it there, but I did."

"I was going to carry it off later, but I forgot," Ms. Crowson said, absently stroking her daughter's hair. "And as for the water in the hole, my husband knows about it, it's something to do with drainage. Not a leak."

Dooley chuckled and nodded. All that trouble, all that worry and risk and deceit, for nothing. Then again, maybe not.

"Well, that's good to hear," he said.

A silence passed. Ms. Crowson, her eyes searching his, asked, "Why did you tell me . . . us . . . Why'd you tell us this?"

He sighed. "I'm not sure." He grinned sadly at Melissa, and then—remembering the cop's request to follow them downtown—turned to leave.

"Mr. Dooley?"

He stopped.

"There's something I need to tell you, too," the woman said.

He waited, watching her thoughtful eyes, her stern expression.

"You've got my vote," she said.

BREAK TIME

Angela Potts was flushed and winded when she crested the small hill and saw the man standing on the pond bank. A handsome fellow in his early thirties, dressed in a work shirt and jeans, tossing pebbles into the still water. He looked up when he heard her, then relaxed and smiled.

"Good afternoon," he said.

"Same to you." She jerked a thumb over her shoulder. "That your car I saw, in the trees beside the road?"

"Yes, ma'am. I wouldn't have thought anybody would notice it there."

"I used to be a teacher. We have sharp eyes."

He seemed preoccupied, but his smile stayed in place. "Join me, if you want to. I'm just taking a break."

"Me, too. I was driving to a friend's house and saw your car sitting there." Angela worked her way down the rise and knelt by the water's edge. She was still breathing hard. "You must be from out of town."

"Birmingham," he said. "This your pond?"

"No, I just stopped because I'm nosy. The pond belongs

to the convent." She pointed at a slate roof above the distant treetops.

He looked in that direction, then said, "That's where I've been today, visiting." He lobbed another rock into the water.

"Really? I don't know many of the nuns—I'm Baptist, myself. You have friends there?"

"Sister Mary Catherine. I'm her brother-in-law."

Angela nodded. "It's good to keep in contact with your kinfolks."

"Better for me than for her, probably," he said, smiling.

A silence passed. The wind picked up a bit, rippling the water's surface. Somewhere nearby, a frog croaked.

"How'd you know about the pond?" she asked. "You can't see it from the road."

"When I drove by, I saw a little boy leaving with a cane pole and two fish on a stringer. I was in no hurry, so I stopped."

"Just as well. There's been some excitement in town today—a bank robbery. Some streets are blocked off."

"I thought I heard sirens," he said. He stretched, yawned, tilted his face up to the sun. After a moment he turned to look at her. "You live around here, then?"

"Yep. Taught school here, thirty years. I'm Angela Potts, by the way."

"Jack Smith," he said. "Pleased to meet you."

"Call me Angel. Most everybody does."

He chuckled. "Maybe I should've brought *my* fishing pole."

"Why's that?"

"I'm bound to be lucky, surrounded by angels and nuns."

She smiled and nodded toward the faraway convent. "I'm afraid all I have in common with those folks is that I'm not married."

"Me either," he said. "Never took the plunge."

"Well, don't get any ideas. I like living alone."

Grinning, they both fell silent. Overhead, the sun eased behind a cloud. A dragonfly flitted past.

Suddenly Angela stood up, fumbled in her pocket, and removed a cell phone. "Excuse me," she said to Smith.

"I didn't even hear it ring."

"It's set on VIBRATE," she said. But as she turned away and held the phone to her ear and said "Hello" as if to answer a call, she instead pressed a button for a preprogrammed number.

Seconds later a voice—unheard by Jack Smith—said, "Sheriff's office, can I help you?"

"Hi, Chunky. What's up?"

"Ms. Potts? What do you mean, what's up? *You* called *me.*"

"I'm doing fine, thanks," she said cheerfully.

She heard a deep sigh. It was a familiar sound, coming from Sheriff Jones. "I'm too busy for games today, Ms. Potts. In case you've forgotten, I'm working a robbery here, and—"

"So am I," she said. Jack Smith, she noticed, was watching her closely.

"You're what? I told you to go home and leave this to me."

"Well, it's a good thing you called. I have a favor to ask," she said.

He didn't sigh again, but Angela could picture him rolling his eyes. "Look, Ms. Potts, you've occasionally been a help in the past, I'll admit that. But it'll take more than an amateur to break this case—"

"I already did."

"What?"

"You heard me."

A long pause. "Are you saying . . . are you saying you know who robbed First National?"

"That's exactly what I'm saying," she said.

Dead silence on the phone line.

"Look, Chunky, when you finish mowing mine, Mrs. Wallace wants you to do her yard too. Do you have time?"

More silence. She glanced again at Smith. He was still watching, and certainly listening. They were standing only ten feet apart.

"I'd really appreciate it," she added.

She could hear the sheriff breathing into the phone. And thinking, hopefully.

"Ms. Potts—is someone . . . *with* you, right now?"

"That's correct."

"And you can't speak freely?"

"No," she said, "but if I don't make it home by then I can pay you tomorrow, for the mowing."

"And whoever it is"—she heard his voice grow tight—"is the *suspect*?"

"Yes, I'm pretty sure of that."

"Good God," he said. A short pause. "Where—can you tell me where you are?"

"At Harrell's Pond. I'm headed over to Millie Simpson's house for a sewing meeting in a little while. And be careful not to mow off my daisies in the back yard, Chunky. They're flowers, not weeds."

"Harrell's Pond," he said. "Got it. I'll be there in five minutes."

"And what about your friends? Are they helping you today?"

"You mean the state police? They just arrived."

"Good," she said.

"You're saying I should bring them too?"

"You're getting smarter all the time."

"Five minutes," he said again, and hung up.

"Okay. And there's an extra can of gas in the toolshed, if

you need it."

Angela put the phone away with a shake of her head. "Busy day," she murmured. "Who ever said retirement was carefree?"

Jack Smith nodded toward her pocket. "Chunky?"

"It's a nickname. I taught him in the fifth grade."

"An odd name, Chunky."

"He's an odd boy."

"And you still keep in touch," Smith said. "That's nice."

She grinned. "Better for him than for me."

Six minutes later the troops arrived, without sirens but with guns drawn and frowns in place. After Sheriff Jones had informed a surprised Jack Smith of his rights and Deputy Fred Prewitt clapped him in handcuffs, the sheriff informed Angela that she'd been correct to call him—the description of Smith perfectly matched information collected from eyewitnesses at the crime scene, and so did later descriptions of his car. The state guys had already sprung the trunk and found the stolen loot inside. Angela and the sheriff watched Prewitt lead the prisoner away.

"Guess he'll get to take a longer break than he thought," she said.

"What?"

"Nothing." She was gazing out over the pond, looking wistful, and when the sheriff started to turn and follow his deputy, what she said next stopped him. "Teddy Pilgrim told me you were sitting right there under those willows when he found you."

Sheriff Jones blinked. "Teddy Pilgrim? Teddy moved to Dallas twenty years ago."

She smiled at him. "One day after recess you didn't come back to class. Remember? I sent little Teddy over here to check, and sure enough, there you were, he said, dangling your feet in the water. He dragged you back to school with your pantslegs still rolled up."

The sheriff took off his hat and scratched his forehead. "How'd you know, Ms. Potts?"

"How'd I know you were here at the pond that day?"

"How'd you know Jack Smith was the robber?"

"I didn't," she said. "But I was suspicious."

"Why?"

"Well, for one thing, he fit the description I'd heard the bank manager give you, earlier. I didn't know then what his car was supposed to look like, though."

"You said 'for one thing.' What else?"

She took off her shoe and shook a pebble out of it. "He wasn't who he said he was."

"How so?"

"He lied about Sister Mary Catherine. Said he was her brother-in-law."

"Sister Mary Catherine?" The sheriff glanced up at the distant convent. "I don't know that name."

"Smith probably invented it, like his own. Anyhow, he told me he was her brother-in-law, and then told me he'd never married. So he would have to be the brother of her husband, right?"

He nodded.

"Funny thing about nuns," she said.

"They don't have husbands?"

"Bingo."

Neither of them spoke while the sheriff thought that over. Finally he said, "Well, I guess if he were smart, he wouldn't have to rob banks, would he?" He put his hat on again and studied her in the afternoon sun. A ghost of a smile crossed his face. "By the way—do you really need your yard mowed?"

"Why?"

"Well, now that we got the robber in custody . . ."

"Chunky Jones," she said, stunned. "What a kind offer. I'm proud of you."

"Least I can do." He hitched his belt higher and turned to head back to the car. "I'll need to get some work shoes first, though."

"You don't have your own work shoes?"

"Not for me," he said. "For the prisoner."

A LITTLE KNIGHT MUSIC

Sheriff Charles Jones was on the phone with the mayor when retired teacher Angela Potts barged into the office. He gave her an annoyed look, which she of course ignored. She'd been barging into his office—not to mention annoying him and ignoring his reactions—for more years than he liked to remember.

"Why's everyone standing around outside the town hall?" she asked, dropping into a chair across from his desk.

The sheriff hung up the telephone and rubbed his eyes. "They had a show there tonight. A rock concert."

"A what?" She'd been out of town for a week—a rare blessing, in the sheriff's view.

"A rock concert," he said. "Makes sense, I suppose—after all, Elvis grew up not far from here, right?"

"But what was the concert for?"

"Fundraiser for the new library."

"That's right," she said, "I forgot about that. Who was the band?"

"The mayor hired them—they call themselves The Southern Knights—from down around Munsen County."

She put both hands around her throat and stuck out her tongue. "Sorry I missed it."

"I heard they weren't bad."

"So you're a rock fan, are you?"

"Hip-hop," he said.

"Yeah, right." Then her amusement turned to a frown. "Wait a minute. If it's over, why's everybody still hanging around in the street?"

A historic moment, the sheriff thought: I actually know a piece of news before Angela Potts does.

"Carol Morgan," he said, "was kidnapped from the parking lot, after the show."

"Kidnapped!?"

"Carjacked, actually." He explained that Carol was released unharmed only minutes after her abduction, and then called the police on her cell phone. Deputy Prewitt, who was in the area anyway, soon spotted her new BMW, gave chase, and forced the car off the road south of town, but the suspect escaped on foot into a patch of woods. Carol's description of him was minimal: male, ski mask, long blond hair.

"How'd she see his hair if he was wearing a ski mask?" Angela asked.

"Because it was *really* long. Shoulder-length, she told me."

"Shoulder-length is pretty unfashionable, nowadays, for a guy."

"You think young men in this town are fashionable?" he said. "Or even know what it means?"

"I'm just saying you don't see that as often anymore."

The sheriff gave the matter some thought. "So you figure it might've been a wig? Or maybe a female?"

"Don't know. But I sure can't think of anyone around here, boys or men, with hair that long."

"Me neither."

"Either," she corrected. "When exactly did all this happen?"

"Two hours ago. After the performance."

Angela fell silent, which gave the sheriff time to think some more. He was painfully aware that they had not a single lead, so far. Prewitt was at the town hall now with the mayor, questioning bystanders, but had found no eyewitnesses to what had happened in the parking lot. And the fingerprints he'd lifted from the stolen car—

"Did Prewitt dust for prints yet?" Angela asked, reading the sheriff's mind. Both of them knew that Fred Prewitt, a former big-city cop, always kept a fingerprinting kit in his glove compartment. All Sheriff Jones kept in his glove compartment were gloves. And maybe a few stale doughnuts, in case of an emergency.

"He did that right away," the sheriff answered. "But the suspect wiped the car down, looks like. Nothing on the steering wheel, gearshift, or doorhandle. All we found were two prints on the buttons of the car radio. The idiot apparently needed some music while he drove."

"You send the prints in?"

He shook his head. "No need to. Both are blurred in the middle. I'd say from a burn maybe, or an abrasion, except that it's on two different fingers. Fred thinks they're calluses."

"Calluses?"

"That's what they look like."

"How do you know the prints are the carjacker's?" she asked.

"Because half the radio got wiped clean, before he had to run from the car. And I figure if he hadn't touched the radio—"

"He wouldn't have bothered to wipe it down at all," she said.

"Right."

Angela seemed to think that over for a moment. Finally she asked, "Where's Prewitt now?"

"I sent him back down to City Hall. He's interviewing folks there, and checking out a couple other leads."

"Like what?"

"Like the security cameras the mayor had installed last year," the sheriff said. "But I doubt there'll be anything we can use, unless one was aimed at the parking lot."

Angela lapsed into silence again, her brow furrowed. The sheriff glanced through the doorway at his other deputy, old-timer Earl Wood. Earl, who had been assigned to make some phone calls in hopes of locating a witness to the crime, was instead working on a crossword puzzle. Good grief.

Finally Angela spoke up: "What about the band?"

"They left not long after the show. What about them?"

"What do they play, these—who'd you say they were?— Summer Nights?"

"Southern Knights. They play hard rock, I'm told."

"I mean what instruments," she said.

"Beats me."

"Well, you said Fred's still down there where the concert was held. Have him ask the mayor."

With a weary sigh the sheriff phoned the town hall, summoned Deputy Prewitt, and relayed Angela's question. While they waited for a response, Earl Wood called out, from the other room, "Hi, Angel. Didn't see you come in."

"Hey Earl," she said. "Making any progress?"

"A little. What's a four-letter word for 'Hawaiian goose'?"

Sheriff Jones drew a long breath, let it out, then heard Prewitt come back on the line. While he listened, Angela turned to face him.

"Prewitt says they're a four-piece band," the sheriff

reported to her. "Drums, keyboard, two electric guitars."

"They have long hair?"

He hadn't thought of that. He passed the question along and waited a moment. When he heard the answer he just looked at her.

She grinned. "They do, don't they."

"All four," he said. "Shoulder-length."

Before he had time to ponder it further, she said, "Ask Fred to see if the mayor remembers the two guitar players. Ask him if one was left-handed."

"What? How would he know that?"

"Guitars are like golf clubs—they're built backward for lefties. Ask him."

The sheriff relayed the question into the phone, and after a pause he repeated Prewitt's answer from the mayor: One of the guitarists had indeed played left-handed.

"Do we have a name?" she asked.

Another wait, longer this time. Then: "The left-handed guitarist is named Neely, Prewitt says. Duane Neely. And he has blond hair."

Angela nodded, apparently deep in thought. "Remember when the state police were looking for all those chop shops for stolen vehicles, last year? Wasn't that south of here? Around Munsenville?"

"Yeah. Why?"

"You told me the band was from Munsen County," she said, looking pleased. "And you said Carol's car was going south when Prewitt stopped it."

The room was suddenly quiet. The sheriff could hear the clock ticking on the wall, the hum of the air conditioner, the distant whistle of the evening train. He nodded slowly.

"These musicians," she said. "They stay here last night?"

"Yep. Starlite Motel."

"So Ben Jonas has their license-plate number, on the check-in form."

"Supposed to."

She rose from her chair. "Chunky, my advice is, get their tag number from Ben, pass it along to the Highway Patrol, find the band's car, and bring 'em back. I believe Mr. Neely's your man."

"How come?"

She held up her hand, fingers splayed. "Professional guitarists always have calluses on their fingers, and they're always on the fingertips of the hand that presses the strings against the frets. For a left-handed player, that would be his right hand."

"And . . . ?"

"And—regardless of which hand was dominant—the driver's right hand would be the one he used to operate the car radio buttons."

The sheriff's eyes widened. That made sense.

"But wait a second," he said. "Prewitt said this guy got away on foot. I assume the band left in a car—or at least a vehicle of some kind."

"So? You think Carol Morgan's the only person who owns a cell phone? My guess is, Neely contacted the rest of his group and had them pick him up someplace, on the way out of town."

After a moment he nodded. "I think you're right."

"Of course I'm right."

"Earl?" the sheriff called, over his shoulder. "Put that damn puzzle down and call Ben Jonas. Tell him I need the license number of the band's vehicle, then connect me with the HP in Jackson." To Angela he said, "How the devil do you know all this, Ms. Potts?"

"What do you mean?"

"Finger calluses, frets, all that. You play the guitar?"

John M. Floyd

"All I play is the radio. But long ago, I used to date a musician."

He grinned. "Let me guess. Nero?"

"Elvis."

She turned and left, and he stared open-mouthed at the closed door for what seemed a long time before she came back and stuck her head into his office.

"Had you for a minute there," she said. "Didn't I."

GOOD SAMARITAN

County Sheriff Chunky Jones pushed through the door of his office, huffed down the steps to the street, popped the last of his breakfast doughnuts into his mouth, and squeezed his considerable bulk into his patrol car. He was inserting the key into the ignition when he heard a voice, from four feet away.

"What's the hurry?" it said.

The sheriff turned, his mouth full, to see his old schoolteacher Angela Potts looking through the open passenger window. Not a welcome sight, this early.

"Murglburfl," he said, spewing crumbs.

She squinted at him with open interest. "You know, I don't think I've ever seen anyone stuff an entire doughnut in his mouth before. Must be a rare talent."

He chewed and swallowed. "Police business, Ms. Potts. No time to talk now."

"I agree." Before he could stop her, she opened the door and plopped into the passenger seat. "Where are we going?"

Arguments with Angela Potts, the sheriff knew from long experience, were a waste of breath. He cranked the engine and pulled out of the lot. As they headed south he reluctantly handed her the notes he'd taken while on the phone to one of his deputies moments ago.

It was a strange case. Several rural houses had lost power during last night's thunderstorm, and one—Helen Noble's—had then been burglarized. Deputy Fred Prewitt, reporting from the scene, had told the sheriff he figured the thief was one of Ms. Noble's four neighbors, since the cluster of five homes was surrounded by dense woods and the only road out was blocked by an oak that had fallen during the high winds.

"So he's saying the stolen goods were too big to carry out on foot?"

The sheriff nodded. "TV, computer, some more electronic equipment." He pointed to the paper. "I also wrote down what Prewitt said about the suspects."

He watched her read his scrawled notes: Neighbor One— Nancy Dill (registered nurse); Two—Al and June Willis (security guard and freelance writer); Three—Carl Laszlo (computer pro- grammer); Four—James and Sue Rylie (owners, Rylie's Hard- ware). All were aged forty to sixty. Laszlo and Al Willis worked at the local bank, Dill at a nearby clinic. All except June Willis had left already for work, their tire tracks furrowing a muddy detour through the ditch to avoid the downed tree. It was a miracle no one had gotten stuck. Mrs. Willis, an early riser also, had assured Deputy Prewitt that the ditch had been free of tracks at dawn.

"So if she's telling the truth," Angela said, "the burglar either left within the past hour, or he's still around here some- where."

"Or hiding in the woods with his loot. Prewitt's gone to borrow Leonard Goodwyn's bloodhounds, just in case."

She stayed quiet a moment. "I agree with Prewitt, Chunky. I bet one of the neighbors did it, so he was able to drive out along with everybody else going to work."

"We'll see," the sheriff said. "When we get there, let me do all the talking."

More wasted breath, of course. As soon as they arrived, Angela immediately asked Helen Noble a dozen questions. Finally he interrupted: "Ms. Noble, how long have you known your neighbors?"

"For years, except the nurse and Mr. Laszlo. They've only been here several months."

"And did you hear anything, during the night?"

"Heavens no. Not above all the noise."

"The noise?" Angela asked.

"Our power went off last night, like I told the deputy," Ms. Noble said, "and that nice Mr. Laszlo loaned me his portable generator so I could use the electric fan in my bedroom."

"A generator?"

"We set it on my patio. It runs on gas, so you can't put it in the house. Something about carbon monoxide. But it still made a terrible racket, all night."

"If you had to leave it outside, how were you able to plug in your fan?" Angela said.

"I left the patio door open an inch or two, so I could run an extension cord inside."

Sheriff Jones was losing patience with all this talk of fans and generators. "You notice anything else missing?" he asked Ms. Noble. "Anything besides the electronic stuff?"

"You bet. My billfold's gone." Anger as well as sorrow passed across her face. "No credit cards inside, but I had some cash in there, and an ATM card."

The sheriff's cell phone rang. He excused himself and stepped out of the house to take the call. Moments later Angela followed him.

"That was Earl, at the office," he told her, when he'd

disconnected. Earl Wood was the sheriff's other deputy. "He says old Bud Zeigler just called in. Bud found some electronic equipment in a roadside ditch between here and town. TV, microwave, PC."

"Must be Helen Noble's," Angela said.

"But why dump it? Whoever it was had gotten away clean."

They stood there awhile, thinking. Finally Angela looked up and smiled.

"What is it?" he said.

"Call Earl back." She checked her watch. "Tell him to hustle over to the bank and watch their ATM. And tell Prewitt to do the same, at the other one."

"The other one? The town only has one bank."

"With two branches."

The sheriff frowned. "What'll I tell them to watch for?"

"Carl Laszlo. Ms. Noble can give them his description."

"Laszlo?!"

"Stealing the heavy stuff was just to throw us off, Chunky. What he wanted was her ATM card."

"But if that's true—aren't we already too late?"

"Not if I'm right," she said. "He'd have to make another stop first, before going to the ATM."

Fifteen minutes later, Deputy Wood called back with good news. Carl Laszlo had been caught leaving the Pine Street branch's ATM, with Helen Noble's card and a thick wad of brand new twenty-dollar bills clutched in his hand.

After accepting Ms. Noble's tearful thanks, the sheriff turned to Angela. She looked like the cat who'd just snacked on the canary.

"What clued you in to Laszlo?" he asked her. "If anything, he was the good samaritan in the group, loaning her the generator and all."

She smiled. "That was one of the clues."

"What?"

"Like Ms. Noble said, the generator had to be located outside, which meant a window or door had to be left open for the cord. That gave the burglar two advantages—one, he could stroll right in through an already open door, and two, the motor was so loud she'd never hear an intruder in the house."

The sheriff digested that as they walked back to the patrol car, then said, "But that doesn't necessarily point to Laszlo. Any of the neighbors could've been the thief."

She looked amused. "You better get your eyes checked, Chunky."

"Why?"

"Because it seems you can't read your own notes."

"What's that supposed to mean?"

"You have an ATM card, right? You know what a PIN number is?"

"Personal identification number," he said. "Why?"

"Well, an ATM card's useless without that secret number, because it's programmed so the cash-machine's computer can recognize it. And the only neighbor with access to Ms. Noble's PIN number would be Laszlo, because—"

"—he's a programmer at the bank."

"Exactly. All their occupations were listed right there on your sheet. Who else could it have been?"

The sheriff frowned. "But I remember you saying he'd have to make another stop, before going to the ATM . . ."

"So?"

"You were talking about his office, at the bank?"

"His office at the operations center," she said. "To get Ms. Noble's PIN."

"My point is, why'd he have to go get it? If all this was planned, why didn't he already have the number?"

"It wasn't planned. He couldn't have known, ahead of time, about the storm, or the power outage. When it happened, he just played things by ear."

The sheriff gazed into the distance a minute, adrift in his thoughts. "So he extemporized all this, on the spur of the moment."

"The word is 'improvised.'"

"That's what I said." He started the engine, eased the big cruiser into the ditch to get around the fallen tree, and aimed them toward town. "Want a doughnut?" he asked.

She smiled. "Solving crimes *is* hungry work," she said.

He turned left at the city limits. As they pulled into the new Krispy Kreme on Monroe Street, the sun came out, peeking through the gray bank of clouds to the east.

It was shaping up to be a good day.

DRY SPELL

Sheriff Charles Jones had just finished polishing his new motorcycle when Angela Potts appeared in his garage doorway. She stood there a moment, scowling like a warden doing a midnight bed-check, then pointed a finger.

"What on earth," she said, "is that?"

"What's it look like?" He opened his mouth wide, breathed on the mirror, and wiped it happily with his handkerchief. Even his bossy fifth-grade schoolteacher couldn't spoil his mood, today.

"Have you lost your mind?"

"What I've lost," he said, grinning, "is my carefree youth. Now, for a modest monthly payment, I've got it back. Want to hear the motor?"

Angela was still staring. "I just hope it doesn't have a weight limit," she said.

"Why? You planning to take it for a spin?"

She gave him a dark look. "What I'm planning, since you asked, is to go talk with Willie Ward."

"Who?"

"Pastor Zeller's new assistant. He was robbed today, near the church."

The sheriff's good mood vanished. "Robbed?"

"Your deputy's there now. He's been trying to reach you, but he said your cell phone's not on." She turned to leave. "You coming, or not?"

He groaned. "It's my day off."

"Keeping the peace," she informed him, "is a fulltime job."

***

They parked in the church lot under a cloudless November sky, Angela in her fifteen-year-old Buick and the sheriff on his new bike. "You don't have a helmet?" she asked him, as they hiked together down the hill past the church and parsonage.

"They cost two hundred dollars. I heard I can get one on the Internet for ten."

She snorted.

"You disapprove?"

"That's up to you," she said. "If you have a ten-dollar head, buy a ten-dollar helmet." She pointed through the trees. "There they are."

Deputy Fred Prewitt and Willie Ward were sitting on a creekbank below the hill, in an oak grove thick with fallen leaves. The sheriff noticed a fresh grave in the nearby church cemetery—old man Larson's, probably. The whole scene was dry as sandpaper; it hadn't rained here in weeks.

William Ward, a young theology student who lived with Pastor Bob Zeller at the Lutheran parsonage, had an egg-sized purple bruise on his forehead. He told them the robbery had happened while on his way to town with the money.

"What money?" the sheriff asked him.

"The proceeds of the church festival yesterday—seven hundred dollars. Since the pastor's away today he told me to take it to the bank for him." Ward was almost in tears.

"And?"

"And I stopped to sit here awhile, like always."

"With the money?"

Ward's face reddened. "It was stupid, I know."

"What happened, exactly?"

"Like I told your deputy, somebody slipped up on me from behind, and hit me." He gingerly touched his forehead and winced. "When I woke up, the cashbox was gone."

"Cashbox?"

"This one was big and metal, with compartments. Pastor Bob borrowed one from the bank, to collect the money in last night."

"Where were you sitting, exactly?" Angela asked.

"Right here, under the trees. Looking at the creek. Whoever it was, he grabbed my hair, jerked my head back, and slugged me."

"Probably the Ellis brothers," Deputy Prewitt said to the sheriff.

"We'll check it out."

Further questioning revealed nothing useful. As everyone rose to leave, Willie Ward asked: "Who owns the motorcycle?"

All of them looked at him.

"I heard a motorcycle up near the church just now," he explained.

"That was me," the sheriff said. "You got good ears." The parking lot was almost a quarter mile away.

"Wish I had good sense," the boy said, with a sad smile.

Angela suggested he go over to the hospital to have them take a look at his forehead, but he shrugged it off. They watched him trudge up the slope to the church.

After a quick discussion Prewitt left to interview the neighbors, and Angela and Sheriff Jones followed Ward up the hill toward the parking lot. At one point, crunching through the leaves with his head down, the sheriff looked up and ducked just in time to avoid a huge low-hanging oak branch.

When he did, Angela noticed something shiny on the ground beside him. A tiny pocketknife, with the initials W.W. on the handle.

For a full two minutes she stood there, studying the knife in her hand, the trees overhead, the leaves, the creek, the cemetery. The sheriff knew she was thinking, and from long experience he knew to keep quiet.

Finally she turned to look at him. A big grin lit up her face.

"Christmas," she said, "just came early."

***

Within half an hour, under Angela's direction, the sheriff had located and dug up the cashbox, with the money from the church festival inside and intact.

Twenty minutes later Willie Ward, when confronted, made a full confession.

The key to the mystery, she told the sheriff as they watched Prewitt lead the boy away in handcuffs, was the dry spell they'd been having. If Ward had stolen the cashbox he would've had to hide it fast, somewhere outside the parsonage. And the best place, since the ground was hard as a politician's head, was in the dirt already piled on the fresh grave. Besides, nobody would think to look for it there, and the cemetery couldn't be seen from the road.

"But why'd he have to hide it fast?" the sheriff asked.

"Because it wasn't planned. I think what happened was, on his way to town Ward bashed his head on that same limb you almost ran into—"

"And lost his knife from his pocket in the process."

"Right," she said. "And when he felt the knot on his head and thought about all that money he was carrying, the idea came to him. Why not? The physical result of an assault would be the only thing hard to fake, and now that he had the injury . . . you get the picture."

"I still don't see why he couldn't have gone back and hidden it in the parsonage."

She sighed. "Because somebody might see him, going up the hill with it. It was natural to carry the cashbox from here to town—but not the other way around. Remember, the box belonged to the bank, not the church."

The sheriff furrowed his brow. "So he hustles down there to the cemetery, which is out of sight, buries the cashbox with the money inside, and reports a robbery—"

"And you jump on your new toy, reclaim your youth, and solve the case." Angela looked at her watch. "Gotta run, Chunky. Sewing circle meets at three."

"Not so fast, Ms. Potts. You always do this to me."

"What?"

"Try to leave without explaining," he said. "The pocketknife on the ground under the limb . . . I mean, that's logical thinking, but not enough to accuse somebody of a felony. Even the money we dug up could've been buried there by attackers, instead of by Ward." He paused, watching her. "What tipped you off?"

She scratched her chin and took on the schoolteacher voice he remembered so well. "Two things. One was the injury itself. Why would someone who attacked him from behind pull his head back and whack him on the forehead? The other thing was where Ward said he was sitting when the assault took place. Think about it—since his hearing was so good and the grove was thick with bone-dry leaves, there's no way anyone could've sneaked up on him from behind."

The sheriff mulled that over, then nodded. "I should have caught that myself," he said.

John M. Floyd

She had already turned to continue up the hill. "You might have—if you were good at listening."

"And you are?"

"Snooping," she informed him, "is a fulltime job."

NAME GAMES

Sheriff Chunky Jones arrived at the bank at the same time as retired schoolteacher Angela Potts. The sheriff was there because he'd been notified of a robbery, minutes ago; Angela was there because (in Sheriff Jones's opinion, at least) she possessed some type of mystical, supernatural radar that sensed trouble of any kind.

As usual, he asked her politely not to butt in, and as usual she treated him as if he were a mosquito buzzing around her head. She even steered branch manager Marva Cunningham into one of the empty offices and started asking her questions. Finally he gave up, took out a notepad, and joined in.

The robber, Marva told them, was a customer of the bank. He had asked for access to the safe deposit box area—a proper request, since he had indeed rented a box two weeks ago, and had his key with him. She had then fetched her keys and accompanied him.

"You always accompany the customers there?" the sheriff asked.

"It's required. I have to insert my key along with theirs in order to open their box. Then I leave."

"And what happened this time?"

Marva swallowed hard. "He pulled a gun, grabbed my keyring right out of my hand, and opened someone else's box instead."

"Whose?" Angela asked.

"Ms. Benton's."

"Bessie Benton?" Bessie was known to be one of the richest ladies in town.

"He cleaned it out," Marva said, her voice shaking.

The sheriff frowned. "I thought you said it took two keys to open any box."

"It does. He had Ms. Benton's key."

Angela nodded. "That makes sense, Chunky. Bessie had her purse snatched last week, remember? He must've planned this whole thing."

"So whoever did it, he's local," the sheriff said.

"That's my guess."

He turned to Marva. "You say you have the robber's name?"

"Right here." She looked at her computer monitor. "Ord E. Porter."

"Ord? Like in Fort Ord?"

"O-R-D." Marva swiveled the monitor so they could see the screen from their seats. According to the information shown there, Porter was single, fifty-two, and employed at Ron Dalden, Inc., in Tupelo. Supposedly.

The sheriff thought a moment, then glanced at a security camera overhead. "Does that thing work?"

They all watched the tape together. As things turned out, it was no help. The guy on the video could have been anyone. Average build, beard, thick glasses.

"Anybody see him leave?" Angela asked Marva.

"One of the tellers did. He was driving a white Camry."

"Did she get a tag number?"

"Afraid not," Marva said.

After several more minutes of fruitless questioning, the sheriff thanked her, left the bank, and was unlocking his cruiser when he realized Angela had followed him out and was standing beside his passenger door.

"What are you gawking at?" she said. "I need a ride home."

"How'd you get here, earlier?"

"I walked. I was next door when I heard about the robbery."

"Well, you can walk home again," he said. "This is police work."

She tucked her purse under her arm as if ready to sprint downfield. "Don't you take that tone with me, Chunky Jones. I realize you didn't learn much in school, but I thought I at least taught you some manners."

He sighed and rubbed his eyes. He could feel an Angela Potts headache coming on. "Just get in," he said.

Halfway down the street she said, out of the blue: "He had to come up with a name, in order to rent the box. Right?"

"Right. Look, Ms. Potts, no offense, but I can handle this without your—"

"So the name's phony for sure, and probably the other info too . . ."

"Probably so," he said. "And speaking of names, I've asked you a hundred times, don't call me Chunky in front of other people, especially somebody like Marva Cunningham. Okay?"

Angela was staring straight at the windshield, deep in thought.

"I mean, I've been Charles ever since grade school. In fact I've been Charles all my—"

"Stop here," she blurted.

The sheriff pulled over to the curb in front of a small brick home.

"What's going on?" he said. "This isn't your house."

"Really? And they say you're not good at detective work." Angela was studying the residence, her eyes narrowed. "This is Ruth McKinley's place."

"I know whose house it is. What are we doing here?"

"She's Ned Ladnor's aunt."

"Ladnor? You mean Pete Ladnor? The newspaper guy, in Memphis?"

"His real name's Ned," Angela said. "After Ruth's brother."

The sheriff nodded. "I remember him. He used to write crossword puzzles for the paper there, didn't he?"

"All kinds of puzzles—mostly nostalgic stuff. Called himself Retro Pedro."

"Pedro?"

"It's Spanish for Peter," she said patiently. "Pete."

"I knew that," he lied.

She kept on watching the house.

"Don't tell me," he said. "You think Pete—Ned—can help us solve this case."

"Well, cases are puzzles, aren't they?"

The sheriff snorted. "I met Ladnor once. He's too cocky, if you ask me. One of those guys who thinks he's smarter than everybody else."

She didn't appear to have heard a word he'd said. "Bear with me, Chunky. Go to the door there, and ask for him."

"Ask for Ladnor?" He did a palms-up. "What makes you think he's here? Or even in town?" Ruth McKinley's Ford, parked in the gravel driveway, was the only car in sight.

"Just humor me, okay?"

With a weary sigh the sheriff got out and slogged through the muddy grass to the front of the home. As he stepped up onto the porch he saw, from the corner of his eye, Angela sneaking around the house toward the back yard. He didn't even bother wondering what the hell she was up to. He'd given up trying to figure that woman out a long time ago.

No one answered his knock, but he could hear noises inside. A minute passed. Then two minutes.

Still on the front porch, he turned to see Angela chugging toward him from around the corner of the house. He'd never seen her move so fast.

"Your bank robber's headed for the garage," she hissed, pointing. "Get back there quick, and arrest him."

"You mean Ladnor?"

"Yes, I mean Ladnor. Retro Pedro himself." She was taking huge breaths, wheezing like a draft horse. "He's probably sitting in his car by now, trying to start it. A white Camry, Tennessee plates."

"*Trying* to start it?"

She showed him a crumpled brown bag from her purse. "You owe me a sack lunch—I stuffed two sandwiches up his tailpipe while he was still in the house. Now hurry up, before he gets out of the car and runs off."

A short while later Ned Ladnor and his aunt Ruth sat scowling and handcuffed in the backseat of the sheriff's cruiser. Most of Bessie Benton's valuables had been found in Ladnor's coat pockets.

Sheriff Jones radioed in and turned to Angela. She was standing on the sidewalk eating an apple that had apparently not been donated to the tailpipe cause. "How in the world," he said to her, "did you know it was him?"

"I didn't know, for sure. I wanted to see if he would run out the back when he realized you were at the front door. Then I saw his Camry in the garage."

"But you were pretty sure, before that."

"Well," she said, chewing, "I'll admit that Ruth's car is usually in the garage, not sitting out front like it is now."

"No, even before that. Before we ever arrived here. Ladnor was in disguise on the tape—it looked nothing like him—and still you suspected him. Why?"

She smiled. "Because of his history with word games. That, and his cocky attitude."

"What do you mean?"

"Think about it. What's Ord E. Porter, spelled backward?"

"Spelled backward?" He pondered that a moment, remembering the letters on the screen—then gasped. "Retro Pedro," he whispered.

"And there's probably no such company as Ron Dalden, Inc., in Tupelo or anywhere else. Ron Dalden, backward, is—guess what." She pointed her chin toward the man sitting in the squad car. "Ned Ladnor."

The sheriff was stunned. After a moment he said, "So he wasn't that smart after all."

"Oh, he's smart," she said. She took another bite of her apple. "But he's not the only one who's good at puzzles."

BATTERIES NOT INCLUDED

The only thing predictable about retired schoolteacher Angela Potts was that she was unpredictable. Sheriff Chunky Jones, one of her long-ago and long-suffering students, knew that well. Even so, he couldn't help wondering why she was running down the middle of Main Street dressed in high heels and Sunday clothes.

He pulled his patrol car alongside her and shouted, through the open passenger window, "You taken up jogging, Ms. Potts?"

She turned, puffing and sweating, and gave him a dark look. Without slowing down, she tossed her purse inside, wrenched the door open, and dropped into the passenger seat. "Flora Williams had her car stolen," she said. "Just over the hill, there."

"How do you know?"

"Because she just called me on her cell phone, that's how. I was walking home from church. Get a move on—if we top this hill in time we might catch a glimpse of the car."

"So you're chasing it?"

"I am now. I was on my way to try to console Flora—understandably, she's in a foul mood." Angela straightened her hat. "Hasn't your office contacted you? I told her to call it in."

"I'm surprised you didn't report it yourself," he said.

"Couldn't. My battery died."

"Your battery?"

"In my cell phone, while I was talking to Flora. Hurry it up, will you please?"

As if on cue, the cruiser's radio crackled. A metallic voice said, "Carjacking at Jefferson and Main, Sheriff. Black '99 Honda Accord." The sheriff acknowledged the call, started to request backup, and then realized both his deputies were out of pocket, redirecting traffic to avoid areas damaged from a freak thunderstorm early this morning.

"I'm on my way," he said into the mike.

Up ahead, they spotted Flora Williams standing at the curb, clearly fuming, fists on her hips and staring west. Following her gaze, Angela sat up and pointed. "There's her car, Chunky! Top of the next hill."

The sheriff saw it too—Flora's black Accord, blowing through a stop sign and then swinging left onto Oakmont, half a mile away. "He's headed for the interstate. We'll never catch him."

"Yes we will," Angela said. "Oakmont's blocked, a mile south. Trees and power lines down, from the storm."

"How do you know that?"

"Mary McCall told me, in church. Her son lives there. Main thing is, our carjacker doesn't know it yet—and Oakmont has no cross streets." She grinned. "We've got that sucker trapped."

"But—what about Flora?"

"What about her?" Angela said. She scooted down in the seat as they blasted past Flora Williams, so her friend wouldn't see her in the patrol car.

"Don't we need to ask her her tag number?"

"Are you kidding? Flora can't remember her birthday, half the time. Just follow the car!"

It seemed to take a long time to reach the point where they'd seen the Honda turn left. And as they cruised Oakmont—a quiet, rain-puddled street—they saw no sign of the stolen Accord.

"You think he spotted us, awhile ago?" Angela asked.

"He might have. I think I saw him slow down a tad, just before he made the turn."

Angela hit the dashboard with her fist. "He's here some-place," she said. "He has to be."

But they couldn't find him. Part of the problem was that Hondas were so commonplace. The sheriff and Angela spotted no fewer than three black Accords at intervals down the street: one in a residential driveway; another with its hood up and sprouting jumper cables, parked nose-to-nose with an old Volkswagen Beetle at the curb; and a third angled into a spot beside a ware-house, its open trunk full of boxes. All three cars seemed unlikely candidates. The first looked too new and too muddy, the second apparently had a dead battery (nothing unusual in this part of town), and even though the third one looked suspicious, parked in front of a closed business on Sunday, it couldn't—if it was Flora's—have been loaded with so much cargo in such a short time. Compounding the situation was the fact that Sally at the sheriff's office couldn't look up Flora's license plate number for them. The computers had been down all morning, since the storm.

"So where'd he go?" Angela said, squinting. They'd almost reached the roadblock.

Suddenly the sheriff had an idea. "Hold on, Ms. Potts—I know where he is."

The cruiser did a screeching three-point turn and roared back up the street. When they reached the car with the jumper cables, it had been disconnected and was backing away from the little VW. With uncharacteristic steel-jawed determination, the sheriff blocked the Honda's escape, hopped out of the patrol car, drew his pistol, and made the arrest. Meanwhile, Angela checked the stolen Honda's passenger seat. Sure enough, Flora Williams's sewing basket and Bible lay right there in plain view.

"That was good thinking, Chunky," Angela said, afterward. She still looked a little flushed and out of breath. "How'd you know the thief was faking a battery-boost to throw us off?"

"I didn't, at first. Then it hit me."

"What hit you?"

"He was trying so hard to fool us, he parked in front of the wrong kind of vehicle."

"The wrong kind?"

"Older Volkswagens' engines—and batteries—are located in the back, not the front," he said, pointing. "Jump-starting couldn't be done with those two cars positioned nose-to-nose."

Angela's mouth dropped open. For once, he had figured something out before she did. He decided to enjoy the moment, since it might never happen again.

She gave him a look that was both amused and—he thought—proud. "I remember, from school, that you didn't learn much about math and science," she said. "I guess you learned more about cars."

"All guys learn about cars."

She looked north toward Main Street. Deputy Prewitt's cruiser, and the prisoner in its back seat, were already out of sight.

"Not all guys," she said.

DIAMOND JIM

"This is exciting," Angela said. "My first stakeout."

County Sheriff Charles Jones turned and gave her a hard look. He and Angela Potts were sitting in his patrol car, across the dark street from a Grandma's Chicken restaurant.

"It's called surveillance," he said. "And you wouldn't be here at all if I had remembered to lock my passenger door."

She grinned. "Scared you, didn't I?"

He shifted in his seat. She *had* scared him, appearing out of the black night a moment ago. He was reminded of the time she caught him pulling Suzie Parker's hair in the fifth grade.

"I was concentrating on the suspect," he said.

"Of course you were."

The suspect, in this instance, was one Jim Nagle, a skinny guy seated at a window table in the fast-food joint forty yards away. He'd been there every Friday night for a month, according to the manager. The same four Friday nights that four nearby homes (nearby enough that their backyards could be seen if not for the wooded field between here and there) had been relieved of their gold and diamond jewelry.

And the sheriff had a theory. He thought Jim Nagle was here for a reason. He thought Nagle knew which families lived on the burglarized street, and if and when he saw them here in Grandma's Chicken, he left and robbed their houses while they were out. The theory had flaws, of course—one being that neither Nagle nor his car had ever been seen in that neighborhood. The other was that the manager said he was pretty sure Nagle always stayed until closing time. And if he were sitting here on his butt he couldn't very well be burglarizing houses a half mile away.

But Jim Nagle—an ex-con—remained a suspect, at least in Sheriff Jones's mind. That's why the sheriff was here now, parked in the dark with his former schoolteacher and watching Nagle polish off his third milkshake of the evening. In fact, the word "dark"—also known as "energy-conscious," Angela said—described most of their surroundings, due to the rising cost of electric power. Almost everybody around here was turning off more lights recently.

"When do we make our move?" she asked him.

"I, Ms. Potts. Not we. I'll move, if that's required."

"What if your move requires shooting something?"

"It won't."

"Good," she said. "I've heard about your marksmanship."

He turned to face her. "What does that mean?"

"Come on, Chunky. Earl Wood doesn't walk with a limp because of his arthritis. He's missing a toe."

He felt his cheeks heat up. "That was an accident. I was cleaning my gun."

Angela looked at the restaurant again, and frowned. The sheriff saw her, and looked too.

Jim Nagle was gone.

"Where'd he go?" the sheriff blurted.

"I don't know," she said. "His car's still there."

Sheriff Jones threw open his door, stopped only long

enough to point a finger at Angela and say "Stay!" and strode across the street to the restaurant. He verified that Nagle's car was empty, then pushed through the front door of Grandma's Chicken and looked around. No Nagle. The sheriff hurried down the back hall to the restrooms. The ladies' room was open and dark; the men's was locked. So that's where he was. Reassured, the sheriff went back outside.

As an afterthought he checked the rear of the building. It was pitch black. His flashlight revealed three garbage cans, an A/C unit, and the two restroom windows. He skirted the building, huffed his way back to his car, and got in.

Angela wasn't there.

Before he had time to savor his good fortune she reappeared, marching toward him from Grandma's Chicken. "Where have you been?" he asked her, when she'd squeezed herself back into the passenger seat.

"Checking the scene. I circled the building, right behind you."

"It was a false alarm," he said. "Nagle's in the john."

"I figured that. He's guilty, by the way."

"Guilty of what?"

"You were right—he's your jewel thief."

He studied her a moment. "You have any proof?"

"We will," she said, "if we wait here till he comes out. I want to see what he does when he goes to his car."

"I imagine he'll drive off."

"No he won't. I hid his keys."

The sheriff sat up straight. "You what?"

"He left them in the ignition. Bad habit."

"Where'd you put them?"

"Under his floormat," she said. "Calm down."

"But why?"

"Consider this: Nagle comes outside, finds his car keys

are missing, and sees your police cruiser sitting here. What would he do next, if he's innocent?"

"Ask me for assistance?"

"That's what I'd do. That'd be normal, wouldn't it? But he won't."

"Because he's guilty?"

"And," she said, "he'll be carrying stolen property."

"What? You think he'd still have last week's loot on him?"

"Not *last* week's, no."

"What do you mean by that?"

"Just have him empty his pockets. Trust me."

Finally the sheriff agreed. Ten minutes later Nagle appeared again at his window seat and an hour after that he swaggered outside to his vehicle. He found his keys gone, saw the cop car sitting nearby, and—as Angela had predicted—ducked back inside the restaurant. He was standing at the pay phone when the sheriff walked up and asked him to turn out his pockets. Nagle bolted, but was tackled by the burly manager and was now sitting sullen and handcuffed in the patrol car, awaiting his fate. A diamond necklace, plus a flashlight and lock-picking instruments, had been discovered in his pockets.

"Okay, Ms. Potts," the sheriff said, afterward. "Explain."

"Explain what?"

"You know what. How'd you figure he'd be carrying stolen goods?"

She shrugged. "Simple. He climbed out the restroom window, ran across the field to the house he'd targeted, robbed it, and came back."

"While we were here? Tonight?"

"The other nights too, probably—I saw dried mud in his car," she said. "But right now he has fresh mud on his shoes."

"But ... you knew this before you saw his shoes, didn't you."

"I sure did." She smiled. "You should have too."

"What?"

"Remember when you went around to the back of the building? It was pitch dark back there—I know because I wasn't far behind you." She put her purse on the floorboards and smoothed her skirt. "If Nagle were still in the men's room there would have been at least some light coming from the window— but there wasn't. He had cut the light off before climbing out."

"Why would he do that?"

She shrugged. "Probably to reduce the risk of being seen, going in or out."

That was logical, the sheriff realized. "So by turning the light *off*—"

"He made clear," she said, with a magicianlike flourish of her hand, "the solution."

He shook his head. "Unbelievable."

"Not really. In fact, in a way, it's commendable."

"Commendable?"

She gave him a sly look. "At least energy-conscious."

John M. Floyd

OLD SCHOOL

Retired teacher Angela Potts gazed with satisfaction at the milling crowd in the high-school gymnasium. Speeches had been made, videos shown, door prizes awarded. Now almost everyone was dancing. Over the south goal a huge banner said WELCOME HOME, CLASS OF 1982.

Angela strolled over to the dessert table. One of the graduates, Sheriff Chunky Jones, stood beside it, his pot belly straining the buttons of a twenty-year-old sportcoat. "Guarding the cakes, are we?" she said.

He shrugged and licked a speck of icing from the corner of his mouth. "I ain't much of a dancer."

"I'm *not* much of a dancer," she corrected.

He nodded sadly. "Me neither."

She sighed and was about to reply when she saw Class President Mary Lindstrom plowing toward them through the crowd.

"Come quick, Sheriff," Mary said, her face flushed.

Angela and the sheriff hurried with her to the snack bar, where Mary pointed a trembling finger: The old safe underneath the counter stood open and empty. All around the room, drawers had been pulled out, cabinet doors left ajar.

Mary confessed, near tears, that she had put the cash from the registration table in the safe only fifteen minutes ago. Someone must've seen her walk in with it. When the sheriff asked how much had been stolen, she bawled like a baby. She wasn't sure, she blubbered—all the reunion attendees had made donations, usually around ten dollars each, but some had given more. The take was certainly several hundred.

"And you didn't lock it up?" he asked.

"It has no lock," Mary wailed, which was true. In the years before the school closed, the snack-bar concession money had always been kept right there in that safe under the counter, open and ready during school hours so Coach Smithfield could make change for students buying Cokes and candy bars. Everyone knew that—and no one had ever bothered it.

"These days, a safe without a lock ain't a safe, Mary," the sheriff grumbled.

Mary Lindstrom bawled louder.

"Actually," Angela said, "we got a break."

"What?" Sheriff Jones asked.

She nodded toward the open cabinets and drawers. "Whoever stole this money had to search for it first. Anyone who went to school here would've remembered where the cash was kept, right off."

"So you're saying—"

"I'm saying the thief's probably not one of the graduates."

He thought that over. "Maybe. Unless somebody's trying to throw us off."

"No offense," Angela said, "but the Class of '82 wasn't all that smart." She turned to Mary, who was still sniffling. "Can you get us a list of tonight's attendees?"

They waited in the kitchen, away from the rest of the

group, while Mary fetched the list from the registration table. After studying all the information, Angela and the sheriff came up with twelve possible suspects: all the spouses and dates who'd grown up someplace else.

"How about tonight's cleaning crew?" he asked.

"You're looking at tonight's cleaning crew," Angela said, indicating herself and Mary.

"So what now?" He grimaced as if about to pass a kidney stone. "I can't arrest a dozen people just because they're not from here."

"Come with me," Angela said. She stomped across the dance floor with the sheriff, ignoring the curious gaze of the crowd and looking hard at the hand-lettered nametags of some of the strangers:

WILMA O'NEIL—BEAUTICIAN
JAN BAIRD—ATTORNEY
JORDAN PERRY—RESTAURANTEUR
SUE LOGAN—FLORIST
EDWARD COOPER—PARK RANGER

Angela had met several of them, tonight: Wilma had married good-for-nothing Butch O'Neil, Jordan Perry had told her he was an English professor before opening his restaurant, Ed Cooper worked somewhere out West. Interesting folks—but all she could think about now was who could've committed the crime.

They pushed through the front doors of the gymnasium. Another retired schoolteacher, outside on a smoke break, verified that no cars had left the lot in the past fifteen minutes, which was good news. After asking the teacher to stand watch, Angela said, "Chunky, get on the P.A. system and tell everyone you're going to search the cars."

"What?" the sheriff said. "I can't do that without a warrant."

"I didn't say do it; I said tell 'em you're going to. Then we'll write down the names of those who object."

"And?"

"And compare them to the list of the spouses and guests who didn't go to school here."

Sheriff Jones frowned. "That's a pretty lame plan, Ms. Potts. You been watching *Matlock* reruns again?"

"You have a better idea?" she asked. They both knew the answer to that. Chunky Jones was not an idea man. His talents leaned toward things like pie-eating contests and afternoon siestas.

The announcement took only a minute—and sure enough, there were several strong objections from the attendees. When all the complainants were noted, three of the names appeared on both lists.

"So you think one of these three is guilty?" Sheriff Jones asked her. At his request, both exits had been sealed.

"Well, right now it's the only lead we—"

And then Angela stopped, staring down at Chunky's nametag: CHARLES JONES—COUNTY SHERIFF. It was printed in such a sloppy hand she could hardly read it.

"Who lettered your nametag?" she asked.

"I did. Didn't you do yours?"

"Yes, but I thought it was because we came early. Are you saying everyone wrote his own information?"

"That's what Mary told me. Why?"

She smiled slowly. "Because I think I know, now, who stole the money."

"What!?"

"You know Jordan Perry? Natalie Poole's date?"

"Well, I know his name appears on both lists."

"Follow me," Angela said. "I'll introduce you."

"Wait a minute, here. You're saying Perry's the thief?"

John M. Floyd

"That's what I'm saying."

He frowned. "Based on what?"

"The classes I taught in spelling, that's what."

"And that means . . . ?"

"It means he lied to us. If he really owned a restaurant—especially if he'd once been an English professor—he wouldn't have written *restauranteur* on his nametag. The correct word is *restaurateur*."

He gaped at her. "I didn't know that."

"Well, then, consider yourself lucky."

"That I've learned a new word—or that we've identified a thief?"

She grinned. "That you have me around," she said.

EYES IN THE SKY

"A stuntman?" Nancy asked.

Fred Penski stayed focused on his laptop. The little computer was white, like the desk and the chair where he was sitting. In fact everything in Fred's office was white, including the walls and the door and the ceiling and the clothes he and Nancy Ross were wearing. The only color in the room was on the computer screen, which showed two men talking on an airport runway at the base of a snowy mountain. Behind them, what looked like a small commercial airliner sat waiting on the tarmac.

"I can't believe it," Nancy said. "Your first assignment is a stuntman." She pulled up a chair, adjusting her wings to keep from sitting on them.

"That's him, on the left," Fred said. "William Sparks."

She squinted at the laptop's screen through her white-framed glasses. "He looks worried."

"I agree. I just tuned in, but I think the guy on the right's trying to talk him into doing something with that airplane." Fred tweaked the volume a little.

"How long are you responsible for him?"

John M. Floyd

"Two weeks," Fred said. "Or until Wimberley gets back."

"Where's Wimberley?"

"Some kind of election, in Florida. After the butterfly ballot thing a few years ago, the Boss sent him to keep watch."

Nancy leaned forward and pushed her glasses higher on her nose. "What's with the third guy, and the camera?" she said, pointing. "Wait, don't tell me—they're about to film a stunt."

"Looks like it. That's what bothers me."

"I think it's bothering Mr. Sparks, too." She glanced down long enough to unwrap a piece of white chocolate she'd taken from a jar on Fred's desk. "You know, two weeks seems like a long time to monitor a high-risk subject. And you're just a trainee."

Fred shrugged, making his white wings rise and fall as he watched the young man on the screen. "Maybe he'll decide to quit and become an accountant or something."

"I don't think so." She studied the subject's face again. "He doesn't look the type."

"Too adventurous?"

"Too dumb," she said, chewing.

Fred nodded. "You may be right."

***

At that moment, standing on the flight line of an airport in southeast Alaska, Billy Sparks stopped talking and frowned.

"What is it?" the man beside him asked.

"I don't know," Billy said, puzzled. "For a second there, it occurred to me that maybe I should just quit all this and go back to school."

"Back to school? For what?"

"I was thinking accounting. You know, do people's tax returns."

"Tax returns."

"Just a thought," Billy said.

Jack Jenson rolled his eyes and blew out a sigh. He was always eyerolling and sighing, as if the weight of the universe were balanced on his skinny shoulders. The only times Billy had ever seen Jack look really happy was when he was sprawled in his director's chair with his bullhorn on the studio lot back home. And this was a long way from sunny L.A., in more ways than one.

"Look, Billy, I don't know what you been smoking," Jenson said, "but it's almost time. Try to concentrate, okay?" He glanced at the plane on the runway. Its nose was aimed away from them, toward a blue lake and a wall of white mountains just beyond. "You got your whip?"

"Got it," Billy said, touching the bullwhip coiled at his belt. An Indiana Jones-style bullwhip, of all things. The movie business was getting crazier and crazier.

"All right. When I give you the signal—"

"I don't know about this, Jack. I mean, it looks pretty dangerous."

"What's dangerous? Just climb up onto the bar above the wheels, like we practiced yesterday in the hangar. When the plane gets to the end of the runway and lifts off, you turn loose and drop into the lake. It's been done before, you know."

"When?"

"Well . . . I think Schwarzenegger did it, in *Die Hard*."

"He wasn't in *Die Hard*."

"Look, just do this, okay? It's good money."

"Not as much as I asked for," Billy said.

The director gave him a pained look. "Is it my fault they cast Julia Roberts? There's barely enough left over for *my* salary."

"I should at least have a parachute."

"You won't need a parachute."

"Or maybe a wetsuit. You know, insulated. That water'll be freezing."

"A speedboat and a chopper are standing by," Jenson said.

John M. Floyd

"We'll fish you out in no time, I promise."

"I could wear it under my clothes, Jack. It wouldn't cost much more, after what you must be paying to rent the plane."

Billy paused, watching the director's face.

"You did rent the plane, didn't you?"

Jack Jenson cleared his throat and studied his fingernails a moment. The cameraman, standing behind them, just looked amused.

"You *didn't*?" Billy said.

"Well, the pilot's a friend of mine, and the control tower crew are friends of his, and since the flight'll be taking off anyway, with or without you—"

"Good God, Jack. They put people in jail for this kind of thing."

"No, they give them Oscars. Just go out there and grab on."

As it turned out, that's what he did. When the director got the go-ahead from the pilot's friends in the tower and gave Billy the signal, Billy sprinted to the idling aircraft, climbed up into the landing gear, and hung on for dear life. At least I'm wearing a crash helmet, he thought—but that was only because the hero he was standing in for had worn one yesterday, when they'd filmed the guy speeding out onto the runway on his motorcycle. In the edited version of all this, it would look as if the star—not a lowly stuntman named Billy Sparks—was the one huddled underneath the plane as it took off, to escape the pursuing killers.

Billy groaned. What a hell of a way to make a living.

Seconds later the thunder in his ears became a roar, and the plane began to roll. Billy Sparks braced his feet, clenched his teeth, and watched the tarmac race past him beneath his perch.

It took less than a minute to reach takeoff speed. The wind was furious, the noise deafening. Billy crouched low, looking ahead through the visor of his helmet. The sun glinted off the lake just past the end of the runway.

Suddenly the plane lifted off. The ground fell away. Billy tensed, and closed his mind to everything except the point in time, only moments away now, when he would turn loose and dive into the shining blue water.

And then something happened. A loud WHUMP, and a tremor that shook his bones—and the bar he was standing on began to move. So did the one he was holding. In fact the lower one had become two bars, joined in the middle and bending, and the wheels beneath him began to fold upward. The landing gear was being raised. Above his head, a panel had opened in the belly of the plane.

WAIT, Billy's mind screamed. This wasn't supposed to happen yet!

The space below and around him was full of whirring machinery, moving up toward him from both sides, collapsing in on itself. In seconds he would be crushed.

What was worse—if anything could be worse—his moment to jump had passed. The lake was behind him now, the plane rising toward the towering mountains a mile to the west.

Thinking fast, Billy snatched the bullwhip from his belt, knotted it to the bar he was holding, and leaped backward to avoid the wheels folding in around him.

His grip on the whip almost snapped his arms out of their sockets. Above him the landing gear disappeared into the bottom of the plane and the door clanged shut, pinning the whip in its jaws. Billy was left dangling in space, the wind tearing at his clothes.

He knew, even in the midst of his terror, what he had to do. The mountains were beneath him now, barely a hundred feet below. Looking down, he saw nothing but white, and remembered the reported ten days of snowfall at the higher elevations. The snow would be incredibly deep in places. Which places? He had no idea.

But it was now or never.

Billy held his breath, turned loose of the whip, and fell.

His fall, of course, was more of a lob—a long, lazy arc that seemed oddly quiet after the roar of the jet engines.

Just before impact he folded his arms over his helmet and stretched his body straight and lowered his head as if diving into a calm white ocean.

And then the world exploded. Moments later, when he woke up, his neck was cold and wet, his arms and head were aching, and everything outside his visor was pitch black. But he was alive.

Not for long, he figured. He had landed headfirst, probably punching a narrow but deep hole in the snow, like a bullet fired into a muddy hill. He couldn't see, he couldn't hear, he couldn't move. Soon he wouldn't be able to breathe.

But, all of a sudden, he *was* moving.

Someone, or something, had him by the ankles and was pulling him backward, out of the tunnel he'd made in the snow.

And then he was free. He was out of the hole and lying on his back, gasping real air and blinded by the sun.

Even as he was trying to figure out what happened, why he wasn't dead, he heard a pounding noise and looked up to see a helicopter hovering far above him. He sat up and waved to his rescuers, received a wave in return, and focused on his surroundings.

He was lying in what looked like a shallow bowl with white sides, and right beside him, at the bottom of the bowl, was the body-sized and now-empty hole he had made in the snow when he landed. And the snow, when he touched it now, was much harder than he'd thought it would be. He had no doubt the impact should have killed him. It should've killed him even if the snow *had* been soft.

And the bowl around him . . .

Its walls were smooth and curved, as if giant fingers had burrowed a crater in the snow, grabbed his feet, and eased him out like a human drainplug.

Billy found himself believing, as he stared at it, that he was in the presence of A Higher Power.

**

He wasn't the only one.

While Billy Sparks was being strapped into a rescue harness, Fred Penski stood in a vast white room, staring at an extremely old man behind an extremely old desk. This particular executive was not, however, the very *Highest* Power. That distinction belonged to an unseen entity aptly referred to as the Boss, who (probably in order to remain unseen) never made contact with underlings, even in matters of discipline. But it was rumored that this office where Fred now stood was the second-highest rung on Jacob's proverbial ladder. When Fred Penski had been summoned here moments ago to meet with the Boss's right-hand man, Fred's blood pressure had spiked high enough to dim his halo. He was still trembling in his white loafers.

The old man behind the desk fit right into the color scheme: white hair, white beard, white robe, crinkly pale-blue eyes. He looked like Gandalf the Grey, or maybe a friendly Max Von Sydow.

He also looked as if he might be capable of being unfriendly, if necessary.

"You must be Fred," he said. His voice, like his face, was warm and gentle, yet somehow formidable.

"Yes sir."

"Well, Fred, what's this I hear about"—he turned, checked a white computer monitor—"William Sparks?"

Fred swallowed. "He's fine, sir. A slight mishap."

"He's one of your charges, is he not?"

"He was assigned to me this morning," Fred agreed. "I came into the situation a little late, though."

"What happened?"

In this setting, Fred decided, honesty was the best policy. "He tried to jump off an airplane, into a lake."

"He what?"

"They were filming a movie."

"Hmm. Didn't Bruce Willis try that, in *True Lies*?"

"I don't think Bruce Willis was in *True Lies*."

"Whatever." The white-haired man checked his monitor again. "Did he make it? Sparks, I mean, not Willis."

"He missed the lake, but he landed in the snow. A deep drift between two ridges. Still, he"—Fred hesitated, and sucked in some air—"he almost died."

"Why didn't he?"

"Someone pulled him out," Fred said.

"Pulled him out?"

"I think so."

A silence passed.

"*He* even thinks so," Fred said. "A few minutes ago, he told one of his rescuers he plans to go to church next Sunday."

"You don't say."

"In fact, he said he plans to go to church every Sunday for the rest of his life. Maybe even on Wednesday nights, and he's not even Baptist."

The old man nodded. "Admirable." After a moment he added, "How long will you have him?"

"Until Joe Wimberley gets back from Florida."

"That should be soon."

"It will?"

"How long can it take to do a hand recount?"

Fred shrugged. "Guess that depends on the lawyers."

"Not really. I told Joe he could turn the lawyers into

frogs, this trip."

Fred wasn't sure that was a joke.

A white printer chattered briefly, and the old man tore off the sheet and read it in silence. From somewhere outside the room, Fred could hear what sounded like rock music.

"It says here," the old man said, "that Mr. Sparks was, for a moment there, considering a career change. To"—he squinted at the page—"accounting?"

Fred's shoulders sagged. "Actually, sir, I might have caused that. Unintentionally."

Fred held his breath as the old man stroked his beard. Even the trainees knew that any interference in a subject's long-range decisions was forbidden.

"You ever been to Vegas, Fred? The casinos? Ever heard of the Eye in the Sky?"

"Yes, sir."

"Well, that's what you are, in a way. It's what we all are. Except we can do more than just secretly watch the players—we can intercede, short-term, for the safety of those in our care. But only when there's no other way."

"I know," Fred said miserably. And he hadn't done it.

"Well," the old man said, with a nod. "Main thing is, your man Sparks is alive and kicking. And you learned something in the process."

Fred cleared his throat. "You're saying . . . the Boss won't have to know about this?"

"He already knows about it, Fred. That's why he's the Boss. But no, there's no need to press the issue." The old man thumbed through some papers on his desk. "Anything you'd like to add?"

"I guess not."

"That'll be all, then."

"Yessir."

"Oh, and on your way out, ask that group next door to hold it down a little, would you?"

"Excuse me?"

"Elvis's group, down the hall. I mean, 'Love Me Tender' and 'Crying in the Chapel' is one thing, but 'Suspicious Minds' . . . you understand my position."

"Yessir. I'll tell him." Fred bowed, turned with a soft swish of his wings, and trudged to the door. His footsteps echoed in the vaulted room. At the door, he turned again. "One more thing, sir."

The old man raised his head. "Yes?"

Fred hesitated. The light through the stained-glass windows painted the white floor with rectangles of every color in the rainbow.

"You pulled him out, didn't you," Fred said.

The white-haired man leaned back in his chair, folded his hands.

"No, more than that," Fred said. "You kept him from breaking his neck. That fall should've killed him, snow or not."

After a long pause the old man asked, "Do you like movies, Fred?"

"Sir?"

"I like movies. Always have. I also like stuntmen. That thing with the chariot race, a few years ago . . ." He shook his head. "Risky line of work, that." He seemed to ponder a moment. "You think I look like Charlton Heston, Fred?"

"Maybe just a bit, sir."

"I think I do." He nodded thoughtfully, then said, "For what it's worth, you were right, about the accounting thing. It wasn't a bad thought. CPA's, unless they work for the mafia, generally live longer than daredevils."

Still shaken a bit, Fred allowed himself a tiny smile before he remembered the look on Billy Sparks's face awhile ago. "You think he'll do it?" he asked.

"Give up stunts? Who knows. I understand your fellow trainee—"

"Nancy Ross."

"I understand she thinks Mr. Sparks might have . . . more guts than brains, shall we say."

"He might have," Fred admitted.

"Time will tell. But I do admire stuntmen." Another pause. "Do you think he knows Jackie Chan? Personally, I mean."

"I couldn't say, sir."

"No, of course not. I'll look it up. Anything else?"

"No sir," Fred said, his hand on the doorknob. The music outside was louder now. "And I'll give your message to Elvis."

"Oh, never mind that. They'll probably do 'Hound Dog' again soon, and I like that one."

"'Hound Dog'?"

"Has a good beat, don't you think?"

"Yessir," Fred said, and then felt his face flush.

The old man chuckled. "Don't worry—a little white lie's okay now and then." He swiveled his chair around, turned his attention to his computer. Fred could hear him humming and tapping his foot.

Fred left quietly, closing the huge door behind him. His tension faded as he strolled through the palm-lined gardens on the way back to his office.

The Eye in the Sky, he thought, and smiled.

He liked the sound of that.

***

Huddled in a blanket inside the helicopter, Billy Sparks sipped warm coffee from the thermos the young paramedic was holding for him. The boat and chopper crews had been expecting a quick water rescue, not a windswept high-altitude operation. It had taken fifteen minutes to lower a man to help him into a harness and then haul them both back up.

"Thanks," Billy said, shivering. "Thanks for everything."

"We'll send you a bill," the rescuer said.

Billy turned to the window. Below them, the mysterious white crater drew his eye like a magnet. He felt himself shiver again, and this time it had nothing to do with the cold.

"I may have a better idea," he said, still staring down at the scooped-out hole in the snow.

"What's that?"

"Who does your taxes?" Billy asked.

THE MOON AND MARCIE WADE

"G'night, Miss Marcie."

She'd been standing in the short corridor, looking up at the numbers above the elevator. She turned now, buttoning her overcoat, and gave him a weary smile.

"Good night, Willie. By the way, take some extra time on Dr. Ellsworth's office, would you? The senator's coming by tomorrow."

The janitor nodded. "Yes'm. I'll do that." He seemed about to turn away, then hesitated, a half-full bucket of soapy water in one hand and a pushbroom in the other. Several yards of black power-cord lay draped over his shoulder like a cartridge belt.

"Something wrong, Willie?" she asked.

He looked embarrassed. "Not really, ma'am. It's just— well, it's awful late. And with what's been happenin' and all . . ."

She knew what he meant, and smiled her thanks. "I'll be all right, Willie. Whoever he is, he seems to be after the kids, not me. I don't qualify."

The elevator dinged. "Good night," she said again.

"Be careful just th' same," he called, as the doors sighed shut behind her.

***

She got off on the first floor, turned up her coat collar, and opened the arched front door of the Administration Building. She made sure it locked behind her, then strode across the flag-stone courtyard, her steps echoing off the building behind her, her breath smoking in the frigid January air.

Marcia Ellen Wade paused at the top of the steps that led down to the parade ground. It was a beautiful night, clear and cold; not a whisper of wind stirred the cedars that lined the twenty-acre drill field and shaded the brick sidewalks. Ivy-laden buildings a hundred years old surrounded the open area like the hotels around Central Park. Off to the left, above the tower of the campus chapel, a brilliant white moon rode the sky. At first glance, the scene was peaceful and natural and normal.

Only one thing was wrong: There were no people. It was barely 9:15 on a university campus of some five thousand students, and not one was in sight. The place looked as deserted as a mudflat in the Bering Sea.

And Marcie Wade didn't mind it a bit. Matter of fact, she was sick and tired of walking through an ill-mannered throng of kids every night she worked late, listening to their foul language and smelling the booze on their breaths and watching them necking or petting or whatever the name for it was these days. How different things were now, she thought sadly. Her father, rest his soul, had been a Pentecostal preacher—old Fire-and-Brimstone, they'd called him. She wondered at times what he would have thought of all this.

Anyhow, on this particular night all the students were tucked safely away in their beds—or at least in their rooms.

Marcie smiled. It was as if she had the whole place to herself. The idea of a totally calm, quiet campus was rather soothing.

The reason for it, of course, was not.

The killings had started in late October, three months ago. The first victims were a couple of sophomores who'd been smoking grass at a roadside picnic area in densely wooded Riverside Park, at the north edge of the campus. Both had been shot in the head at close range. The next was a senior math-major from upstate, jogging in those same woods a month later, grooving to both his iPod and what was later determined to be a fair amount of cocaine. He had been found the following morning, with a bullet through the back of his skull. The latest two murders had taken place during Christmas break, when a guy and his date were out parking beside that same section of road. Causes of death: gunshots wounds to the head, fired at point-blank range through the driver's window.

The police department was, by its own admission, baffled.

Only one clue had surfaced: The murder weapon was a .45-caliber handgun, probably a revolver since no shell casings had been found at the scenes. Everything else was conjecture, and—since the newspapers, naturally, were having a field day with the whole thing—groundless rumors had spread like California wildfires. Some said a cult of devil worshippers had been hiding out at the edge of town for months, boasting about the murders and promising more. Others swore they had all been suicides and were being covered up due to pressure from rich parents. Still others suggested the killings were tied to the cycles of the moon.

Whatever the truth was, some definite action was now being taken.

Three things had happened as a result of the two most recent homicides: (1) the campus security force had been doubled, and was supplemented by units of city police, (2) a nine p.m. curfew had been put into effect, and (3) the sale of handguns in the adjoining town of Millboro had quadrupled.

This last development was an item of real concern to the local authorities. People were getting trigger-happy. One elderly woman had already shot her husband by accident as he slipped in the back door late one night. *Caution is your best weapon*, the local P.D. announced to the public. *Carrying a gun can cause more trouble than good.*

No one paid much attention to their warnings—especially Marcie Wade. The police, as far as she was concerned, could go spit in their hats. She'd been carrying a pistol in the glove compartment of her car for the last thirty years, and she had no intention of changing things now.

Besides, nobody told her what to do. Nobody. It was, she realized, one of the reasons she had never married.

Burrowing deeper into her overcoat, Marcie clomped down the steps and set off along the paved but shadowy path that wound between the EE labs and the library. Her hard-soled loafers made sharp, slapping sounds in the brittle air as she walked.

Then she stopped. She stood very still for a moment, looking around. Something was wrong.

***

A thick cedar hedge lined the sidewalk, and somebody was on the other side, to her right. She couldn't see anyone, but he was there. She had heard him moving.

She stood there several seconds longer, then kept going. Be reasonable, she told herself. So what if someone was there? It would take a lot more than that to scare Marcie Wade. She hadn't made it to the age of fifty-six by going to pieces at every little thing that went bump in the ni—

A man stepped from the shadows. She stopped in her tracks, clutching her purse in a deathgrip and holding her breath.

A flashlight snapped on; its beam found her face,

blinding her.

"Sorry," a voice said. The light clicked off. "What are you doing out here, ma'am? There's a curfew, you know."

Marcie blinked, her pulse pounding in her ears. "Officer...?"

"Lawson. Millboro Police."

She was silent a moment, waiting for her heart to slow down. "Officer Lawson," she said finally, "do you know Dr. Robert Ellsworth?"

"The president of the university?"

"I'm his assistant. And curfew or not, it's also the week of accreditations. I've been working a little late. Now, if you don't mind—"

"Ma'am, these aren't easy times," he said. "The rules are for everybody."

Marcie sighed. Her head was beginning to hurt. "You're right, of course. I'm sorry."

"I'll walk you to your car," he offered, switching the light on again.

She nodded tiredly. "Very well. It's just over there, in the dorm lot—"

A sharp buzz made them both jump. The officer took his radio handset from the clip on his belt. "Lawson," he answered.

The voice on the radio was metallic but clear: "Quinlan here. We may have something. A guy hiding in the bushes, behind Bradley Hall. We're in pursuit."

"I'm on my way." The officer turned to Marcie Wade. "You go straight to your car, ma'am. Understood?" Without waiting for a reply, he sprinted past her and back down the path toward the buildings Marcie had just left.

She stared after him. "I was thinking of taking a dip in the fountain first," she called. With a shake of her head she turned and continued toward the dormitory parking lot. She'd left her car there for the past three days, while the administrative lot was being resurfaced.

Ten seconds later she saw it, a white four-door Chevy parked in the next-to-last space. She dug her keyring from her purse as she walked, her mind on the police officer and his radio message. What a goat rodeo, she said to herself.

Behind her to the west, in the direction of Bradley Hall, she heard the wail of a siren. She hesitated a moment, standing beside her car and listening. The sound faded. She pushed the button to unlock the driver's door and climbed inside.

She sagged backward against the headrest, breathing deeply, her eyes closed. For a minute or more she sat there motionless, bone-tired, then opened her eyes and stared at the windshield. With a final sigh she put the key into the ignition; the motor whined and then caught. She pulled slowly out of the lot and onto College Drive, following it through the main gate and onto River Road, where she hung a left toward home.

It was a five-minute drive, much of it through the winding roads of Riverside Park. Like the campus, it seemed deserted. There was never much traffic through here anyway, and even less now, after the killings. It was just not a very smart place to be anymore. And certainly not at night.

She was halfway through the park when she heard a sound behind her. A heavy thump, like the noise a clod of dirt might make against the underside of the car.

Something made her glance up at the rearview mirror, and when she did—

She looked straight into his eyes.

***

Marcie screamed, and her muscles locked. The car was at that instant in the middle of a curve; she felt it leave the highway. Without thinking she stabbed her foot down on the brake-pedal, and the Chevy ground to a stop in the grass twenty feet from the road. Dazedly she looked again at the mirror. This time she saw nothing.

Then she heard a groan, and the owner of the voice lurched into view in the back seat, holding his head with one hand.

It was a boy. A young man, actually, in his early twenties. His eyes were squeezed shut. He looked about as dangerous as a Beagle puppy.

Finally Marcie Wade found her voice. "What are you doing in my *CAR*?" she shouted, veins standing out on her forehead.

The boy moaned again and shook his head as if trying to clear it. At last he opened his eyes—the glazed blue eyes that Marcie had first seen moments ago in the rearview mirror.

"I was asleep," he murmured. "Where are we?"

She just stared at him. "Asleep?"

The boy spread his hands wide, looking confused. "I locked myself out of the dorm. It was cold, and nobody was around. I was . . . tired."

"You were *drunk*," she said, smelling his breath. Her voice was as icy as the night outside the windows.

"Your back door was unlocked," he said, still groggy. "I, ah, guess I kind of crawled in." He seemed to lose track of his thoughts for a moment, then focused on her once more. "Where are we?" he asked again.

"We're in the middle of Riverside Park."

That brought him around. "What?" He rubbed his eyes and squinted out the window. "Oh hell," he said. "Get us outa here."

Sure enough, the woods seemed to have closed in around them, the bare branches of the oaks stark and ominous in the moonlight. The silence, broken only by the soft ticking of the cooling engine, was unnerving.

"I'll tell you what I *should* do," she snapped. "I should drive you straight to the police sta—"

She stopped talking. Her eyes focused on the passenger window.

The boy blinked. "What is it?"

She said nothing for a moment, watching something in the woods to the right. Without looking at him, she whispered, "Get out of the car."

"What?"

She licked her lips, still peering out the window. "Get out the door on this side and run to the edge of the trees. Crouch down there and wait for me. We'll be okay, I've got a gun in the glovebox."

He stared at her, speechless, as she leaned over and popped the glove compartment. She groped around for a second, her eyes fixed on the window, then found the pistol and hauled it out. As an afterthought, she reached above her head and adjusted the switch for the dome light. That would keep it from coming on when the door was opened.

"Do what I said," she hissed, over her shoulder. "But wait for me there. I can't see much in the dark."

The boy swallowed once, loudly, and did as he was told. The door eased open. She heard him hurrying softly across the wet grass.

Only then did the tension leave her face. In its place was a tight, bitter smile.

She looked down at the gun in her hand. It was a big one—a Colt .45 revolver that had once belonged to her father. She cocked the hammer, watching the smooth movement of the cylinder and thinking about the boy.

The sinner, she corrected herself. Sleeping it off in the back seat of her *car*, of all things. The very thought disgusted her.

Well, one thing was sure: This would be the easiest one so far. Certainly better than sneaking around in the cold shadowy woods like before, waiting for them to come to *her*. Her luck was changing.

The timing was even right, she told herself.

The moon was almost full . . .

John M. Floyd

ONE-WAY TICKET

"I just wish you weren't going," the girl at the window said.

She stood with her back to the room, staring out at the street. The look on her face was at least as sad as her voice, which sounded as if she were about to lose her last friend. Actually, that wasn't far from the truth: She and Mary Lou had been roommates for the past two years.

Mary Lou Foster paused and glanced up from her packing. "I have to, Annie. You know that."

"You don't have to," Annie Hopkins said, without looking at her. "I mean, you could just . . . well . . ."

"Throw the ticket away?"

"Or sell it." Annie turned from the window, her face brightening. "That's it, you could sell it. There's still time—"

But Mary Lou's look silenced her. "I don't want to sell it, Annie. I want to use it. We've been over this a dozen times."

Her friend slumped into a chair beside the window. Behind her, the late-morning sun shone down on the hats and caps and turned-up collars of the people in the street. A few glanced through the window of the little apartment as they passed, but most stared straight ahead. As usual, no one smiled. Even the brightness of a fine spring day wasn't enough to cheer up this dreary part of town. On the other side of the room, Mary Lou continued with her packing, placing two folded nightgowns into her open suitcase and returning to the closet for her shoes and her one good sweater. She was having trouble concealing her excitement. While sad to be leaving her longtime friend, she was anything but sad to be leaving the city.

"And it's not just to get away," she added, trying to find an empty place for the shoes. "It'll be a chance to see Uncle Clyde again. He's not getting any younger, you know."

"Phooey," Annie said, with a frown. "I remember your Uncle Clyde—he's healthy as an ox. He'll live another fifty years."

"Yes, but I might not. Especially as hard as Mrs. Billings works me around here."

The two girls shared a knowing look. Old Mrs. Billings was a fair employer, but her strict and overbearing manner had always been a sore spot with Mary Lou. It never seemed to bother Annie, who had worked here almost five years now, but then again, nothing ever seemed to bother Annie. By her own admission, she could put up with almost anything. Well, not me, Mary Lou thought. Being a maid was never easy, but—as in most jobs—it would be a lot easier if you liked your boss.

"Whatever," Annie said, studying the hooked rug at her feet. "I just don't want you to go." Her frown deepened. "I'll probably never even see you again."

"Of course you will, silly. I'll be coming back to visit—"

"No you won't. And you know it's true. You'll find a job there, and probably a beau too."

"A beau?" Mary Lou smiled. "How do you figure that? I sure haven't found one here."

"That's what I mean. You're overdue. With your luck, it's

just a matter of time—"

"That's a lot of bunk," Mary Lou said, and went back to her packing. But she knew exactly what Annie meant.

Mary Lou Foster *was* lucky. She was probably the luckiest woman on earth.

That was an exaggeration, of course. In at least two areas—love and wealth—she had been decidedly unlucky. But in most everything else, she seemed to lead a charmed life.

It was spooky, almost. Everyone who'd ever known her, even as a child, had commented on it. She was always the one who won the parlor guessing-games and caught the wedding bouquets and received the door prizes at social gatherings.

And it didn't seem to be limited just to material things. Several years ago, when she worked in a house on the really affluent side of town, she had been on her way to the kitchen one morning and had stopped just outside the doorway to tie her shoes. Unknown to anyone, there had been a gas leak in the newfangled cookstove that morning, and as Mary Lou knelt on the side porch to see to her shoelaces one of her colleagues struck a match in the kitchen to start preparing breakfast. The explosion took off the roof and destroyed the entire rear section of the house. Mary Lou spent a week in the hospital and couldn't hear a sound for almost a month afterward, but at least she recovered. Three other servants did not.

There were plenty of other instances as well, though none quite so spectacular. But her reputation was firmly established: Mary Lou Foster had a guardian angel watching over her.

The Ticket was only the latest occurrence. She'd won it three weeks ago in a church raffle, the first raffle of any kind she'd ever entered. Even the purchase of the chance itself had been lucky: She had thought the coins she'd placed in the hand of the deacon that morning was a regular Sunday offering. (She had always believed, ironically, that all gambling was wrong—

even church raffles. If she'd felt otherwise, she could probably have been rich at an early age.) At any rate, she had in fact purchased the chance and, not surprisingly, won the prize: a travel ticket valued at more than she could earn in six months' time.

Her first thought when she discovered she had won, though she didn't tell Annie this, had been to sell the Ticket. After all, it was only one-way, and to buy a return fare would have been far beyond her means. But after thinking it through, she realized she had stumbled upon an unbelievable opportunity. The fact that it was a one-way ticket was, she decided, symbolic as well as practical. It was God's way of telling her it was time for her to leave here, and leave for good. She even had an ace in the hole: Her only living relative, a dear uncle named Clyde Marsten, had moved West two years ago, and would welcome her as his own. Once there, she could begin a new life.

Mary Lou looked at the old watch she kept in the pocket of her skirt. It was almost time. She closed her suitcase, cinched and buckled the straps, picked up her little blue valise, and turned to face her friend.

"Gotta go," she said.

Tears were shining in Annie's eyes now, and Mary Lou felt a sudden wave of affection for this kind girl with whom she had shared a room for so many months. They hugged for a long moment, and when they separated Annie said, sniffling, "Let's go get Willie. He'll give you a ride down."

Mary Lou smiled and dabbed at her eyes with the back of her hand. "Willie said he'd be off today, remember? I'll walk."

Annie gasped. "You can't walk. It's at least a mile—and this isn't the greatest part of town, in case you forgot."

"My stars, Annie, I grew up here, I know that. I'll be fine." She hefted her small suitcase and valise; her purse hung from a shoulder strap. "See? I'm traveling light." Which was true. The only heavy item in either of her bags was a tiny iron skillet, and she wasn't about to leave that behind. It had taken years to season it properly. "Besides," she added, lifting her chin, "I'm young and strong and capable."

"What you are," Annie said with a sigh, "is stubborn. And I suppose it's a little late to change that." She gave her friend another hug and walked her to the door. "God bless you, Mary Lou Foster," she said in a shaky voice. "Have a good trip."

Mary Lou took a long look around her, gave Annie a final wink, and stepped out into the bright April morning. The breeze was cold but pleasant, the sun warm on her face. The smell of soot and woodsmoke hung in the air. Sparrows twittered and played along the rooftops.

I'm free, she said to herself.

As she headed south on the littered sidewalk she felt a mixture of sensations—relief and excitement, mostly, but also a little tingle of apprehension. This was, after all, a drastic step she was taking. As if for reassurance she pressed the inside of her elbow against the purse hanging from her left shoulder. Inside it was the Ticket, and all that it represented: adventure, independence, a future. Face it, girl, she thought, maybe you really are favored by the Almighty. And now it would finally pay off.

The lighthearted mood didn't last long. By the time she'd traveled three blocks she knew someone was following her. At first it was just a feeling; then she turned and caught the eye of a dark, shabbily-dressed man twenty or thirty yards behind her. He looked away and ducked into a storefront alcove—but a minute or so later she saw him again, much closer and still watching her. As the seconds flew past she thought of asking someone to help her, but knew she would get little aid here. Pedestrian traffic was sparse, and there was a fair chance she might even be robbed by those whose assistance she needed.

Just as she was about to turn and confront the man, she noticed a small bakery shop just ahead. Breathing hard, she made it to the door and ducked inside. Half a dozen sad-faced women and children stood at the counter, waiting to make purchases. Mary Lou found a table in one corner and sat down with her bags to watch the front door.

Minutes passed. The man didn't appear. She waited ten more minutes, then rose and inched out onto the sunlit sidewalk. Her back near the door, she looked up and down the street. No sign of him. Apparently he had given up on her.

With a quick glance at her watch—she had only a short time now until the scheduled hour of departure—she hitched her purse higher on her shoulder and started walking.

It was as she passed the entrance to an alley a block from the bakery that she realized her mistake. The man who had been following her earlier leaped from the shadows and clamped a grimy hand over her mouth; his other hand bound her arms to her body. Within seconds he had dragged her into the darkness of the alley and behind a pile of rubbish.

His left hand over her mouth, he let go with the other long enough to draw a short, wicked-looking knife. When she felt the cold tip of its blade against her throat she tensed and was still. He took his hand from over her lips and spun her around to face him.

"All I want's your purse, Missy," he hissed, grinning. "Hand it over."

Trembling, Mary Lou turned a bit to her right and lowered her left shoulder as if to offer him the purse-strap. As he reached for it, though, she swiveled suddenly, bringing the small, flat suitcase in her right hand up and around with all her strength. The case was almost horizontal when it reached the attacker's head; its hard metal side caught him an inch above the left ear. His head, after bouncing off the suitcase, bounced off the brick wall of the alley. His knife went spinning away into the gloom.

The blow didn't quite knock him unconscious, but it did nothing to improve his mood. Dazed and bruised and cursing, the man staggered to his feet, pulled a gun from his belt—

And shot her.

There was no way he could miss, at that range. Mary Lou cried out and fell flat on her back. Her assailant fled into the shadows.

She lay as still as a stone on the cold brick pavement. Her eyes were closed, her left hand still clutching the little valise to her stomach, where it had been when her attacker had fired the shot. As luck would have it, it was that bag—actually the small iron skillet inside the bag—that had taken the bullet meant for Mary Lou, but she did not yet know that. Simply put, she thought she was dead, and so did the old man who had witnessed the struggle from the second-floor window above the alley. Only the fact that she was still breathing proved otherwise.

A full thirty minutes later, the wife of the old man, having carried Mary Lou and her luggage into their apartment and doused her with attention and damp washcloths, discovered that the only bullethole to be found was in one of the girl's carrying-bags instead of in the girl.

Ten minutes after that, Mary Lou was sitting up in the old couple's bed, dazedly sipping ice-water and offering them embarrassed thanks for their trouble. But along with the profound relief of being alive came another realization. It hit her like a slap in the face.

The Ticket.

She jerked her pocketwatch out so fast she spilled the rest of the water in the drinking glass. Her eyes stared at the watch dumbly, her heart pounding. Twelve-fifteen.

Departure time was twelve noon.

Mary Lou suddenly felt short of breath. Her vision blurred; spots swam before her eyes.

She was too late.

She sprang to her feet, grabbed her bags, and without another word of thanks (and to the amazement of her rescuers) dashed through the door and down the rickety steps and out into the street. She took a moment to get her bearings, then took off like a rocket. Her feet flew, her breath rasped in her throat, hot tears stung her eyes. She streaked down the narrow sidewalk as if all the hounds of hell were snapping at her heels.

At 12:26 she rounded the last corner, sprinted across Canute Road, and ran puffing through a forest of telephone poles and cranes and sheds and boxcars . . .

And then she was there.

And what she saw, fifty yards away, told her the whole story.

The crowd, which she had heard would be huge, was only twenty or thirty people now, and even they were beginning to disperse. The show was over.

Woodenly she crossed the open space, her face slack, her eyes blank and faraway. Her breath made little white clouds in the chilly air. Near the edge of the platform she stopped and stared out over the shimmering green water. For just an instant she thought she saw it—a long dark shape, huge even at this distance—as it turned the corner and headed out into the main channel.

Very slowly Mary Lou lowered her head and looked down at the purse dangling from its shoulder-strap. With unsteady fingers she opened it and removed the Ticket, then stood and stared at it, knowing that now it was of no use to her—or to anyone else.

Printed on the rectangle of thin cardboard were the words:

- ONE (1) SECOND-CLASS CABIN -
THE MAIDEN VOYAGE OF THE
R.M.S. TITANIC
- THE BRITISH WHITE STAR LINE -
SOUTHAMPTON TO NEW YORK CITY
April 10, 1912

She fetched a sigh, brushed away a final tear, and turned to start the long walk home.

So much for luck, she thought.

GREASED LIGHTNIN'

For once, the Swede was speechless. He sat with his elbows propped on the poker table, his eyes narrowed in disbelief, his cards forgotten in his hand. He was staring at the stranger sitting on the other side of the table.

"You're either joking," he said finally, "or you're drunk. And I don't think you're drunk."

Jesse Dobbs grinned at him over his cards. "I'm dead serious. It'll happen tomorrow morning, at sunup."

All four men at the table with Dobbs exchanged glances. Nobody seemed very interested in the game anymore.

The Swede hesitated, then leaned forward and spoke in a hushed voice. "Folks around here," he said, "don't take kindly to backshooters."

"Who said anything about backshooting?" Dobbs took a slow sip of his beer, apparently enjoying the attention. "I'm calling him out. Fair 'n square."

If anything, that corner of the saloon grew even quieter. Dobbs's words seemed to hang there in the dead silence. Somewhere in the street outside the swinging doors, a buckboard rattled past. A horse whinnied.

The Swede had opened his mouth to say something when the doors parted and a tall gray-haired man came in. He was dressed in chaps and a black vest, and looked as weathered and rugged as the hills south of town. After a moment he spotted the group at the table and stomped over, slapping the dust from his clothes with a worn brown hat. He nodded to Dobbs, then turned to the others at the table. "Wagon's loaded, boys, let's get back to the ranch and—"

He stopped when he noticed the looks on their faces. All of them were still staring at Jesse Dobbs.

"What's the matter with you fellas?" he said.

The Swede glanced up at him, then went back to looking at Dobbs. "Our friend here says he's taking on the Marshal tomorrow. Head to head."

The older man regarded Dobbs a moment. "That true?"

Dobbs answered by tilting his head in the direction of the bar. "Man in the back office is already taking wagers. I'd bet on me, if I was you."

The gray-haired man eased into one of the extra chairs, keeping his eyes on the stranger. His fingers toyed with the hat in his lap. "You know how many men he's killed, young fella?" he asked. "I hear twenty, and that's prob'ly low." He shot a questioning glance at the Swede, who nodded agreement.

"That don't matter," Dobbs said.

"I'd say it matters. I'd say it matters a hell of a lot."

Dobbs took another swallow of beer. "That was a long time ago."

"Billy Allgood wasn't a long time ago. Case you ain't heard, Billy decided to murder a bank teller and help hisself to the cash drawer. Ryan shot him between the eyes, if I remember right. From all the way across the street."

"I heard. I also heard Ryan wasn't all that fast. Allgood

was just no challenge for him."

"And you are?"

Dobbs set his beer down, smiled at it for a moment, then raised his eyes to look at the faces around the table. His gaze stopped on each one in turn, and came to rest on the gray-haired man. "That's right. I am." Carefully Dobbs put his cards face-down on the tabletop, pushed his chair back a couple of inches, and held his hands up in front of him, palms out. "The Marshal's old and he's tired and he's slow," he said. "I'm young—"

No one at the table actually saw Dobbs' right hand move. Suddenly the gun was just . . . there. It was in his hand, cocked and ready and pointing at the older man in the chair across the table.

"—and I'm fast," Dobbs finished.

Five pairs of eyes stared at the gun in his hand. Then, almost as quickly as it had appeared, the pistol spun in a circle and streaked back into its holster. Dobbs' right hand, empty once more, picked up his beer mug and brought it to his lips. He looked pleased with himself.

Almost everyone at the table exhaled, and there were several loud swallows. Only the gray-haired man remained impassive, and even he seemed to be looking at Dobbs with a bit more respect than before. "That you are," he agreed.

Their gazes held for a long time. The silence at the table dragged out. Finally the older man said, without breaking eye contact, "Let's go, boys. Foreman wants us back before dark."

Four chairs scraped on the wooden floor. Winnings were gathered; half-empty glasses were finished and set down. It took a while—everyone was watching Dobbs and no one made any sudden moves. When his partners were all standing and waiting, the gray-haired man rose also, his eyes still locked with the stranger's.

"Maybe the Marshal *can* be beat," he admitted. "But I

sure wouldn't want to be the one to try it."

Jesse Dobbs's grin widened. He was leaning back in his chair, legs crossed, both hands cradling his beer. "I agree. I wouldn't want you to either." He glanced up at the others then, and for a moment his smile turned cold. A wild light burned in his eyes.

"You men remember this day," Dobbs said. "You can tell your grandchildren you once met the man who killed Stone Ryan."

The old cowhand gave him a long, measuring look. Slowly he put on his hat, turned, and marched out of the saloon. The others followed.

Dobbs watched them leave, then sat motionless at the table, gazing out at the dusty street as the batwing doors swung back and forth on their hinges. After a minute or so he chuckled to himself, raised his mug, and drained it. He turned his head to call for another beer, and that was when he saw the boy.

***

He was sitting on a stool in the small space between the wall and the end of the bar, about twenty feet from Dobbs's table. He sat perfectly still, and his dull clothes and dark brown skin made him all but invisible in the gathering shadows. His eyes were what caught Dobbs's attention. They were narrow and bright and piercing, and something in those eyes made the hair stand up on the back of the gunfighter's neck.

"What you lookin' at, boy?"

At first the youngster didn't move, or change expression. Then, very slowly, he got up off his stool and approached the card table, his eyes fixed on Dobbs and his hands tucked deep into the pockets of his homemade overalls. At that moment Dobbs understood the feeling he'd had a minute ago: The kid was part Indian. And it wasn't just his eyes or his color. He even moved like one.

"We need to talk, Mister," the boy said.

Dobbs snorted. "No offense, kid, but I don't talk to red-skins. And right now I'm busy." He turned again to look for the bartender.

"This time tomorrow you could be dead," the boy said, "if you don't listen to me."

The gunman blinked. "What did you say?"

The boy took his hands out of his pockets and stood up straight. "I heard you talking a minute ago, about the gunfight. And I know Mr. Harley's been taking bets all day today."

"How is it you know Harley?" Dobbs asked, suspicious now. The kid looked to be twelve or thirteen at the most. "For that matter, what are you doing in here at all?"

"I work here, after school. I sweep up in the back, and see to the ashcans and spittoons." The boy raised his hand, caught the bartender's eye, and pointed to Dobbs' beer mug. The bartender nodded.

"And just help out in general," he added.

Dobbs regarded him in wary silence for a moment. "Okay," he growled. "I'm listening. Make it quick."

The youngster licked his lips and swallowed. "Like I said, I heard you talking. And I saw—" His eyes shifted to the holstered gun and back again. "I saw what you did just now." He drew his brows together in an expression that would have been almost funny in other circumstances. But his voice, when he spoke next, was low and deadly serious: "You could be in big trouble tomorrow, Mister, whether you know it or not. Marshal Ryan might be old, but he's not tired. He's fast as greased light-nin'. Faster maybe."

Dobbs felt a twinge of amusement. "Faster than me?"

The boy hesitated, as if remembering the draw he'd just seen. "It'd be close. But yeah, I think he is."

Jesse Dobbs studied him a moment. The kid might be a

redskin, he thought, but he's no dummy. That much was clear.

"Tell me something, boy—"

"My name's Jake. Jake Longbow."

"Tell me then, Jake Longbow: What's your interest in all this?"

The boy seemed to consider that, then said, "I want you to win."

"And why is that?"

"Because I'm going to bet on you," Jake said. "Tonight, when I finish up here, I'm going to go get every penny I own, and as much as I can steal from my parents, and bet it all. Tomorrow, when I win, I'll pay my folks back. The rest I'll put in the bank. And when I'm old enough—"

The bartender came with Dobbs' beer, and Jake fell silent. When they were alone again, he said, "When I'm old enough— and it won't be long now—I'm leaving here. Forever." He paused, and a shadow seemed to cross his face. "I'm a half-breed Sioux in a white man's town, Mr. Dobbs, and that's the bottom of the barrel. What I win tomorrow'll be my way out."

The gunfighter was quiet a minute, but not in contemplation of Jake Longbow's station in life. His mind was on other things.

"Let me get this straight. You think the Marshal's faster than I am—"

"Not by much," Jake interrupted.

"But you think he's faster."

"Right."

"—and still you're going to bet on me."

"Right."

Dobbs spread his hands. "Why? If you think he can beat me, why not bet on *him*?"

"I'm risking too much money for that. There's no room for chance—it has to be a sure thing."

"And you think I'm a sure thing?"

The boy raised his chin and said, "You will be. With my help."

Dobbs' eyes hardened. "With your help."

"That's right," Jake said. "I thought of it this morning, really—when I first heard about the wagers—but I wasn't sure it'd work. Then I saw you draw, a few minutes ago. Then I knew."

Dobbs just stared at him.

"I can show you how to beat him," Jake said.

***

Twenty minutes later, Jesse Dobbs stood alone on the rim of a dry wash just outside town. The sun was behind him, low on the horizon; his jagged shadow was printed on the opposite wall of the ravine. Beyond the wash, a rolling sea of cactus and scrub and sagebrush stretched away as far as the eye could see.

Dobbs heard a sound, and turned to watch the boy stride toward him from a stand of dead willow trees fifty yards away. "I was about to give up on you, kid," he said as Jake approached.

"My mother was home. I had to sneak past her to get to Pa's workshop."

"Well, let's see it."

Jake Longbow reached into his pocket, then paused and looked in all four directions. Precautions were, of course, unnecessary: Not only was there no one within earshot, there was no one within a quarter of a mile. Satisfied, he withdrew a small container from his pocket and held it up for display.

It was a short glass bottle with a wide mouth and a metal screw-on lid. Dobbs frowned at it doubtfully.

"It's a lubricant," Jake explained. "My father's a handy-man; people pay him to fix things. He uses this on machine parts."

Dobbs was clearly trying not to show his interest. But he couldn't seem to take his eyes off the container. "What's a lubergant?"

"In our case, it's speed," the boy said. "Speed in a bottle." He pointed to the holstered pistol. "Hand me your gun."

Dobbs tensed, drew back a step.

"I'm not gonna hurt it," Jake said. "And if you behave I won't shoot you with it."

Dobbs gave the boy a hard look, then seemed to make up his mind. He pulled the gun, twirled it once, and held it out butt-first. Jake took it.

With the pistol in his left hand, the boy opened the bottle and stuck two of the fingers of his right hand inside. His fingers came out covered with a thick, colorless glob. Very carefully, as Dobbs watched, Jake applied the greasy substance to the top and sides of the revolver.

"We have to be sure not to get any on the grip, or the trigger, or the hammer. You'll be touching those. It's got to go only on those places that come in contact with the holster."

When he was done, most of the front section of the gun was evenly coated with the stuff. Still holding it by the grip only, he handed it back to Dobbs, who let it slide back into its leather scabbard. It went in quietly, cushioned by the thin film of goo. Once inside the holster, the gun looked normal.

"Nobody'll notice anything funny tomorrow if you leave it be," Jake said. "Besides, you have to let it set for twenty minutes anyway."

"Let it set? Why?"

"How should I know? That's just the way it works. My pa taught me how to use it: You apply it and then leave it alone for at least twenty minutes." Jake looked around in the gathering twilight. "C'mon, we'll use the time to walk down the wash for a ways. You'll want to practice a little, and down there nobody'll hear the shots."

They left the rim and picked their way along a footpath to

the bottom of the ravine. It was cool and shadowy here, and quiet as a church. Saying nothing, they trudged along the sandy floor, heading away from town. When twenty-five minutes were up, Jake pointed out a target and sat down on a rock to watch.

Dobbs took a comfortable stance, facing a sandy clump of brush thirty feet away. He stood there poised and ready in the lingering twilight for ten seconds or more, flexing the fingers of his right hand as they hovered near the handle of his pistol. The gunshot, when it came, was so sudden and loud Jake Longbow almost fell off his rock. A fountain of sand erupted from the target, but neither of the onlookers even noticed it. Both were thinking only of the blurry speed of the draw itself. Dobbs stared at the gun in his hand.

"Fantastic," he said, under his breath. He looked up at the boy. "It's like the holster wasn't even there." Slowly he lowered the revolver and eased it back into its scabbard. It made no sound as it slipped in.

Jake nodded. "That's because there's no drag. No friction."

Dobbs assumed his stance and tried again. The result was the same: The act of drawing the weapon, thumbing the hammer, and squeezing the trigger happened in the blink of an eye.

"It's like you said," Dobbs murmured, smiling. "Greased lightnin'."

"No pun intended," Jake said.

Dobbs gave him a puzzled look. "No what?"

"Never mind." Jake nodded toward the target. "Try again."

Dobbs did try again, and again, and again. The pistol roared, the sand flew, and the gunman's wicked grin grew wider still.

Finally he turned, holstered his weapon, and gave Jake a triumphant look. "Well, kid? Whaddaya think?"

The boy nodded. "Good," he said, still staring at the gun.

"Very good." Then he looked Dobbs in the eye. "It's not just the lubricant, you know. It helps, sure—the draw's smoother, easier. But part of it's the confidence it gives you. It *feels* better, so *you* feel better. And perform better." He nodded again. "You're faster than before. Not by much—but enough. That's the edge."

"So now you think I can take him."

"Yeah. I think you can."

They looked at each other a moment, then Jake broke the spell: "Come on, let's clean it up." He pulled a damp rag from his hip pocket and motioned for the gun. This time Dobbs handed it over without argument.

"You have to wipe the stuff off afterward," Jake told him, mopping the barrel and cylinder down with the cloth. "Like this. In fact, you should break it down tonight and clean it like always." After a few minutes he exchanged the wet rag for a dry one, and polished all the places where the grease had been removed. Then he went through the same routine with the inside surfaces of the leather holster.

Dobbs watched, no longer hiding his interest. "What'll happen tomorrow, exactly?"

"We'll meet here in the morning, half an hour before sunup. I'll have the bottle with me, and we'll grease the gun down the same way we did a while ago. That way you'll have time for the stuff to gel for twenty minutes before the show-down." Jake paused to refold the cloth, then went back to work. "You can practice all you want if you get here before me, but once we apply the goo you're not to touch it at all till you square off with Ryan." Jake finished and looked up at him. "Understand?"

"Got it." Dobbs frowned. "But why can't you just leave the stuff with me now?"

"My pa might miss the bottle. I have to return it to its place in his shop tonight, then sneak it out again in the morning.

Don't worry, everything'll work fine."

"Yeah," Dobbs said dreamily, toying with the handle of the gun. Jake knew he was still remembering the feel, the perfect gliding ease, of the draw. "I believe it will." He raised his eyes and studied the boy, who was rolling up the used rags now and stuffing them into his pockets along with the bottle. "You done good, kid."

Jake felt a sudden twinge in his gut. So far he'd tried hard not to think too much, or too long, about the death he was about to cause. He kept his head down and his hands steady, intent on his task.

"What I'm doing," he said, frowning, "is for me. Not for you."

Dobbs just smiled. He spun the cylinder, reloaded with fresh shells, and dropped the gun back into its holster. It was almost full dark now, and they could barely make out each other's faces. Jake looked up at the purple sky and shivered; the wind had grown chilly. Stars gleamed down at them from above the black rim of the wash.

"Any questions?" Jake asked, turning to Dobbs. "If not, I'll see you around five-thirty."

The gunman regarded him a moment, and even in the darkness Jake thought he could see strange little lights glittering in his eyes.

"I'll be here," Dobbs said.

***

The next morning at 5:10, almost an hour before sunrise, Jake Longbow crawled out of bed, dressed quickly, and made a cautious and silent trip down the hallway to his father's workshop. After a moment he pocketed his treasure, returned to his bedroom, and climbed out the window.

Forty minutes later he was back. The first hazy lights of dawn crept in with him through the bedroom window. He could

207

smell breakfast cooking at the other end of the house. He tiptoed down the short hallway to his pa's shop, then stopped outside the doorway. His father was there already, tinkering at his workbench. Replacing the bottle this time would have to wait.

Jake turned and followed the smell of frying bacon all the way to the kitchen. He kissed his mom on the cheek and sat down at the table, thinking happily of the events of the past half hour. Everything had gone according to plan. All he had to do now was bide his time.

He was pleased to find that he had no misgivings like those he had suffered yesterday in the dry wash. He fully understood the fact that he had just guaranteed a man's death. It was a hard world, as his father had so often stated, and you had to stand up and think for yourself now and then. His father, of course, wouldn't have approved of something like this; neither would his uncle. But some things you had to do just because they needed doing. This was one of those times.

He was still sitting there, watching his mother's reddish hair as she worked at the cookstove, when they heard the gunshot, flat and sharp and clear in the early-morning stillness.

His mother glanced up at the window, a look of mild curiosity on her face, then went back to her cooking. Jake rose and looked out across the beanpatch toward town.

"I'll be back soon, Ma," he said, and slipped out the door before she could reply.

This time he was gone for more than an hour. The sun was over the back fence, breakfast was finished, and his father, he found out later, had already fixed old Mr. Taylor's coffee-grinder and was working on a rocking chair the local schoolmarm had brought in yesterday. Jake could hear the sounds of a saw and hammer all the way from the back steps. As the screen door slapped shut behind him, Jake took a lumpy feed-sack from under his arm and set it down in the corner. Then he turned to face his mother.

"Young man," she said, "where'd you run off to in such a hur—"

She stopped and snapped her mouth shut, her green eyes fixed on his hands. Her gaze shifted to his face (which was grinning like an idiot's) and then back to his hands again.

"What's that?" she asked.

Jake spread his fingers, fanning the stack of bills like an oversized deck of cards. "It's money, Ma. More money than we ever dreamed of."

She just stared at him.

He stepped forward and handed her the thick roll of bills. "It's for you. Twelve hundred dollars. Some of it's mine, I want you to hold it for me. Put it in the bank."

"Hold it . . . ?"

He drew his back up straight, the way he had done in the saloon the afternoon before. "I'm gonna be leaving someday, Ma. Maybe pretty soon now. My share can get me started." He paused. "And God knows we can use the rest of it, right?"

She felt the beginnings of tears in her eyes. This was indeed a gift straight from heaven. "But . . . how—"

"There was a gunfight a while ago. Last night I bet on it, at odds of six to one. I won."

She blinked. "A gunfight?"

"It was a new guy in town. Jesse Dobbs." Jake paused. "Him and the Marshal."

"Oh, no—" Her eyes widened, and her right hand flew to her mouth and stayed there, pressed tight to her lips. Stone Ryan wasn't just the Marshal, or a neighbor, or a good friend—he was her older brother. Jake's uncle. She had always tried not to worry about him; he was a brave and capable man, everybody knew that. But in a gunfight . . . Well, everybody also knew he wasn't as quick as he used to be—

"Uncle Stoney's fine, Ma. Dobbs is deader'n a bedbug."

His mother exhaled and closed her eyes. "Thank the Lord."

"I asked him just now if I could have the dead guy's gun and gunbelt," Jake said, with a wave toward the sack he had set down in the corner. "But I'll have to give it back later if a relative turns up to claim it."

A voice from the other side of the house—the work-shop—interrupted them. "Emily!" Jake's father called.

Jake glanced at the hallway door, then back to his mother. "Maybe you better be the one to tell Pa. I'm not sure he'll like the fact I've been gambling."

"I'm not sure I like it either," she said. "But you're right about one thing, son: We can sure use the money." Her face softened, and she gave him a smile. Bright tears were shining now in her eyes.

He smiled back, and when his father called again he said, "I better go, Ma, or I'll be late. See you after school." With that, he grabbed a bookbag from a hook on the wall and took off out the door. His mother watched him, her heart swelled with pride, till he rounded the other end of the garden and disappeared. Then she turned and walked, a little unsteadily, down the corridor to her husband's workroom, where she stopped outside the door-way to wipe her eyes.

Thank God the Marshal's okay, she said to herself. I guess he hasn't lost his touch after all. And twelve hundred dollars . . .

It was almost too much to believe.

She sighed and cleared her throat. "What is it, William?" she asked as she entered the room. The money was, for the moment, tucked out of sight in the pouch of her apron.

William Longbow glanced up from his cluttered worktable. "Emily, you haven't been cleaning in here again, have you? I told you, I—"

"Nobody's been in your things, Will." Her mind was still on her brother.

"Nothing's ever gone," her husband muttered, "until I need it the most. And then—"

She forced herself to pay attention. "Well, what is it? What's missing?"

Before answering, he raised his finger and pointed to a row of short glass containers on a shelf above his workbench.

"My glue," he said. "A bottle of my best glue."

John M. Floyd

ILLUMINATION

"Mr. Boatwright? I'm Judy Keszler, from Channel 10."

"I know who you are, Miss Keszler."

She lifted her chin and studied him a moment. "This had better be good, you know."

He smiled. "Won't you come in?"

The living room was small but neat, with books and plants and family photographs covering every flat surface. The air smelled of Pine-Sol. On the far side of the room an elderly woman sat in a blanketed wheelchair, her eyes closed in sleep.

"My wife," Boatwright said. "Multiple sclerosis."

Judy Keszler gave the old lady an impatient glance.

"We can talk in the back yard," he said. He led Keszler through the house and out the back door. A long metal swing and a lawn chair stood near the center of a fenced lot. Boatwright waved a hand toward the swing, waited while she was seated, and picked up the folding chair. He took his time positioning it, then sat down and faced his guest.

Just as she was opening her mouth to speak, he took a small device from his pocket and pointed it at the back fence. A hidden sprinkler system began peppering the long flowerbed that bordered the rear of the property.

Judy Keszler raised one eyebrow.

He shrugged. "I'm a scientist. It's my hobby as well as my profession. In addition to this"—he tipped his head toward the hissing sprinkler—"I'm working on a wristwatch roadmap system for motorists, a portable air-conditioning unit, a pocket-sized device for the filtering of secondhand smoke—"

"Mr. Boatwright," she said, "this is not what I came here to discuss."

For a moment he studied the remote control, turning it over in his hands. "I wasn't sure you would come at all."

"I started not to. I mean, all this mumbojumbo about keeping everything secret and taking the bus and not bringing anyone with me . . ." She picked a speck of lint off her skirt. "Rather strange requests, don't you think?"

"So why did you come?"

"Three reasons. One, you sounded fairly safe, on the phone. Two, even if you're not, I carry a gun in my purse. And three, I couldn't resist the chance—the *chance*, mind you—that you might actually have some worthwhile information about this case."

The old man nodded. "Tell me, Miss Keszler—"

"Ms."

"Tell me, Ms. Keszler, are you always this . . . abrupt?"

She gave him a cold stare. "What I am, is a professional. I have no time for pleasantries." She shifted position in the swing. "And I'm not looking for anyone's approval."

"What *are* you looking for?"

She seemed to consider that. "Illumination," she said.

He smiled again. "Illumination?"

"That's right."

"By camera lights, I suppose." He leaned back in the lawn

chair, watching her. "Or should I say limelight?"

"I am referring, as I think you know, to the quest for answers, and knowledge, and enlightenment. But in my case, yes, it has led me to my share of the limelight."

"Has it also led you to harass the relatives of innocent victims, Ms. Keszler?"

"What do you mean?"

"I saw your report last night. On the freeway accident."

She glared at him. "And?"

"I saw you ask a woman, 'How do you feel about the fact that your child was decapitated just now?'" He paused. "How can you *do* that, and still look at yourself in the mirror?"

A silence passed. Her dark eyes glittered like chips of coal.

"You're pretty abrupt yourself, you know."

He sighed. "Frankly, Ms. Keszler, there are two types of people I have absolutely no respect for. TV news reporters are one of them."

"And is that supposed to bother me?"

"Not at all. I just wanted you to know."

Judy Keszler leaned forward, her elbows resting on her gleamingly stockinged knees. "Let me give you some advice. There are hundreds of reporters in this city. There's only one of you. Save your breath." She raised up again, her face flushed. "And just for the record—was there any truth at all in what you told me on the phone?"

He frowned. "What?"

"I came here for information, Mr. Boatwright. Remember? You said you knew something about the two missing journalists."

"The missing TV reporters," he said. "I don't consider them journalists."

"Do you know something about them?"

"Of course I do. I know why they're missing."

The words seemed to linger there in the sudden silence. Slowly, without taking her eyes off his face, Judy Keszler removed a notepad from her purse, flipped it open, and uncapped a pen.

"Then tell me," she said, "why they're missing."

"They disappeared," he answered.

Her face darkened. "I know that. I want to know *why* they dis—"

"I don't mean they disappeared in the usual sense. I mean they vanished."

She narrowed her eyes. "What?"

"I've studied that kind of phenomenon, you see. Under certain conditions, light that has been focused and reflected through a perfect convex prism can cause what appears to be a deterioration—a vaporization, almost—of the basic materials that make up—"

"Get to the point," she said.

He shrugged. "They vanished. Poof. Body, clothes, shoes, everything but the rings on their fingers. One minute they're here, the next they're not."

She sat and stared at him, her notebook and pen apparently forgotten in her hands.

"And this," she said, "is what you said would be 'exclusive information' for Channel 10 News?"

"That's about it, yes." His voice had turned bored and distracted. It was a warm, clear day; he tilted his face skyward, squinting at the progress of the sun across the heavens.

She watched him a minute longer, then snorted. "You're a fool, Boatwright. And you've wasted enough of my time."

She replaced her pen and notepad, and started to rise.

"Just a moment." Still staring up at the sky, he raised the remote control and aimed it over his shoulder at the house. "I want to show you something," he said, and pressed a button. Behind him, in a sunlit window on the upper floor of the house, a tall mirrorlike device began to glow like a hot ember. A high-pitched whine filled the air. A second later, a beam of reflected white light passed within a foot of Boatwright's left shoulder and lit up the swing and the woman sitting in it.

For an instant she sat frozen in the eerie spotlight, her mouth open in wonder. Then she was gone.

Once again, he pressed the button on the remote. The device in the window went silent and dark. The beam winked out.

The empty swing moved slightly in the breeze. Scattered in its curved metal seat were a pair of earrings, a wristwatch, a keychain, a small black revolver, and a single gold filling from a tooth. The old man gathered them up and dropped them into a plastic bag he had taken from his pocket.

The air smelled faintly of ozone.

As he walked back to the house, Boatwright thought of something Keszler had said earlier:

There are hundreds of reporters in this city.

She was probably right, he decided.

Maybe it was time to move on to lawyers . . .

SPEED DIAL

Eddie Vance took a final look at the streetmap, folded it, and tucked it into his pocket. The grass of the hillside was soft and cool on the seat of his jeans, the sun warm on his face. He could smell honeysuckle somewhere nearby. This is how it feels to be free again, he thought.

Eddie remembered a movie he'd seen in the prison gymnasium a few weeks ago, a casino heist film with that Clooney guy from *ER*. He'd especially liked the ending, the hero serving his time and getting out, good as new. Unlike the movie character, though, Eddie Vance had emerged from the tall iron gates into the sunlight this morning to find nothing waiting for him. No stolen money, no girl, no friends. All he had was a plan.

He slid his cousin Ned's Luger automatic from his waistband and checked the clip. Nine rounds. More than enough.

He would only need two.

Eddie replaced the gun and looked down at the winding suburban street at the base of the slope, the view unobstructed by bars or walls or razor-wire. He knew that what he was about to do might send him back inside, for life this time. But he also knew he wouldn't go. What would happen would happen. If he got away with it, fine. If he got caught, that was fine too. He'd just use three bullets instead of two.

He drew a long breath of summer air and checked his wristwatch, a cheap digital he'd bought earlier today. Normally he didn't care what time it was. This afternoon he did.

Jack Mason would be leaving from work right about now.

Eddie rose to his feet, brushed off the seat of his stiff new jeans, and limped down the hill.

***

"May I help you?"

"You must be Mrs. Mason," he said. She was dressed in a cotton blouse and slacks and was drying her hands on a dishtowel.

"That's right," she said. "And you are . . ."

"A friend of your husband's."

Her smile was polite but cautious. Eddie figured Ann Mason's husband—like most cops—had more enemies than friends, and she probably already knew the friends. Besides, people just released from the Big House had a look about them.

"I'm afraid he's not home now," she said.

"I know." Eddie Vance took out the gun. "Step back inside, please."

He followed her through the front door, then locked it and put the security chain on. Her eyes stayed fixed on the pistol.

"Anyone else here?" he asked.

She took a breath, cleared her throat. She seemed shaken but not terrified. "No."

"Let's take a look anyway."

He steered her through the house, room by room. He of course knew they had no children, knew she was a writer and worked at home alone, but he had to be sure there were no visitors here, no friends or relatives or repairmen. Nothing could be left to chance.

The house was small, the tour short. Everything tidy and clean, beds made, clothes folded, bathrooms gleaming. So this is where Jack Mason spent his time while I was in an eight-by-ten cell, Eddie said to himself.

He'd seen enough. He made sure all the windows were locked and the back door was chained, then they retraced their steps to the kitchen, where she tossed her towel onto a counter-top covered with neat rows of silverware. They continued into the front room, a sort of living room with a couch, a pair of chairs, video and audio equipment, and two desks. One was wedged into a corner, the other positioned in front of a huge window. On an endtable beside the couch was a large purse made of some kind of meshed fabric. He wondered how you kept things from falling through the little holes in the material.

Eddie pulled the shade, blocking out the late-afternoon sun, and sat in a chair facing the entranceway. Ann Mason perched on the edge of the couch beside the endtable. He looked away from her long enough to inspect the darkened room more closely: framed photos, worn carpeting, TV/VCR/CD cabinet, old Pioneer speakers, book-lined walls. He could easily imagine Jack Mason and his wife sitting here together in the evenings, watching sitcoms and reading the newspaper—

"What do you think you're doing?" he blurted. He had turned to find her rummaging through her mesh purse.

"Looking for my cigarettes," she said.

"Put it down. Get away from there." Eddie motioned to her with the gun and watched her replace the purse on the table and move away. She sagged into the cushions at the other end of the couch and sat there looking at him, her face expressionless.

"No cigarettes, no moving around, no tricks," he said. "Just sit still." As it occurred to him, he added, "I didn't know you smoked."

She crossed her legs and gave him an icy look. "How would you know if I smoked or not?"

"I know a lot about you," he said.

"How?"

"We've talked quite a bit, your husband and me."

He saw something change in her eyes. "You're Vance," she said. "You're Eddie Vance, aren't you."

"Apparently you know things about me as well," he said.

For a long moment they sat and stared at each other. He knew what she'd heard. Three years ago Eddie and his older brother Dwayne had robbed a bank not far away. They had the money and were on the way out when they heard sirens and, against Eddie's protests, Dwayne took a female teller hostage. Moments later there was a standoff with police in the street, and Dwayne threatened to kill her if they weren't allowed safe passage.

Sergeant Jack Mason was at that time a police sharpshooter—a nice way of saying sniper, Eddie thought. And Mason didn't wait long for the Vance brothers to consider the bullhorned requests to lay down their weapons. All he waited for was an opening, and when Dwayne Vance took his gunbarrel away from the woman's temple long enough to wave Eddie toward the car, Jack Mason placed a bullethole in the center of Dwayne's forehead, and relocated what few brains he had onto the glass doors of the Midland Merchants Bank building. Eddie, who had already thrown down his pistol, turned to dive for it and felt his right leg explode. Mason's second shot had shattered his kneecap.

Could Mason have killed Eddie as easily as Dwayne? Of course. Eddie knew that. He also knew Jack Mason had crippled him and taken his brother's life, all in the space of five seconds, and sent him to prison to boot. He swore to get even.

But Eddie, unlike Dwayne, was not stupid. Almost from the day of his conviction Eddie had followed a sketchy but effective plan: He would devote every waking hour to plotting his revenge. He started by finding out the name of the teller Dwayne had tried to kidnap (she was physically unharmed but suffered an emotional breakdown) and sent her letters of apology, and even a portion of the pay Eddie received each week for his work in the prison laundry. Then he approached Mason himself, via letters and messages, offering his sincere regrets for what had happened and his assurance of a change of heart. He asked Mason to come visit, which he did, and within three months they were meeting regularly. Somewhere in the process, Eddie's secret generosity to the teller was revealed—as Eddie had known it would be—and further boosted his credibility. The cop/inmate relationship evolved into an odd friendship; for more than two years they talked about everything from books to hobbies to religion. Mason even told Eddie he would help him find work, if and when he was paroled.

But Eddie didn't stop there. Inside the granite walls he searched out those who had known Sergeant Mason or known of him, and who could supply or verify knowledge of his job, his family, his daily routine. As a result of that—and of hours spent online in the prison library, checking access routes and commute times—Eddie now knew, as well as any outsider could, what Mason's usual movements were, on any particular day. Because Jack Mason, it turned out, had two faults: (1) he was too trusting, and (2) he was a creature of habit. Dangerous traits, for a law officer.

When he arrived home today, Eddie would be waiting.

Ann Mason tilted her head and studied him in the dim light. "You're going to kill him, aren't you," she said. It wasn't a question. "You're going to kill me, too."

He didn't reply. Instead he looked again at his watch. 5:13. Mason would be getting off the freeway soon.

"I suppose you know where he is," she said. "And when

he'll get home."

"Yes."

"You went to a lot of trouble."

"It'll be worth it," Eddie said.

The room was quiet. Somewhere nearby he heard a clock ticking. A truck roared by in the street outside.

"Let me ask you something," she said. "If you were so chummy, the two of you, why didn't you just call and come over? Have dinner with us, maybe? No forced entry, no risks. Then you could murder him—both of us—at your convenience."

He felt himself smile. "You want to know why?" he said.

"That's what I'm asking, yes."

"Because I'm tired of secrets," he said. "Make no mistake, I hate your husband, Mrs. Mason, I've hated him since the day he killed my brother and shot me and put me away. But for the whole time since then, I've had to be the model prisoner, the reformed sinner. I'm changed, hallelujah, I've seen the light." He shook his head. "I'm sick of playacting. Of being somebody I'm not."

She watched him a moment, as if thinking that over. Then she nodded. "Me too," she whispered.

"What?"

"Nothing."

Eddie looked again at the time. 5:20. About now Jack Mason should be pulling into Bernie's Tavern on Nowell Street for a drink with the other cops, as always, and twenty minutes later he would leave the bar and continue via surface roads to the house. Eddie knew the route by heart. Mason should arrive here at a quarter to six, give or take a few minutes.

Right on schedule.

Still, Eddie felt his hand sweating on the grip of the automatic. The thing with the purse had spooked him. He was comfortable with his overall plan; he was locked away in secret in the very den of the lion, and all he had to do was wait. Even if his presence here became known by others (and it wouldn't), they couldn't see him or what he was doing, or get to him without endangering the wife. But the wife worried him. He would have to be more careful of her. If there'd been a gun in that purse of hers he'd be dead now.

She spoke up then, interrupting his thoughts: "How'd you do it?"

"What?"

"Some of the things you had to know, to do this," she said, "Jack wouldn't have told you. How'd you find out so much?"

He shifted the gun to his left hand and wiped his damp right palm on his thigh. "We live in a pushbutton world, Mrs. Mason. Remotes, Tivo, speed dial, one-touch recordings—"

"What are you talking about?"

"Technology." He wiggled his fingers like a typist. "Google. E-mail. It's easy to find things out, if you know who to ask and where to look." He grinned. "Even in prison. The websites they block weren't the ones I wanted anyway."

He paused then, listening. A siren wailed in the distance. Getting closer. He tensed and sat up straight. Then it blew past, the sound fading. He wiped a trembling hand across his brow.

Ann watched him in silence. Finally she said, "I understand why you hate my husband. I know the story. But what about me?"

"What?"

"Why would you hate me?"

"I don't hate you."

"But you'll kill me anyway."

He hesitated. "Not because I want to."

"Well, you don't have to," she said.

Eddie felt another ripple of unease inch its way up his

spine. He had misjudged this lady, he knew that now. He hadn't thought she'd be this calm. Here she was, her life hanging in the balance, sitting there looking at him as if considering whether to hire him as a lawnboy.

"What do you mean, I don't have to?" he said.

"I mean killing me is not only unnecessary—it would be the worst thing you could do."

"Why's that?"

"Because I can help you."

"You can what?" he said.

"I can offer you something."

There she went, doing it again. Surprising him. He had a fixed agenda, everything mapped out. He didn't want, or need, surprises.

Still, he had to ask. "Offer me what?"

She sat back and smoothed the fabric of the couch. "You say you've been gathering information about us," she said. "Have you ever heard of us going someplace together?"

"Going someplace?"

"You haven't, have you. That's because we *don't* go anyplace together. Not anymore." She held up her left hand. The ring finger was bare. "I've been playacting, too, for a long time. We're having problems, Jack and I. Do you understand? Big problems. I bet he never mentioned that."

"Look, I really don't care if—"

"What I'm telling you is, if you're here to kill him . . ." She leaned forward, elbows propped on her knees, her face hardening. "If you're here to kill him, more power to you, Eddie Vance. I won't stand in your way. But there's a good reason not to kill me too."

Eddie was watching her closely now, his wristwatch forgotten.

"What's the reason?" he asked.

"It's right here." She rose to her feet and took two steps toward the heavy oak desk in the back corner.

"Hold it!" he said. "Sit down."

She stopped, gave him an exasperated look, and went back to her seat.

"And don't you make another move," he said.

"You get it, then." She pointed. "That's his desk. Top righthand drawer."

Eddie hesitated, thinking hard. Nothing about this was going the way he'd figured. Hostages were supposed to be scared, dammit. And something else was bothering him too, something about the room. About the whole house. But he couldn't pin it down.

"Go ahead," she said.

Slowly he sidestepped across the room and opened the desk drawer. He took his eyes off her long enough to look inside.

"The insurance policy," she said. "It's on top."

He took it from the drawer, turning a bit so he could hold it with one hand while keeping the gun on her with the other.

"It's a whole life policy, on Jack. Five hundred thousand." She leaned back into the couch cushions, her eyes focused and unblinking.

He scanned the information, looking back and forth from her to the papers. Even in the gloom he could make out the amounts. He felt his heartbeat quicken.

"I'll split it with you if you let me live," she said. "A quarter million apiece."

He studied her a moment, dropped the policy onto the desktop, and returned to his chair. Watching her the whole way.

"You hate him that much?" he asked.

"No. I just can't live with him any longer." Her face was still calm, her voice steady. "And since you're set on killing him, and I need to save myself—"

"This would work out for everybody," he finished.

She shrugged, a tiny rise and fall of her shoulders. "You get revenge, I get freedom, we both become moderately wealthy."

"I'll think about it," he said. He checked his watch again. Almost five-thirty. Mason would still be at Bernie's, having a Miller Lite. Plenty of time yet.

But maybe not so much time. Eddie had decisions to make. The woman's proposal was interesting, provided it was true. But he still couldn't shake the feeling that something was out of place here. He glanced around the room. The tabletops, the desktops, the purse, something was amiss . . . but he couldn't put it together.

"So what happens next?" she asked.

"We wait. When he gets here, you stay put and stay quiet."

"How're you going to know when he gets here? You can't see him with the windowshade down."

Eddie blew out a sigh. He wished she'd stop talking and let him think.

"The shade's down so *he* can't see *us*," he said. "I don't need to see out—I told you, I know what time he'll get here. Besides, I'll hear him unlock the door."

"But you put the chain on. He'll know something's wrong."

"Don't worry about it, okay? I'll slip the chain before he arrives. And when he gets inside—"

"You'll shoot him."

"That's the plan," he said. "Now shut up."

Ann gazed off into space a minute, then faced him again. "One more thing."

"What?"

"There's something I don't understand, about your plan."

Her brow furrowed like a child's. "If you intend to kill me too, why didn't you do it right away? What good could it do to let me—"

She paused, and her frown faded. She nodded slowly.

"Well, well," she said. "I think I do understand." She actually smiled a little. "You're keeping me alive in case he calls home."

Eddie just watched her. He made no reply.

"You say you've studied us, but it's not enough, is it? There's no way you could know whether Jack calls me sometimes from Bernie's, or from his car on his way home. Maybe to ask if he should pick up a loaf of bread, a gallon of milk. Isn't that right? And you need me here to answer the phone if he calls today."

He smiled too. "Your husband told me you were smart."

"Smarter than you, it seems."

"What do you mean?"

"What if he calls my cell phone? Have you thought of that?"

He blinked. "Your cell phone?"

"Everybody has a cell phone, Mr. Vance. I'm no exception. And Jack has both it and the house phone on his speed dial. What if he calls my cell instead?"

Eddie thought a moment, licked his lips. "Where is it?" he asked.

"If I tell you, would that convince you?"

"Convince me?"

"That I'm sincere about this. About helping you."

He felt the beginnings of a headache. "Just tell me," he said, through clenched teeth.

She let several seconds pass. Then: "It's in my writing desk. The one in front of the window." And before he knew what was happening she stood again, cool as could be, and headed for the little desk backed up against the lowered windowshade.

"I told you not to move!" he said, raising the gun. "I'll get it."

She sat down again.

"And stay put." Glaring at her, Eddie limped across the carpet to the writing desk, stood in front of it, pulled on the only drawer. It opened with a loud creak.

He looked inside.

"There's no cell phone in here—"

And in that split-second, as the words passed his lips and he looked at the drawer, empty except for writing paper and pens and a tray full of paperclips, the answer hit him. He realized what was bothering him about this room.

There were no ashtrays.

Why would she have cigarettes in her purse and no ashtrays around? He'd seen the whole house—there were none anywhere. The house didn't even smell like cigarette smoke.

And another thing: When she'd returned to her seat just now, she hadn't sat on the couch like before, opposite the window. She was in one of the chairs.

And just like that, everything clicked into place. He knew where the cell phone was. And why she was sitting in a different chair.

She was out of the line of fire.

That knowledge hit him the same instant the bullet did. It punched through the glass and the drawn windowshade and took him square in the chest, knocking him backward; the second and third plowed through his neck and shoulder. He went down hard, on his back, and lay there on the carpet, his ears ringing and his eyes staring up at a ceiling that was spinning like a roulette wheel.

Then he saw Ann Mason standing over him. She had picked up his gun and was pointing it at him. Her jaw was set, her back ramrod-straight.

He drew a painful breath. "It was in your purse the whole time, wasn't it?"

"What was?" she said. Her voice seemed to come from somewhere far away.

"Your cell phone. You turned it on at the very first, when you looked in your purse."

Ann stared down at him. From the edge of his consciousness Eddie heard something slam into the front door. The chain was still on.

"Your husband heard every word we said, didn't he?" Through that damn little mesh purse. Eddie coughed, felt something tear inside him. "He heard us and came straight home. No stops, this time." Her husband had also heard the familiar creak of the writing-desk drawer, as she'd known he would. Eddie couldn't believe it: She had set him up, positioned him right in front of the darkened window while Mason waited outside, finger on the trigger, listening for that creak.

Still Ann said nothing. Her eyes were tiny slivers of coal.

"But how?" he asked. "You had no time to place the call—"

"It's a pushbutton world, Eddie. You said so yourself."

He swallowed, then understood. "Speed dial," he said.

She nodded.

Unbelievable. Then he had another thought, something about the kitchen counter, and tried to focus on her hand. "Your wedding ring?"

"Under the dishtowel," she said. "I was polishing it, along with the silver."

This time he was the one who nodded. Mistakes galore. He was about to close his eyes when he heard the splintering of wood in the entranceway and saw Jack Mason burst into the living room, his sniper rifle smoking and his face pale as a tombstone. His wife handed him the pistol and stepped into his open arms.

The two of them, locked in an embrace, was the last thing Eddie Vance saw.

And as his limbs grew numb and his chest tightened, as everything began to dim out, he looked up at Jack Mason and said, "You were right."

"Right about what?"

"She's smart," Eddie said.

ELEVATOR MUSIC

Sally Pritchard believed in Fate. She believed that those who are meant for each other will be drawn together. Whether they remain together is another matter, of course; all Fate does is ensure that their paths will cross. She figured it's up to the participants to take it from there.

But Sally's mind, when she stepped into the elevator on the first morning of her new job, wasn't on Fate, or on men. It was on her watch, and her appearance, and the butterflies in her stomach. Still, she couldn't help noticing the blond man standing beside her—and the fact that he had a problem.

He had his collar upturned and a suitcoat draped over one arm, and was trying to tie a necktie using the mirrored back wall of the elevator. He wasn't having an easy time of it.

Before going back to his task he gave her a sheepish grin—a grin that made Sally feel she knew what he must have looked like as a little boy. It also made her say something that, under different circumstances, she would never have dreamed of saying.

"Fashion problem?" she asked him.

The grin reappeared. "Fashion crisis. I have a sales meeting in eight minutes, and I spilled coffee on my tie in the car." As he spoke he loosened a lopsided knot and started over again.

"I don't see a stain," she said.

"This one's a spare, from my glove compartment—but it's ten years too old and an inch too wide."

She pushed the button for eighteen and studied his profile as the doors eased shut.

"Here, let me try," she said. "I have three brothers."

Fifteen seconds later she finished off a passable half-windsor, gave it a final tug, and smoothed his collar. "There. You have a perfect dimple."

"You have two of them," he said.

She looked up to find him staring at her.

"I meant in your tie," she said, smiling.

The elevator car slowed, then stopped. Both of them blinked and faced forward. Sixth floor.

The doors opened; nobody there. Seconds later they closed again.

The blond man pulled his jacket on. "Thanks for the help," he said.

"You're welcome." Sally flicked him a glance, then watched the digital floor numbers above the door.

"Do you work here in the building?" he asked.

"It's my first day. Actually, I'm a little nervous." She turned to look at him. "What about you?"

"Am I nervous?"

She grinned again. "Do you work here."

"Twelve years," he said.

That made sense, she thought. He looked about her age, early- to mid-thirties.

"What do you do?"

"I'm a salesman." He was staring at her again. She felt

her face getting warm.

"What do you sell?"

"Anything the company makes," he said.

The elevator stopped again, on nine. A middle-aged woman got on, struggling to balance a stack of books and a potted plant. She got off on ten. Sally held the elevator while he helped the woman carry her load to an office across the hall.

When he returned Sally said, "One of your customers?"

They both smiled.

"Everybody's a customer," he said.

Amused, she stared at the closing doors. "You like to speak in generalities, don't you."

"I suppose I do. Generally speaking."

A silence passed.

"I can be specific, you know. If I try."

"Let's hear it," she said.

"Antonio's. Corner of Hamilton and Fourth."

"I beg your pardon?"

"Go to lunch with me," he said.

She turned and looked him in the eye. He appeared to be holding his breath. After a moment she smiled again. "Okay."

He exhaled and grinned from ear to ear.

"Should I meet you there?" she asked.

"I'll stop by your office. Where do you—I mean, where will you be working?"

"Eighteen. Accounting."

He blinked. "You're with Cameron Enterprises?"

"How'd you know that?"

"We have the top three floors."

Her eyes widened. "You work there too?"

"Don't look so shocked."

"I'm not," she said quickly. "It's just . . ."

He waited.

"I wondered if they might frown on . . . you know—"

"Fraternization in the ranks?" he asked.

She blushed a little.

"You tied my tie," he said, "and I asked you to lunch. We're not engaged or anything."

"Darn," she said.

She looked up at him, and their eyes locked. If this were a movie, she thought, violins would be playing.

This is wild, she told herself.

She drew a deep breath and concentrated on the floor numbers. She assumed he was going to nineteen; it was the only other button lit up.

"What time?" he asked.

She knew he meant lunch. "I'm not sure. I have a meeting at eleven on the twentieth floor."

"With the brass?"

"I guess. Introductions, they said."

He nodded. "Standard procedure, the first day."

"The twentieth floor," she repeated, half to herself. "It sounds intimidating."

"It is, in a way."

"Are you there a lot? As a salesman?"

"As little as possible."

She frowned, thinking that over. "They're not a bad bunch, are they?"

"They're pretty good folks, actually. Everybody here is."

"Generalities again. You sure you're not a lawyer?"

"Positive." He studied her awhile, his eyes twinkling. "11:45," he said.

"What?"

"I'm being specific again. That's when I'll pick you up."

The elevator glided to a stop. Eighteenth floor.

"What if they're not done with me by then?" she asked as

the doors opened.

"Tell them they have to be."

She smiled. "You're a little crazy, you know that?"

His face turned serious. For a moment time itself seemed to stand still.

"Only since you rescued me," he said.

They stood there a second longer, looking at each other. She swallowed. "I'm Sally," she said, her voice low.

"Tom."

The doors started to close. She held a hand out to stop them. "Accounting," she said, backing out into the hallway.

"I'll remember."

The doors closed between them.

***

During the next three hours, Sally learned that Cameron Enterprises had sixty-two employees, twenty of whom were in marketing, on the nineteenth floor. And only one of the salesmen was named Tom.

"Tommy Fordham," a young lady named Deborah informed her, as they sat in the break room over cups of hot chocolate. "He's an okay guy, I guess."

Sally was instantly alert. "Just okay?"

"Don't worry, he's not out on parole or anything. He's just not too . . . reliable."

Deborah gave no further explanation, which did Sally's nerves no good at all. She stewed over it the rest of the morning. She finally decided, as she took the elevator to the twentieth floor at 10:55, that Deborah was wrong. Sally knew nothing about Tom, really—and yet she did. She thought Fate had had a hand in this, with or without violin music.

An attractive older woman met her outside the CEO's office on twenty. "I'm Mary," she said. "Mr. Cameron's assistant."

Sally followed her through a mahogany door and into a

huge corner office. Beyond the floor-to-ceiling windows was a panoramic view of the mountains west of the city. The head of the company rose from his desk as they entered.

"Ms. Sally Pritchard," the assistant said, "Mr. Thomas Cameron."

Sally's jaw dropped as Mary left the room.

"Tom?" she murmured.

"I got three compliments on the tie," he said. "How are you at fixing budget problems?"

Sally broke out a slow smile. "I thought marketing was on nineteen," she said.

"It is. I met with them there, this morning."

"You said you were a salesman."

He grinned. "Everyone here's a salesman." He walked around the desk and took her hands in his. "Generally speaking."

She swallowed. "Do you believe in Fate, Tom Cameron?"

"I believe in early lunches," he said.

She realized, as they left together, that her nervousness was gone.

CLARA'S HELPER

The doorbell chimed. Somewhere in the house there was the sharp clocking of footsteps on a wooden floor, then the release of a latch and the creak of a door as it opened wide. Sunlight flashed off the long blade of a butcher knife.

Jim Holliman took a step back, almost to the edge of the porch. "Ms. Vanetti?" he asked.

"That's me." With two quick swipes of her dishtowel the lady in the doorway finished drying the knife, then pointed it off to her right. "The mower's around back, if that's what you're here for."

"Excuse me?"

She studied him a moment. "Didn't you come to look at the lawnmower?"

"No ma'am." He flashed his badge. "I'm Inspector Holliman, from downtown. I wanted to ask you some questions about Ms. Endicott."

"Oh." The knife drooped. "My mistake." She took a long look at his outfit, which consisted of blue jeans and sneakers and a leather bomber jacket. "You're not . . . what I expected."

John M. Floyd

"Neither are you," he said, pocketing his badge. It was the name, for one thing. The yellow-aproned woman in the doorway was sturdy and blond and blue-eyed, like a girl you might see drawing a stein of beer in a German travel poster. She didn't look like a Vanetti. Also, she seemed too young to have been Clara Endicott's housekeeper for thirty years, which was what he'd been told by one of the neighbors. Holliman asked her about it as he followed her down the dark hallway toward the rear of the house.

"I started here when I was twelve," she said. It sounded like the kind of joking remark often heard when the subject is age and the number of years on the job, but Holliman saw that she was serious. "I came over on afternoons and weekends until I graduated," she added, "and by that time my folks were gone and I was married and I needed the money even more than before."

The hallway led to a large, old-fashioned kitchen, where Ruth Vanetti tucked the knife away in a drawer, draped the towel over the rest of the waiting dishes, and waved her visitor toward a chair at the table. "How about a glass of tea?" she asked.

"No, thanks." Holliman shrugged out of his coat and sat down, taking a quick glance around the room. "You were saying . . . ?"

"Oh. Yes." She took a seat across the table from him. "By that time I was married, but I just stayed on the payroll, so to speak. Every day I came over and did the laundry and cooked her meals and swept the floors and so on." She paused and adjusted the tablecloth. "A few years later, when my husband died, I more or less moved in with her."

"You moved in here, you mean? In this house?"

"That's right. Clara was getting pretty frail even then, and needed me more than just part-time." Ms. Vanetti paused again, as if remembering happier days. During the silence Holliman took a ballpoint pen and notepad from his pocket and flipped to a clean page.

"Were you her only housekeeper, during all that time?"

She blinked and looked at him. "Yes. I was."

"So you were close, the two of you?"

"I'm not sure anyone was very close to Clara Endicott. We got along, I guess you'd say."

He clicked his pen and made a note in the pad. "So there were disagreements, then?"

"We were both women, Inspector Holliman. Of course there were disagreements. But as I said, we got along most of the time."

Holliman stopped what he was writing and studied the result as if regarding a rare piece of artwork. "How did your husband die, Ms. Vanetti?"

She didn't reply right away. Finally he raised his head, and their eyes met. "An oil rig accident," she said. "In the Gulf."

"I see. And afterward, you said you moved in here."

She shrugged, and for an instant Holliman saw the sadness underneath the composed outer shell. "I had no choice. Creditors took our trailer, and Paulie wasn't much on the idea of life insurance."

"And you've been here ever since?"

"Going on eighteen years."

"Were you with her the night she died?"

She sat there and stared at him for a long time.

"Is something wrong?" he said.

"Inspector, you said you wanted to ask me some questions about Ms. Endicott."

He leaned back in his chair. "I thought that's what I was doing."

"All your questions so far have been about me."

He sighed. "I'm a detective, Ms. Vanetti. I just like to get all my facts strai—"

"The doctor said she died of natural causes, Inspector. Isn't that right?"

"That's what he said, yes."

Neither of them spoke for a moment. Outside the kitchen window, the branches of an old cedar tree nodded in the breeze.

"Why did you ask me how my husband died?" she said.

"I told you, I only wanted—"

"Inspector, I'll be direct." Her expression was no longer composed, or even sad. There was a challenge in her eyes now. "It doesn't sound to me like you're investigating what you think is a death from natural causes. It sounds like you're investigating what you think is a murder."

Slowly Holliman closed his notepad and held it flat between the palms of his hands.

"I'm not sure it was a murder," he said. "It might have been suicide. But it was one or the other."

She stared back at him in disbelief. The defiance in her eyes had disappeared as quickly as it had come. Her pretty round face had gone slack, her cheeks pale. Even her bright blond hair seemed to have lost its color. It was as if someone had waved a wand and suddenly rendered her Old.

"But . . . she died in her sleep."

"She died, yes. In her sleep? Possibly. But not of old age." He paused, then said, "She was poisoned."

This time Ms. Vanetti just blinked. Otherwise her face remained frozen with shock. Holliman watched her closely. If she was faking, she was the best actress he'd ever seen.

"Poisoned," she repeated.

He nodded.

"But the doctor said—"

"He didn't know. The coroner noticed it later. Smelled it on her breath."

Ruth Vanetti gaped at him.

"Sorry," he said. "Bad choice of words. He smelled it on her mouth. The poison was something called strophanthus, and he had run across it before, in his work with the Peace Corps. It's an arrow poison, like curare. The effects are blurred vision, then circulatory failure, then death." He rubbed his forehead. "At any rate, the coroner caught it, and did an autopsy. Definitely strophanthus. Taken orally, in this case."

Ms. Vanetti swallowed hard, as if demonstrating the procedure in question. She looked dazed. "I . . . don't quite know what to say."

Holliman opened his pad once more and raised his pen. "Were you with her," he asked again, "the night she died?"

"I was here in the house, yes."

"But not with her?"

"I . . . found her. Afterward."

"In her bedroom?"

"That's right."

The inspector flipped back through notes he had made when talking to the other officers. "That was on the twelfth? Two nights ago?"

"Yes." Her face had regained some of its color now, but she was still shaken. She seemed to be having trouble focusing her thoughts.

"What time would that have been?"

"What time?"

"When did you find the body, exactly?"

She frowned. "Around midnight, I think. Maybe a few minutes before."

"I see." The pen scribbled a note. "Did she cry out, then?"

"What?"

"I asked if she cried out, or called to you."

"No, she didn't call to me. I told you, she died in her sleep. Or so I thought, anyway."

Holliman looked up from his pad. "Then I'm a little confused, Ms. Vanetti. If you weren't summoned, what were you doing there with her, at midnight?"

At that, her face seemed to sag even further. She looked as if she might be about to burst into tears. Holliman didn't know if it was because of her memory of what had happened or because of the fact that he had asked her about it.

She drew a shaky breath, then said, as if each word was painful to her: "My room's down the hall from hers, and I always watch TV till late. Before I went to bed myself, I always went back in to check on her."

"Why was that? Did she have trouble sleeping?"

"It was just my routine." She seemed a little irritated. "She couldn't see well enough to read much, so I read to her every night around 9:30. It usually took half an hour or so. I would leave her room around ten, she'd go to bed at eleven, and I'd come back to check on her at midnight." She stared dreamily down at the tablecloth for a moment. "I look in on her again at seven every morning. She's always asleep both times, but I check on her just the same."

Suddenly Ruth Vanetti's face changed again. She looked surprised, and embarrassed. Her right hand came up to cover her mouth. "Oh my," she whispered. "I said that as if . . . as if everything were still the same."

Holliman thought he saw tears shining in her eyes.

"I can't believe she's really gone," Ruth Vanetti said.

Neither of them spoke for a while. As he waited Holliman could hear sparrows playing in the trees behind the house. Somewhere nearby a dog yapped, and what sounded like a large truck rumbled past in the street.

"Could I see her room?" he asked.

***

Clara Endicott's bedroom was bright and warm and spotless. Inspector Holliman stood in the center of the room with his hands in his pockets for a full five minutes or more, scanning everything, trying to picture the scene as it had been two nights before, when the old woman was alive and breathing and lying there in the bed after Ruth Vanetti had left and returned to her own room. The coroner had been emphatic about one point: That particular poison took perhaps an hour to do its work—an hour and a quarter at the most. If what the housekeeper had told him was true, Clara Endicott must have ingested the poison between ten and eleven o'clock. The question was, how had it happened?

The bedroom was simply, almost childishly, furnished: bed, dresser, wardrobe, nightstand. The bed was large but plain, covered with a thick flowered spread with ruffles around the hem. Small pictures in wooden frames littered the top of the dresser; most were old and black-and-white, and the few that were in color were of small children holding pets or dolls or Christmas presents. The nightstand was a large bedside table stocked with a vase of dried flowers and a clock and a cupful of pens and pencils. No phone, no radio, no TV. Sunlight filtered into the room through thin pink curtains.

Holliman frowned. Something about the room bothered him, but he couldn't put his finger on it. Finally he nodded and followed the housekeeper out the door and down the stairs to the kitchen.

"Ms. Vanetti," he said when they were seated again at the table, "was anyone else here that night? Did she have any visitors at all?" He had taken her up on the offer of tea this time, and sipped from his glass as he waited for her answer.

"No," she said. "Only me."

"What about during that day?"

She shook her head. "No one ever comes here anymore, Inspector. Certainly not to visit."

He pondered that for several seconds. "Let me make sure

I have something right. You left her at ten, watched TV till twelve, then went back and found her dead. Correct?"

"Yes."

"Did she have a bedtime snack, possibly? Or anything to drink?"

"Not to my knowledge."

"What do you mean by that?"

"I mean I didn't bring her anything. There's always the chance, I guess, that she went and got a snack or glass of water on her own, but I doubt it. She doesn't—didn't—get around very well, and I don't think she'd have tried to tackle the stairs by herself."

Holliman ran a finger along the rim of his glass, thinking. "I suppose you ate together that night, the two of you?"

"Yes, we did. Right here at this table, matter of fact."

"Could she have carried something to her room with her afterward, that you didn't know about?"

The housekeeper sighed. "She could have, I suppose. Again, I doubt it. She just didn't do those things."

A silence passed. Ruth Vanetti was looking more weary with every passing minute. For the first time, Holliman realized he could hear the soft chiming of a clock somewhere in the house.

He took another drink of iced tea, then set his glass down and studied it a moment. Finally he asked, "You and Ms. Endicott were the only two people in the household for many years, is that right?"

"That's correct."

"Who bought the groceries?"

"The groceries?"

"Did you go out and buy them yourself, or were they brought in?"

"I bought the food myself. I wrote checks on Clara's account, then paid her back for my share." For an instant the challenging look returned to her eyes. "I was very careful about the accounting."

"I don't doubt that, Ms. Vanetti. Bear with me, here." His notepad was out again now, and open. "It has been established that she died of poison, taken orally. That means, to me, food or drink. Did you buy *all* the groceries?"

"Yes."

"Well then, did you buy anything that she ate and you didn't?"

That caught her by surprise. She seemed to give it some thought. "Not that I remember. I ate some things she didn't, but not the other way around."

"Even drinks? Sodas, lemonade, grape juice—"

"Clara only drank water. Nothing but. Morning, noon, and night." Ruth Vanetti allowed herself a weak smile. "She said it was the secret to a long life."

"And you're sure someone else couldn't have given her something?"

"Everything went through me, Inspector Holliman. I think I wish now that it hadn't."

"And you're positive no one else came to the house that day?"

"No one but Freddic. He comes every day, but only to the front door. He gives everything to me."

Holliman narrowed his eyes. "Freddie?"

"Freddie Barton. He works now and then at the filling station around the corner. Before I started here full time, Clara used to pay him to run errands for her. Afterward, we just kept it up. He didn't have much else to do, and it was kind of handy."

Holliman took down the name. "What kind of errands?"

"All kinds. Dry cleaners', bank, post office, Wal-Mart, anything she needed. Even when she didn't, he brought the mail and the newspaper."

John M. Floyd

"And he gave it to you?"

"That's right."

"And you gave it to Ms. Endicott?"

"Inspector, I told you—she saw no one but me. She wanted it that way."

"But he did come that day?"

"Freddie? He comes every day." Ruth Vanetti seemed to be tiring of this, and it showed on her face. "You want some more tea?"

"No, thanks." He paused for a beat. "Why didn't she want to see anybody?"

She heaved a sigh. "That's quite a story. She was a very wealthy woman, you see, before the medicine started taking all her money—"

"Wait a minute," he said. "The medicine?"

"Her heart medicine. Expensive stuff, that was."

"She was taking heart medication? How often?"

"Three times a day."

"Including late at night?"

She shook her head. "Only before meals. And we had supper at seven that night, like always."

"Could she have smuggled some to her room with her? Taken it without telling you, maybe, before turning in?"

Another sigh. "I guess it's possible, Inspector, but it would have been totally out of character for her to do that. I gave her all her medicine. I never found any in her room in all these years."

He thought that over. "What kind of medicine? Liquid, from a bottle?"

"No, they were pills."

"Capsules?"

"Some of them. Others were tablets."

"But if some were capsules . . ." Holliman pondered

that for a moment, remembering the old commercials for "time-released" headache relief. That could be a possibility. "Where were the prescriptions filled? Here in this area?"

"That's right. Robinson's Drugs. Surely you don't think—"

"We'll check it out. Right now I'd like to go back to something else. You said Ms. Endicott was wealthy before she got sick . . ."

"Right. But it's the *way* she got wealthy that caused the problems. You see, there used to be a cotton gin out on Highway 12, and a meat-packing plant over in Redford, and a bank and a lamp factory downtown. They were all Clara's. Actually they were her husband's, but he left them to her when he died." A sad look crossed her face. "Those are gone now. Torn down, or sold and revamped. She got rid of them all. Before she was through she put half of this side of town out of work."

"So you're saying a lot of people around here never forgave her?"

"I'm saying a lot of people around here hated her guts."

"What about the druggist, Robinson? Was he an admirer?"

She chuckled without humor. "Even the ones who didn't hate her weren't admirers, Inspector. But to answer your question, Hiram Robinson had no special grudge against her. Not that I know of, anyway."

Holliman glanced at his notepad. "And . . . Freddie Barton?"

"That's a different story. Freddie's sister had a stroke and died the day she was laid off from the packing plant."

"Is that so. And he had had recent contact with the deceased."

"Well, indirectly. Through me."

Jim Holliman stayed quiet a moment. "The thing that really bothers me is the poison. After all, it wasn't strychnine, or arsenic, or anything common. It was rare and exotic, practically inaccessible." He chewed on his lower lip, then asked: "Could Freddie Barton have had any history or connections outside the country? Relatives in foreign service, vacations abroad, that kind of thing?"

"People around here don't take vacations abroad, Inspector. Freddie went somewhere way off with a church group a while back, but I don't know where."

"A church group? Like missionary work, you mean?"

"I think so."

"Where? Africa, maybe? South America?"

"I really don't know, Inspector. You'd have to ask him."

"I will." Holliman mulled on that awhile, then rubbed a hand over his eyes. "Okay," he said. "Can you think of *anyone* else who might have come here to the house that day? Salesmen, a minister, a repairman . . ."

She looked pained. "No. Certainly none of those. Clara hated salesmen with a vengeance, all preachers were off-limits, and there hasn't been a repairman here since the day the pipes froze under the house last winter."

Holliman gave her a stare. "You thought I had come to fix the lawnmower," he reminded her.

"I thought you had come to *buy* the lawnmower. It's out back, in the shed. Besides, you would have been the first to answer the ad."

Holliman reached up and scratched his cheek with the end of the pen. "Hmm. So you're sure Clara Endicott never had a moment's contact with anyone the day of the . . . the day of her death."

The housekeeper shook her head. "Not face to face. She wrote to her kids and grandkids all the time, and a few old acquaintances from her hometown back East—"

"I thought she couldn't see well enough to read."

The irritated look returned. "I said she couldn't read, I

didn't say she couldn't write. It was mostly chicken-scratching, but it did the job, or so she thought. Anyhow, it didn't matter much—nobody ever wrote back to her." Ms. Vanetti drew a long breath and exhaled. "The truth is, she was a lonely, pitiful old woman, right up to the very end. She had no real family and no real friends." As she spoke these last words, Holliman could once more see tears in her eyes.

This was one complex woman, he told himself. Over the past half hour he had seen her demonstrate every emotion from fear to anger to surprise to sadness, with very little transition time from one to the other. But the strangest thing was that all these emotions seemed to be genuine. Holliman sighed. He was no psychologist, but in the course of his career he had become good at recognizing a killer when he saw one. This lady was no more guilty of murder than his great-aunt Mildred.

Finally he closed his notebook and put it away. "Well, thank you for your time, Ms. Vanetti. I'll be in touch."

They stood.

"Aren't you going to tell me not to leave town?"

He smiled. "Don't leave town."

She swallowed, looked around at the kitchen, then turned to face him again. "It's the house, isn't it? That's the reason."

"I beg your pardon?"

"The fact that she left it to me. It was a total surprise, you know. It never entered my head she would do something like that. I never even knew she had a will." A tear spilled onto her cheek, and she brushed it away with the back of her hand. "Then again, I guess we spent a lot of time here together, she and I."

A response really wasn't required, and he didn't make one. He just stood there and watched her, waiting.

Finally she straightened up a bit and stared him in the eye. She looked as thoroughly miserable as anyone he had ever seen.

"I watch a lot of TV, Inspector," she said. "From the

police point of view, I'm the ideal suspect. Opportunity and motive. Am I right?"

He started to say something, changed his mind, then said it anyway.

"I think you'll come through this fine, Ms. Vanetti. I shouldn't be telling you that, but I think you will. If I'm any judge at all, that is."

She gave him a sad smile. "Maybe so," she said.

They walked together down the gloomy hallway. As he was about to leave, he turned to face her. "One more thing. You told me you read a book to her that night, until around ten o'clock."

"That's right."

"And then you went to your room."

"Right."

"And you came back at midnight to find her dead. Two hours later."

"We've been over all this, Inspector—"

"Hear me out. Is what I've said correct?"

"Yes."

"And you also told me she went to sleep around eleven o'clock every night."

"That's right."

Holliman stayed quiet a moment, deep in thought. "When you took me to see her bedroom," he said, "there was no TV there. No TV, no radio, no record player, no telephone."

"Right again."

"Well, that's what's bothering me."

She just looked at him, puzzled.

"What did she do in the meantime?" he asked, turning his palms up. "What did she do for that hour every night, between ten and eleven?"

"Oh." Ruth Vanetti smiled a little, as if at a fond memory.

"She wrote her letters."

"Her letters?"

"They were always there on her nightstand every morning, sealed up and addressed and ready for me to carry down and give to Freddie to take to the P.O." A look of sad reality passed across her face. "Like I said to Freddie a while back, those were just about the only two things left that she could do all by herself."

Holliman frowned. "Two things . . . ?"

"Writing letters," she said, "and licking stamps."

THE WADING POOL

Susan Weeks had never seen a monster before.

At the time it happened, she was sitting alone at the kitchen table, eating an afternoon snack of chocolate cookies. Her school gear lay in a pile near her right elbow: a writing tablet, a set of colored pencils, two third-grade textbooks, and a lunchbox. To her left, had she cared to look in that direction, a window offered a view of the vegetable garden that bordered the woods behind the house.

Susan finished her second cookie and licked her fingers. This was a good day, she decided. School was done, her aunt and her sister Darlene had gone shopping, the breeze through the open window was cool and pleasant, and—best of all—Uncle Felix wasn't home yet.

Susan Weeks hated her uncle Felix. So did her sister. They had good reason: Felix was almost always drunk, and when he was drunk he was a problem. Susan, who was nine, had endured regular beatings during the six months she and Darlene had spent with their aunt and uncle since their mother's death. Darlene, who was fifteen, had endured a different kind of problem—or at least the threat of it. And though Susan didn't really understand it all, she was old enough to know there was something very odd about the look in Uncle Felix's eyes whenever Darlene was around.

But right now Felix wasn't home, and it was a good day, and the spring sunshine was warm and tingling on her left shoulder. Susan popped the last of the chocolate cookies into her mouth and leaned back in her chair.

She could never remember, afterward, what made her turn and look out the window, but when she did she saw a sight that stopped her chewing and froze the blood in her veins.

Something terrible was standing at the edge of the woods.

It was about the height of a tall man—between six and seven feet—but all resemblance ended there. Its head was huge and misshapen, its body hairy, its snout long and pointed like a wolf's. The face itself reminded Susan of pictures she had seen of mandrills and baboons. Fangs three inches long lined its grinning mouth.

And it was staring at her.

It was standing there in the weeds beyond the garden, completely motionless, its head slightly lowered . . . and it was watching her.

After a long moment the creature turned away—a grotesque statue come to life—and shuffled toward the woods. Just before it melted into the shadows, it turned and gave her one last look.

And something about its eyes . . .

Sitting there at the kitchen table, Susan Weeks felt a chill that reached to the core of her soul. Only when the monster had vanished did she realize she'd been holding her breath. Instantly her muscles unlocked; she clapped her hands over her eyes, spat out her half-chewed cookie, and gasped for air like a drowning sailor. Her head began to clear a little, her heart began to slow down. She forced herself to peek out the window again, this time through the trembling spaces between her fingers.

Nothing there. Just the woods and the weed-choked garden, basking peacefully in the sun.

The thing—whatever it had been—was gone.

But the image was there, burned into her brain. The fearsome, grinning face, the teeth, the matted hair, the somehow *knowing* look in its eyes.

It was the eyes that had kept her from screaming.

Suddenly she heard something move behind her, and this time she did scream, her face contorting as she grabbed the edge of the table and swung around in her chair—

"What the hell's the matter with you, girl?" Felix Bowman said. He scowled at her a moment, gave the window and the ejected cookie a suspicious glance, then looked at her again. Susan couldn't tell if he was drunk or not, which usually meant he was. She had often wondered how a kind, sweet woman like Aunt Helen—her own mother's sister—could have married a slug like Felix.

"Answer me," he growled. "What mischief are you up to?" As he spoke, his narrow eyes swept the room, searching for evidence. His big fists clenched and unclenched.

Still trembling, Susan opened her mouth to tell him about the monster. But nothing came out.

His eyes narrowed even further. "Ha! Something *is* going on, ain't it?" A crooked smile stretched his face. "What've you done now, little gal?"

Again she tried to speak, to tell him of the horrible creature she had seen through the window. Again, no words came.

In the blink of an eye Felix's belt was off, hissing snake-like through the loops of his jeans. He doubled the belt in his fist and slapped it hard across the tabletop, two inches from Susan's right hand. The sound was like a pistol shot in the small room.

"Tell me!" he bellowed.

Yes, Susan thought, tell him. So she opened her mouth and said, clear as crystal, "She's in the woods."

Felix's coal-black eyebrows drew themselves together. "What?"

Susan just sat there, stunned. The four words she had just spoken were not her own. She had uttered them with her own mouth, her own tongue, but someone else had put them there. She didn't even know what they meant.

Even Felix, no Rhodes scholar, apparently knew something was amiss. Probably because her voice sounded different. He cocked his head to one side, like some overgrown, evil puppy. "Who's in the woods?" he asked.

"Darlene," Susan heard herself say. "She's taking a bath."

Felix blinked. "She's what?"

"There's no water in the house. Darlene wanted to take a bath after school, and she couldn't, so she got a bar of soap and went out to the wading pool in the woods." Susan swallowed. "I'm supposed to watch, make sure nobody goes down the path."

Just for a moment, as this strange message was being told, Susan saw a gleam in her uncle's eye. Then his better judgment, what little there was of it, seemed to take over.

"What are you trying to pull?" he said, curling his lip. "There ain't nothing wrong with the water."

Susan was well aware of that. She had washed her hands at the kitchen sink fifteen minutes ago. For an instant, all thoughts of the monster and of the strange voice disappeared as she considered the beating she was about to get. Felix hated to be lied to, and Susan and his belt were old acquaintances.

But all she could do now was watch as her uncle marched to the sink and, to prove his point, twisted the handle of the hot-water faucet.

Nothing happened.

"Well, dern," he said, and tried the cold tap.

Not a drop.

Susan Weeks didn't say a word. After the things she had seen and heard over the last few minutes, she was beyond surprise. More than anything else she wanted to cry.

But she didn't cry. She didn't even change her expression. Just as the monster's eyes had a moment ago forced her to keep silent, the odd voice inside her head now told her to do the same. And to try to act naturally.

Ten feet away, Felix Bowman had come to a startling conclusion. "The water *is* off," he said, as if to himself.

Slowly he raised his head, and their eyes met. Then he turned to the window, staring hard at the narrow path that led from the garden to the forest. He had a weird smile on his face, and Susan could almost read his mind. She knew he was picturing her sister Darlene, at the wading pool just past the edge of the woods. His eyes were fixed like a laser on the spot where the path melted into the shadows.

Susan looked too. And even though she could see nothing in the dark, leafy foliage, she knew—somehow she *knew*—the creature was there, crouching near the pool, just out of sight.

Felix turned to face her. The goofy smile was gone. "I got something to do, girl," he murmured. "You go to your room and stay there." He held the folded belt up for emphasis.

"Yes, sir." Without another thought she stood and scooped up her scrap of cookie and her books. It occurred to her, as she fled through the hallway door, that those last two words had been spoken in her own voice. Felix didn't seem to have noticed. He was still gazing out the window toward the garden.

Once in her room, Susan dumped her things onto her bed, counted to fifty, and hurried back to the kitchen. She arrived just in time to see her uncle creeping like a thief into the shadowy woods. Then he vanished from sight.

Susan eased herself into her chair. For a full thirty seconds or more she sat there, watching. She didn't really know what she was watching for, or waiting for. She saw nothing but the forest.

Then she sensed, rather than heard, movement behind her. For the third time that afternoon Susan felt her heart leap into her throat. She whirled around in her chair.

Her sister was standing in the doorway.

"Darlene," Susan said, exhaling. With an effort, she resisted the urge to run and hug her. "I thought you were shopping with Aunt Helen."

"I've been over at Debbie Olson's, listening to music." Cautiously Darlene entered the room, her eyes glancing everywhere at once. "Who were you talking to, a minute ago?"

"Uncle Felix," Susan said.

"I know that. But who else? I heard another voice."

Susan hesitated. "It was just me. What . . . what exactly did you hear?"

Darlene studied her sister a moment, then seemed to relax. She crossed the room and took a drinking glass from the overhead cabinet. "Not much. I heard someone—you, I guess— say something, then I heard Felix say he had something to do, and he told you to go to your room. He sounded a little funny, so I hid in the bathroom for a while." She gave the door an uneasy look. "Where is he, anyway?"

"He's gone," Susan said. She found herself watching with interest as Darlene held her glass under the cold tap and turned the faucet handle. Water jetted into the glass. Somehow this didn't surprise Susan at all.

Darlene shut off the water and looked at her younger sister, who was still staring at the faucet. "You make it sound like he's gone for good," Darlene said.

Their eyes met and held.

"What if he was?" Susan asked.

Darlene's face darkened. "Then I'd start believing in miracles."

"And what about Aunt Helen?"

"I think she would, too."

The kitchen had gone quiet. Darlene stared into her water glass and Susan stared out the window, at the path leading to the forest. Somewhere down the street, a dog barked.

After a minute or so Darlene drained her glass. "I gotta get back to Debbie's," she said, patting her shirt pocket. "I just came home to get some CD's." She paused. "You are okay, aren't you?"

Susan sighed. "Yeah. I'm okay."

Darlene started to say something, seemed to think better of it, then nodded and walked to the door.

"Darlene?"

She stopped in the doorway.

"Who did you think you heard?" Susan asked.

"What?"

Susan felt strangely calm. "You told me you heard another voice. Who did it sound like?"

A silence passed.

"It sounded like Mother," Darlene said.

This time it was Susan who nodded. Very slowly, lost in her own thoughts, she turned and looked out the window again. The breeze had died down now, and the shadows were longer.

Nothing stirred at the edge of the woods.

KNIGHTS OF THE COURT

"Is he still out there?" Patty asked.

She was making a ham sandwich on top of the bar between the kitchen and the living room, stopping now and then to glance at the TV. The seven o'clock news was on, and at the moment an Afghan terrorist was staring back at her from the screen. Not a sight to help the appetite, she thought.

Thirty feet away, in the darkened bedroom of Patty's apartment, Stephanie Waltman peeked carefully out the corner of the room's only window, looking down at the street. Stephanie was Patty's best friend; she lived two blocks away, on West Maple. They also worked together, downtown—Stephanie was the receptionist for Patty's boss, which meant the two women reported, actually, to the same person.

"He's still there," Stephanie answered.

After a moment Patty Nichols put the top on her sandwich, licked her fingers, and walked into the bedroom. She felt her way quietly through the dark to the window and crouched on the floor beside her friend. Together they stared down at the dimly-lit sidewalk that bordered the parking garage on the far side of the street.

Standing with his back against the wall of the garage, smoking a cigarette, was a tall man in a black coat and hat. Mostly he seemed to be watching the traffic in front of him, but now and then he would turn his head and glance up and down the street. Occasionally he looked at his watch. It had been misting rain, and his coat was wet and shiny in the light from the streetlamp on the corner of Maple and Livingston.

"You sure it's him?" Stephanie asked, for the third or fourth time.

Patty frowned, studying the dark figure below. "I think it is," she said. "I told you, it's too dark to be sure, from this angle." She took a bite of the sandwich.

"But he's the guy you saw in the courtroom?"

"It looks like him," she said, chewing. "He sat in the back, on the left side."

"And you saw him again later, you said. In the hallway, talking to Calucci's lawyer?"

Patty took another bite and nodded, her mouth full.

Stephanie hunched forward until her forehead rested against the windowsill. "This is crazy," she murmured. "This kind of thing just doesn't *happen*." She looked up again at her friend. "Have you called the police, like I asked you?"

Patty swallowed. "What would I tell them, Stef? That there's a man standing in the street outside my building? Is that against the law?"

"How am I supposed to know what's against the law? You're the lawyer." Stephanie took another look out the window. "But if he works for Frank Calucci and he's come to kill you, I'd say that's worth a phone call, yeah."

Patty stood up, sighed, and headed back to the living room. After a minute or so Stephanie followed. She left the bedroom door open so they could continue to check the situation every so often. He'd been out there for twenty minutes now.

"It could be, you know," Stephanie said, as Patty slouched down on the couch with her sandwich. "It's not impossible. I can't believe you're not taking this more seriously." Stephanie began to pace worriedly back and forth on the carpet. "I don't know Mr. Calucci personally, but I doubt if he's really big on tolerance and forgiveness, especially when it involves being sent to prison for about a hundred years."

Patty was watching the TV screen. The coverage of the trial had started, and she wanted to see it. To her friend she said, "Look, Steffy, I'm only the Assistant D.A. If anybody's worried it should be Ferguson, not me."

"So? For all we know, this guy's already killed Ferg, and is on his way to all the jurors' houses tonight too."

Patty turned back to the screen, trying to concentrate on the action there. It wasn't easy, with Steffy carrying on this way. And the truth was, Patty thought, she probably *should* be taking this more seriously. After all, the man outside really did look a lot like the guy at the courthouse today. What if he did work for the mob?

She knew she should probably blow the whistle, and loudly. The cops could be here in ten minutes, and if the guy checked out, fine. If he didn't, he could take a ride downtown, and there'd be one more of Calucci's gang behind bars.

The problem was, Stephanie had been reading too many Robert Ludlum novels. She had an overactive imagination to begin with, Patty thought, and all it took was something like this to send her into a tizzy. Sure the guy down there might be a mafia hitman, but the odds were against it. He was probably harmless. Patty had already been told, to her astonishment, that a large number of the attendees in the courtroom these past few days had been there not to see the defendant but to see her. The trial of Frank Calucci had been a media circus, and Patty Nichols—the young and solemn and beautiful young lady sitting at the prosecutor's table every day in front of the cameras—had become something of a public figure. As Assistant District Attorney she had played a major role in the preparation of the state's case (a fact that had been well-publicized) and as a result the infamous Frank Calucci had this afternoon been pronounced guilty of eleven counts of racketeering and extortion (a fact which had done nothing to hurt her celebrity status). Three teenagers and a housewife had asked her for her autograph on her way home tonight.

So the guy standing in the street, as crazy as it might sound, was quite possibly just one of her newfound fans, hoping to catch a glimpse of her in her natural habitat. She had even suggested this, with considerable embarrassment, to Stephanie, back when they had first spotted him outside the window. Steffy would have none of it. She was worried sick, and it worried her even more that Patty wasn't worried.

"If you want to know what I think," Stephanie said, standing with her arms folded now and watching the TV as she spoke, "I think you should consider finding another occupation. I know you like the research and the preparation and the strategy and all that, but I also know you hate the actual courtroom stuff. You're good at it but you hate it, and you don't even like all the media hype and hoopla. Besides, your salary's not that great—and don't look at me that way, I see all the payroll sheets, and I know." She paused, gnawing at a fingernail. "And worst of all, there's this." She waved a hand first at the TV screen, where D.A. Brad Ferguson was talking grimly into a nest of microphones, and then in the direction of the window in the next room. "There's always the chance that some friend of a friend of the lowlife you're trying to convict will decide to come gunning for you."

Patty turned and looked Stephanie in the eye. The sandwich was gone now. "So you're saying just quit and let them take over? That's what you're saying?"

Now Stephanie was the one to sigh. "I'm saying you should face the facts. The people you go up against have a different set of standards from yours, and a very different regard for the value of human life." She paused and leaned closer. "You're a knight with no armor, Patty dear, you and Ferguson both. You're fighting a war you can't win."

"We won today," Patty said.

"Maybe. We'll see."

Patty gave her a hard look. "Boy, you really are good for my morale sometimes, you know that?"

"I'm trying to save your life, honey. Somebody has to." Stephanie walked over and dropped onto the couch beside her, frowning. "Tell you what," Steffy said. "At least think about leaving town for a while, until all this blows over. Maybe go up to your dad's cabin on the la—"

There was a knock at the front door.

Steffy turned, her eyes wide as golfballs, and stared at the door.

"Don't have a seizure," Patty said, as she rose from the couch. "It's Sue Biggers, from work. Have you seen my glasses?"

Stephanie blinked. "Sue Biggers?"

"She said she'd come by tonight. I'll be out tomorrow, and she has some papers I need to sign."

"Just a minute," Steffy said. "How do you know it's Sue?"

Another knock, louder this time.

"Because she never uses the doorbell," Patty said, rummaging through the clutter on an endtable.

Her friend sighed. "At least let me check, okay?" Without waiting for an answer, she hurried into the bedroom, stayed a minute, then reappeared in the doorway. "You're right," she admitted, relieved. "He's still there."

"What a surprise," Patty said. Eyeglasses in hand, she marched into the foyer, unlocked the door, and reached up to take hold of the deadbolt. She hadn't yet gotten around to installing a chain or a peephole; that was another thing Steffy was always on her about.

Maybe it was time for both of them to grow up a little, she thought.

She released the deadbolt.

***

Still a little annoyed, Stephanie stomped back to the other room and settled into the darkness beside the window so she could keep watch on the man across the street. Never in her short life, she decided, had she met a more stubborn woman than Patty Nichols. She was pondering that fact as she heard Patty shoot the bolt and turn the knob and pull the front door open.

At that same instant Steffy happened to glance again at the street, and when she did she saw, to her horror, that the dark figure she had been watching wasn't the same man. This was old Mr. Greenbaum, waiting on the bus to take him downtown to his lodge meeting.

She whirled around. "Patty!" she whispered.

But she knew her friend couldn't hear her from here. And it wouldn't matter anyway, now—the squeak of unoiled hinges had been proof that the front door was open. Her heart thudding, Stephanie hurried through the darkness to a spot near the doorway to the living room, where she could listen without being seen.

***

In the other room, Patty Nichols stared into the face of the young man standing in the front doorway. His black hat was off now, held meekly with both hands in front of him as if he were here to ask for a loan. He was in fact, she realized, the man she had seen at the trial—but he looked different too, somehow.

The face that had seemed dark and grim in the courtroom was lit up now by a bright, friendly smile. "Patricia Nichols?" he asked.

She stayed quiet a moment, to give herself time to think. She could still slam the door, of course, and if she was quick enough she could probably get it locked and bolted before he could react, and then could call the police. But what more could she tell them now than she could have told them earlier, when she saw him outside the window? He looked more like a college basketball star than a hired killer.

"I'm Jack Pearson," he said quickly, when he saw her hesitate. "From the *Tribune*."

She gaped at him.

"I missed you at the trial today," he added. "Could we talk for a minute?"

Of course, she thought. A reporter. That would explain not only his presence in the courtroom, but also his later conversation with the defense lawyer in the hallway.

Patty felt like a fool. She cut a glance at the bedroom doorway, but saw nothing. Her friend was nowhere in sight.

What the hell, she decided. "Sure. But just for a minute."

Steffy had probably just wet her pants, Patty thought.

The young man stepped through the door and looked around. "Nice apartment," he said.

She shrugged. "It's home." She tucked her glasses into a pocket and pointed toward the living room. "Won't you sit down?"

"No thanks," he said, holding up a hand. "I just have a few questions." He dug a pen and a spiral-bound notebook from his coat pocket. "Actually, I hung around outside for a while, hoping I'd catch you on the way in or out. I hated to bother you at home."

"No problem," she said tiredly. Actually, she was a little intrigued by the man. They were still standing in the foyer, and several seconds passed before she realized he was still holding his wet hat in one hand. "Here," she said, taking it from him. She hung it on the ornate wooden coat-rack beside the door.

His eyes lingered for a moment on the coat-rack. "An antique?" he asked.

"I suppose it is, yes. It belonged to my grandfather."

A silence passed while they stood and looked at each other. The man glanced once more at the heirloom, then blinked and focused on the matter at hand. He clicked his pen and flipped open his notebook. As he turned to a fresh page Patty took a couple of steps backward into the living room and leaned back against one of the armrests of the couch, watching him thoughtfully.

"How did you know where I live?" she asked, before he could get started.

He glanced up at her. "A friend at the paper told me." He paused, looking a little guilty. "Actually, I wasn't that worried about bothering you. I was outside in the street because I didn't think they'd let me get through to see you. As it was, I finally just snuck past them."

She frowned. "They?"

"The police. Sometimes they're not too crazy about reporters."

"The *police*?"

"Look, don't get me wrong," he said. "I think it's a good idea. I mean, these days you never know—"

Her frown had deepened now. "What exactly are you saying, Mr. Pearson? *What's* a good idea?"

The reporter blinked, looking confused. "Protection," he said. "Guard duty."

"But . . . there are no police here. I'm not under guard."

"You might not realize it, but I think you are," he said. "The two men I saw waiting in the lobby didn't look like they belong around here, if you know what I mean. And I heard them mention your name a time or two. That's when I decided to go out and wait in the str—"

He broke off when he saw the look on her face. She had gone grayish-white.

Suddenly he seemed to understand. His jaw tightened. "Surely you're not thinking—"

But Patty *was* thinking, fast and fiercely. If there were people downstairs and they weren't cops—and she knew, somehow, that they weren't—then it didn't take a genius to figure out who they were. Names danced in her mind, flipping past each other like flashcards: Carlo Brasi, Ed Gruber, Johnny Russo . . .

Famous names, at least in the files of the police and FBI, but names with no faces. Those who had seen their faces had not lived to describe them.

Steffy had been right after all, Patty thought; she'd just had the wrong man in mind.

"What am I going to do?" Patty asked in a weak voice.

Swiftly Jack Pearson put his pen and notebook away. "Call the police," he said. "Now." He glanced around like a man looking for a rock to throw at a bear. "I'll stay with you until they get here."

She didn't need to be told twice. She found herself wishing fervently that she had taken similar advice ten minutes ago. She snatched up the phone on the endtable, started to dial—and froze.

The line was dead.

She just stared at him, eyes wide with fear. She didn't have to tell him what had happened.

"Dear God," he said.

He hesitated for a moment, then drew in a long breath and exhaled loudly. "I'll go for help," he said, turning toward the front door. Then he stopped and looked at her. "No," he added.

"First you have to get someone to stay with you. A friend in the building, maybe . . . ?"

"Someone's here already," Patty said, a little guiltily. "Steffy?" she called, over her shoulder.

The reporter blinked. His eyes flicked toward the empty bedroom doorway. Sure enough, Stephanie appeared there a second later. Her face was as pale as Patty's.

The women's gazes met and held for a long moment.

Patty gave her a weak smile. "I guess you heard," she murmured. Keeping her eyes on her friend, Patty said to the reporter: "This is Stephanie Waltman. Stef, meet Mr.—"

As Patty turned toward him, her gaze stopped for an instant on the coat-rack beside him, and she realized then what it was that had caught his attention a while ago. She hadn't even noticed it before.

Hanging beside his black hat was Steffy's jacket— Steffy's jacket, still damp from the rain and a full three sizes smaller than her own . . .

Patty felt her stomach turn over. Her eyes went immediately to Jack Pearson's.

And then she saw the gun. It was short and black, with a thick silencer fitted to the barrel—and it was pointed straight at her. Pearson looked pleasantly calm and satisfied, as if he had just solved a simple but troublesome problem.

"Now that I'm sure we're all here together," he said, "allow me to introduce myself properly."

Slowly he raised the gun, and cocked it.

"My name is John Russo," he said. "Pleased to meet you both."

THE WINSLOW TUNNEL

The scariest day of my life—and the most wonderful—happened when I was ten years old. The time was summer, the location northwest Arkansas. It was a place I'd never been before, and have never been since, but what happened there on that Saturday morning in August forever changed the way I would look at the world.

When that day started out, of course, none of us had any inkling of what Fate had in store for me. If we had known, would I have done anything differently? I don't think so. Would my parents? You bet they would. My dad would have put Delores, Arkansas, in our rearview mirror, and faster than you could say Jack Sprat. What happened was harder on them, I think, than on me.

But the fact was, I had no idea I was about to experience something amazing and terrifying and marvelous. Or that what I was looking at through the car window would turn out to be far more than it appeared.

All I knew was that Dad said—

***

"It was my great-grandfather's train."

The three of us—Mom in the front seat, Jenny and I in the back—sat and stared at him.

"It was what?" my mother asked.

Dad grinned. "I'm serious. He worked here, for this railroad, for twenty years." He pointed through the windshield at the dusty station and the shining tracks and the long cars lined up behind the locomotive. "This was his train."

"You mean he was the *engineer*?" I asked. At ten years of age, I was young enough to be excited and old enough not to want to show it. Jenny, who was fifteen and half-asleep anyway, had no such problem. She just rolled her eyes and yawned.

"He was the conductor," Dad said. He nodded toward the first passenger coach, the one just behind the engine. "His place was on that car, right there. It's been rebuilt now, the folks in the ticket office said, but underneath all that it's the original car." Dad couldn't seem to stop smiling. "How about that?"

How about that, indeed? I thought. So this was what Dad was leading up to, when he suggested this little side trip yesterday. We had stopped for a bathroom break at the Arkansas welcome station on I-40, on our way back to Nashville from Amarillo, when Dad spotted the "Great Railway Adventures" brochure in the rack at the information desk. Ten minutes later he'd talked us into a detour, called ahead to book a room at the Delores Holiday Inn, and aimed the car north on Highway 71 into the heart of the Ozarks.

And now here we were, the only people in the station parking lot at seven a.m. on an overcast Saturday that also happened to be my tenth birthday, holding tickets Dad had purchased a moment ago in the little building next to the tracks and staring at the train. And, for three of us at least, trying to adjust to this unexpected information from the cobwebs of our family history.

"At eight sharp," Dad was saying, "we'll board the train and—"

"Eight o'clock?" Jenny groaned. "We could've slept another hour."

"We'll board the train," Dad said, fixing her with a stare, "and take the front four seats. That's why we're here early, so we can be first in line. Understood?"

Jenny sighed and leaned her head against the window-glass. Dad glanced at Mom, who was still pondering all this, and then at me. I just nodded. Most of my attention was focused on trying to control my rising excitement. He could have instructed us to pull our pants down and dance the Bossa Nova in the dining car, for all I cared. I just wanted to get on the train.

During the next hour, as the sun climbed into the gray clouds above the town of Delores, Mom and I asked Dad a hundred questions about this newly discovered ancestor. We found out, among other things, that the old man had not only spent most of his working life on the train, he had died on it as well. On the afternoon of July 4, 1910, the train sitting before us had derailed and crashed into the White River. There were no survivors.

"They think it was the Langtree Gang," my dad said. "A tree was down across the tracks, and the engineer couldn't stop in time."

"You mean like, Owen Langtree?" I asked.

"That's him. Not long after that, he and his brothers—"

"Murdered all those kids, at the Brineyville school-house," I said. "I saw it on the History Channel." Sitting there, safe in the car with my family, it was a sobering thing. The site of the famous massacre wasn't far from where we were, actually, though we'd made sure to avoid it on our trip up from the interstate. Rows and rows of tiny gravestones weren't my mother's idea of vacation fun. But the tragedy was still morbidly fascinating, probably because of who had caused it. The notorious Langtree brothers had been the scourge of the early 1900's.

"Anyhow," Dad said, "the train wreck was what killed your great-great-grandfather. Not far south of here."

At that point in my dad's narrative, while he paused in thought and my dumb sister snored like a drunk sailor beside me, my mother said, "You never even mentioned *having* any relatives in Arkansas, Robert."

He gave her a sad smile. "I didn't, after that. Six months later his widow and the rest of the family moved to Tennessee."

"My great-great-granddad," I said, half to myself. "Was he a Franklin, like us?"

"No, he was my father's mother's father. His daughter—my grandmother—married a Franklin." Dad paused again, remembering. "His name was Burnside. Cecil Burnside."

I repeated the name to myself, rolling it over on my tongue. I think I was even more affected by this whole business than Mom was. It stayed on my mind as other passengers began to arrive in the parking lot, and as we locked our car and took our places at the head of the line. I tried to picture what all this would have looked like, so many years ago.

"I wish I could've lived back then," I said.

Dad raised an eyebrow. "What about computers, and video games, and rollerblading?"

I looked up at him. "What?"

"It's your birthday, Timmo," he said, with a grin. "Be careful what you wish for."

"All aboooooard!" a voice yelled, from somewhere behind us.

Obediently Jenny and I followed our parents up the metal steps and into the lead coach. Once inside, we passed through a small front compartment and then into the passenger area, which looked big enough for forty or fifty people. Dad motioned Mom and Jenny into the front seat on the starboard side of the aisle. He and I sat together in the seat behind them, with me at the window. The four of us were quiet for a time, watching the other passengers file past us into the car. Jenny, still yawning and frowning, brightened a bit when she saw a uniformed young lady bring a tray of food into the forward compartment. Apparently we were to be served breakfast on our little outing.

While my sister watched the food and Dad watched the passengers and Mom gazed out the window, I looked around the interior of the coach. It was impressive. I would learn later that Dad had been correct: this was the original car, one of three that had made the countless mountain runs up and down the Ozarks during the early years of the twentieth century. It did not, however, look its age. I remembered what Dad had said about the restoration. The bench-style seats were now padded with a green leatherlike material, their arms and backs capped with ridges of gleaming brass, and all the woodwork around the windows and in the seats and side panels was mahogany. Old sepia-toned prints were framed and displayed on the bulkhead wall.

Several minutes after the last of the passengers were seated, our conductor came on board. His nametag said THOMAS HARDY, and he wore a black uniform and a pillbox hat and a stiff white shirt. He even had a pair of round spectacles on his nose, which made him quite believable, I thought. Every conductor I'd ever seen on TV or in the movies had worn those same little wirerimmed eyeglasses. There was something, though, that seemed wrong about him as I watched him standing there in the front doorway. Something missing. I just couldn't place it.

After studying the assembled passengers a moment, he sat down in the front row on the other side of the aisle, across from my mother and sister. With practiced ease he took a "reserved" sign off the seat and tucked it into his pocket, then picked up a little black box—it turned out to be a portable PA system—and unhooked a microphone from its side.

"Ladies and gentlemen," he said into the mike, "welcome to the Ozark & Arkansas Railroad." Mr. Thomas Hardy was, it appeared, our tour guide as well as our conductor.

He spent the next few minutes briefing us on the history of the railroad and the train itself and our upcoming day's agenda. We would, he explained, be departing soon for the city of Van Buren, Arkansas, seventy miles south. The trip would take about three hours. Once in Van Buren we would have some free time in the downtown historic district, to shop and have lunch. At around two o'clock we would reboard the train for the return trip, and would arrive back here in Delores at five p.m.

"But the first order of business," he said, "is breakfast, to be served in the forward section of the coach. Please help yourselves." With that, he clipped the mike to the side of the box and left the car. Since we were in the front row of seats we were the first in line again, and Jenny led the charge. The meal consisted of strawberries, grapes, cheese, croissants, muffins, juice, and coffee, laid out on a small buffet table in the front compartment. We ate on little paper plates in our laps and stared out at the window at the railyard and wondered when we were going to get the show on the road.

We didn't have long to wait. As soon as the last passenger was served and re-seated the train made a sound like a huge exhale, then started to inch forward. Within minutes we were bumping and clacking through the southern outskirts of town, the warm August wind riffling our hair. Even though we continued our meals, every eye stayed on the spectacle outside the open windows. We were underway.

"It's easy to imagine my mom's granddad doing that," Dad said. Neither Mom nor Jenny had heard him above the noise of the tracks, but I did, and turned to look at him. He was staring up at the conductor, who had reappeared in the coach's front doorway. Dad grinned at me. "Except for the speaker system, of course. Doubt that was around, back then."

I was a little surprised by the emotion I saw in my father's face. "What else do you know about him?" I asked.

"My great-grandpa? Only what my mother told me, when she was in a reminiscing mood." He paused. "She said he let her ride with him sometimes, but not often. That was a different era, Tim—they thought girls belonged at home. Besides, she always suspected he wanted a grand*son*, not a grand*daughter*. A boy to talk to and take along on runs and maybe even teach about the business. He never had one, and that bothered him. Or so she thought."

I waited for Dad to continue. Mom, oblivious to our conversation, turned and smiled at me, then faced front again. She seemed to be having a good time. Jenny just kept eating. I wondered idly how many times they'd let her go back for refills before they threw her off the train.

"My mother loved him anyway, of course," Dad went on. The conductor seemed to be taking a headcount. Both of us watched him as Dad kept talking.

"She used to tell me about his little hat, and glasses, and mustache, and cologne. And most of all . . ." He broke off, frowning.

"What, Dad?"

He turned to face me. Tipping his head toward Mr. Hardy, he said, "Look at his watch."

I did, and saw immediately what it was that had struck me as odd a while earlier. On Mr. Thomas Hardy's left wrist was a black digital watch. An old-timer, I thought, with a new timepiece. I was disappointed. To my way of thinking, a conductor was supposed to wear—

"A pocketwatch," I said.

Dad nodded. "Right. That's what's missing. And that's

what my mom always remembered most about her granddad. His big thick railroad watch, with a copper case and a gold chain and a little key for winding and setting." He shook his head sadly. "It's a shame she never got it, afterward."

"After he died, you mean?"

"Yeah."

"Who did get it?" I asked.

"Nobody did. It was lost in the wreck."

I was still thinking about that when I saw Dad watching me. "What?" I said.

"This is something, isn't it, Tim?" He waved a hand to encompass the coach, the passengers, the whole adventure. "All this, I mean."

"It's a surprise, for sure. Really cool, Dad."

He grinned. "Birthdays," he said, "are good times for surprises."

He seemed to be about to say more, but a sudden change in the rhythm and noise-level of the train interrupted him. Everyone looked at each other. The ride had gotten rougher, and the clacking and rattling of the wheels was louder now. When Mr. Hardy picked up the PA box to explain, we learned that two things had happened. First, we had crossed over onto the older-style tracks; second, we had reached our maximum cruising speed of 35 miles per hour.

The conductor went on for a while with more information about the train. Today, he said, since it was a Saturday, it would be carrying passengers only. On weekdays it handled both passengers and freight. He also furnished some interesting stories about the countryside. Outside our windows, the terrain had become hilly and wooded, with swift streams and tall mountains visible in the distance. Twice we spotted deer at the edge of the woods. The slate-gray clouds grew darker.

Every few minutes Mr. Hardy picked up his black box

and faced the passengers. On one occasion he pointed out the strange-looking bois d'arc trees used by the Osage Indians to make their bows and arrows. Even now, he said, farmers in the area often search out the straightest of the trees to cut and sell to the makers of archery equipment.

Some of the best stories, though, were the legends and superstitions and trivia surrounding the little towns we passed on the way. Each of them—Greenland, West Fork, Brentwood— had its own unique history, and to a city boy the tales of rugged mountain men and their primitive farms and settlements were fascinating.

The village of Winslow, for example (our approximate halfway point to Van Buren) was known for having the highest altitude of any incorporated town in Arkansas. Built at the crest of the divide between the White and Arkansas Rivers, the conductor told us, it had long ago been a summer resort and a booming lumber town. Even now, as we passed, I imagined horse-drawn wagons plying the muddy streets, and could almost hear the ring of axes on timber in the clear mountain air.

I was sitting there gazing out the window, drinking in these mental images, when I heard Mr. Hardy unclip his mike again.

"In a few moments, the train will pass through a tunnel— the only one on our trip today. It was built in 1882, and is about half a mile long. It'll take a full minute to get through it, and it'll be totally dark inside." He paused to make sure he had every- one's attention. "One word of caution. Since there are several couples on board, I don't want to hear about any hanky-panky in the tunnel."

Several people chuckled, and he added, "I didn't say there couldn't *be* any hanky-panky. I just don't want to hear about it."

Now everybody hooted laughter. Smiling, Mr. Hardy replaced the mike and took his seat.

And then, while I sat there in our comfortable coach, feeling the pleasant summer wind in my face and staring out at the green mountains and wondering how fantastic it would have been to live in the Olden Days, the train entered the tunnel.

***

It happened fast. One moment we were in daylight, the next we were plunged into a sudden and noisy darkness. It was a scary feeling—the wind whistling around my head, the wheels clanging and roaring against the rails. The noise seemed to come from everywhere at once. No one spoke. At one point I held my hand up in front of my face and couldn't see it. The conductor had been right: it was pitch black in the car.

After what seemed much longer than a mere sixty seconds, we emerged into bright light. In fact it seemed even brighter than it had been, before we'd entered the tunnel. An instant later I realized why: The sun was out. Out and blazing away, lighting up the fields and the mountains under a brilliant blue—

I blinked.

A brilliant blue sky.

I leaned to the right, hanging out the window, looking for clouds. There were none. The sky was clear.

Puzzled, I turned to my left to see what my dad thought of this. After all, you don't normally go from overcast to sunny in the course of half a mile.

But my father was gone. In his place was a kindly-looking old lady in a green dress, staring straight ahead and murmuring to herself. When I looked around, I saw that Mom and Jenny were missing also. Their seat, right in front of me, was empty.

And something else was funny too. Their seat wasn't just empty—it was *brown*. A dark, worn brown, with cuts and splits and stains in the material. A quick look around showed me that the other seats were the same. Even my own seat had changed in color from green to brown. And there were no brass or mahogany trimmings, either.

What *is* this? I thought. And where were my folks?

I looked across the aisle to where the conductor had been sitting, but he too was gone. And there were no framed prints hanging on the forward wall anymore. Just old, grimy boards, with a few posted notices and a calendar.

What was *happening*?

I felt the first little tingle of panic, deep in my gut.

And then the conductor came back into the coach. The sight of his black uniform brought a heartfelt sigh of relief.

But the sigh died in the bottom of my throat.

This wasn't the same conductor.

Even his outfit was different. Black suit and cap, all right, and white shirt, but all similarity ended there. This uniform was smudged with what looked like oil or soot. And he wore a little string tie and hightopped shoes, and no nametag. Only the eyeglasses were the same: round wire-rimmed spectacles.

But the biggest change was the face behind the glasses. This man was about the same age as Thomas Hardy had been, but had a thin nose and blue eyes and a gray mustache. In fact, he looked vaguely like an older, tireder version of—

The thought hit me like a punch to the stomach.

He looked like my father.

Before I could give myself time to think about it, I whirled around and looked at the other passengers. They couldn't see me well, since I was so short and tucked away beside my old-lady seatmate, but I could see them. And what I saw almost stopped my heart.

There were less than two dozen passengers aboard. We had had a full car before. And these people had something in common: They were dressed in clothes straight out of a history book. Or at least out of an old colorized movie. Everyone wore a hat, for one thing, and the men's suits and ladies' dresses were all a zillion years out of style. Old-timey clothes, my Uncle Jack used to call them. Even the elderly woman beside me was wearing a bonnet and a pair of lace-up shoes.

I looked at the conductor again, my pulse pounding so hard I could barely think. As I gaped at him he pulled a watch from a fold of his vest, a big copper pocketwatch with a gold chain and a winding slot instead of a stem, and when I saw it the last shred of doubt left my mind. I didn't yet know how it had happened, or why, but I understood at last what was going on, and where I was.

The conductor—the man standing there looking at his watch—was my great-great-grandfather, and I was on his train. And the time was long, long ago.

Be careful what you wish for, Dad had said . . .

I squeezed my eyes shut, took a deep breath. When I opened them again I looked down at my own clothes, and was somehow surprised to discover I was still dressed in the blue jeans and T-shirt and Reeboks I'd put on in the motel this morning. Oddly enough, the sight was comforting. It suggested that maybe—just maybe—I was still in the present after all, and was dreaming all this.

But when I reached up and pinched my earlobe, it didn't wake me up. All it did was hurt.

I sat there trying to process all this newly-acquired information. It didn't work. Nothing made sense.

Suddenly I tensed. The train was slowing down. For a moment I thought of the Langtree gang and train robberies and tracks blocked with fallen trees, but when I looked out the window again I saw only a tiny depot and a row of houses. Cordwood was stacked against the loading platform, the ends yellow-white and freshly cut. There was no sign on the depot.

When we'd groaned to a stop, I saw a young man who'd been waiting on the platform climb onto the train and into our coach. He nodded to the conductor, who was on his way out, and then came to my row and leaned down to speak to the old lady sharing my seat. I caught the name "Mrs. Derryberry" and something about Rufus and Esther being at the house, waiting.

She nodded. Her glassy eyes had not moved; they still stared straight ahead. After the boy had gathered her things he helped her up and led her slowly out the door and down the steps to the platform, where an older man met them and guided her down to the street and into . . .

I swallowed hard, staring dumbstruck at the scene outside the window.

They helped her into a buckboard.

My God, I thought. What year *was* this, anyway?

Even as the question entered my mind, and as the train puffed and wheezed and began to pick up speed, I remembered what Dad had told us about his great-grandfather's death. I didn't know yet what date this was, but I knew one thing: it had to be before July 4, 1910.

I found that thought disturbing, on several levels. I glanced again at the conductor (he's not only my relative, I thought—he's my *ancestor*) and wondered what I should do. The depot was behind us now, and he was sitting there looking out his window. Should I try to identify myself to him? Boy, would *that* get a reaction. I wondered what they did in this day and time to people, especially kids, who show signs of mental instability. Lock 'em up and drop the key down a well, probably.

But if I knew the exact day and date that this man sitting ten feet away from me was scheduled to die . . . was I not in some way obligated to inform him of it? To warn him?

Maybe not. Maybe I had no right to. Having watched a hundred reruns of *Quantum Leap* and *Back to the Future*, I wasn't so certain I would even be *allowed* to do it. Tampering with the events of the past could alter the present, couldn't it? Maybe such a thing was forbidden.

But if it was, what was I doing here?

I sighed and closed my eyes again. This isn't fair, I told myself. I'm ten years old. I'm too young to have to face decisions like this.

This time when I opened my eyes again I looked around the swaying car very carefully, searching for anything that might help me sort this out. My gaze stopped on the calendar on the bulkhead wall. I had noticed it earlier but hadn't given it any real attention. Now that I better understood my role as time-traveler, the sight of a calendar made my heart skip a beat.

I leaned forward in my seat, squinting.

The top half of the calendar was a painting of the mountains in springtime—pretty but irrelevant. The bottom half, though, was exactly what I was looking for.

It was a simple grid of the month of May, 1908.

I stared for a long time at the words and numbers.

May. 1908.

A hundred years ago.

I sucked in some air, blew it out, and concentrated on the back of the seat in front of me, thinking hard.

I was riding on a train through the Ozark Mountains in May of 1908.

How exactly had it happened? Logistically speaking, that is. Had I just appeared here, from nowhere, during the train's passage through the tunnel? At first I hadn't thought so. My modern-day attire would certainly have been noticed by the other passengers. Now, however—now that I realized my elderly seatmate had been blind the whole time, and since she'd been shielding me from view anyway—I realized it probably *had* happened that way. I must have appeared instantly, out of thin air. One minute my seat was empty, the next minute I was here. Presto. Had I also vanished, I wondered, from my seat on the train with my folks, to come here?

For whatever reason, I was here now, like it or not. And now that Mrs. Derryberry had gone, my foreign presence was exposed to anyone who cared to look in my direction. Even as that thought occurred to me, a middle-aged farmer in the seat across the aisle began staring at my colorful outfit. I was trying to make myself smaller when I happened to look up into the eyes of the conductor.

He rose from his seat in front of the farmer and crossed to the row ahead of me, where until twenty minutes ago my mother and sister had been sitting. That recollection was enough to bring tears to my eyes. I was beginning, slowly but surely, to realize the gravity of my situation.

"Hello, young man," my dad's great-grandfather said to me.

I just looked at him. My only conscious thought was that this, then, was final proof that this was no dream. I had actually been spoken to, aloud.

He studied me a moment. "Could I see your ticket, son?"

I blinked. My ticket? I remembered vaguely, from another lifetime in another world, my dad handing out the little printed rectangles of cardboard and telling us to keep them safe in our pockets in case they were requested. The fact that it was now a hundred years earlier than the date of purchase was something none of us had planned on.

I pulled the ticket from my jeans pocket and held it out for inspection.

The change in the conductor's face would have been comical under other circumstances. He examined the ticket, frowned, and held it closer to his spectacles. Then he raised his eyes to look at me. "Where'd you get this?"

I hesitated, then said truthfully, "The Delores station."

He waited a long time before speaking again. When he

did, his voice was firm but not unkind. "Someone's played a joke on you, my boy. This ticket's a fake. The company address is right, but unless I'm crazy there's no such thing as the Ozark & Arkansas Railroad Company."

"Not yet, anyway," I said.

"What?"

I just shook my head. What was there to say?

He gave me back the ticket and regarded me a moment.

"Where you from, son?"

"Rogers," I said, voicing a name I remembered from the Arkansas roadmap. I decided the truth—Nashville—might not be such a good idea. Rogers was local.

"And where are you going?"

"Van Buren. With my fo—" I paused. "To meet my folks."

He nodded toward the ticket in my hand. "Your folks get that for you?"

"Yessir," I said, then remembered, too late, telling him I had gotten it in Delores. At any rate, he didn't seem inclined to press the issue. He just kept looking at me.

"What's your name, young man?"

"Timothy Franklin." I was glad to be answering something honestly for a change.

He raised his eyebrows. "My daughter's engaged to a Franklin fellow. He's from Harmon, though, if I remember right."

"I wouldn't know," I said. My head was beginning to hurt. It didn't take a genius to realize he was talking about my dad's grandfather.

"My name's Burnside, myself."

I almost said *I know*, but stopped just in time. I nodded dumbly. "Pleased to meet you."

Both of us were quiet a moment. At last he sighed and rose to his feet, still watching me. In his blue eyes I saw a mixture of feelings. Curiosity, mostly, but something else too. When he spoke next, his voice held a note of warmth that hadn't been there earlier.

"You been on a train before, Timothy Franklin?"

"No, sir."

"Come over here," he said.

I spent the next hour sitting beside him in the conductor's reserved seat, looking out the window with him as his finger pointed out a world I'd never seen before. Like Thomas Hardy had done earlier that same day, this stern but kind man told me a hundred fascinating tales about the countryside and the railroad that passed through it. The difference was, these stories were for me alone, and geared to the level of a ten-year-old boy who wanted to learn everything about everything. He told me how an engine works, and what a cowcatcher is, and how a fresh snowfall paints the rocky slopes beside the track, and what it feels like to sit on the back platform of a caboose watching the rain blow out and away from you as the train slices at full speed through a thunderstorm.

Together we looked down off hundred-foot-high trestles and out over deep vistas and along foaming blue-white mountain streams while the wheels played their strange rattling music on the rails. At one point he showed me the old route taken by the St. Louis-to-California Butterfield Stage Line, where women passengers were often warned to cover their eyes on some of the steeper roads. When there was nothing particularly interesting about the landscape he told me about his days of driving spikes and his travels up north after the war, and his dreams of owning a home on one of the taller mountains. He told me also of dozens of different rules of the railroad, like the special rhythm of the whistle when approaching a crossing: two longs, one short, one long. "That rule'll never change," he said. "It'll be the same a hundred years from now." When I looked up at him sharply, he didn't appear to notice.

He also talked of colorful characters like Judge Isaac Parker and Butch Cassidy and Owen Langtree and John Wesley Hardin and a dozen more topics he knew would interest a young boy. He even mentioned the fact that odd things had been known to happen back down the track a ways, around the town of Winslow. Something about an Osage burial ground, and lights in the sky, and sightings of Civil War soldiers camped in the valleys years after the war ended. Once more he ignored my questioning glances, but I think he sensed my concern, and the eerie feeling that broke my arms out in gooseflesh as we sat there together on that swaying brown seat in the coach.

I think he also, though there was no way he could have known, sensed the relationship between us. Now and then I saw a peculiar expression on his face, and every time I saw it I was reminded of a similar look I'd seen on the face of my father last night, when we'd entered the rest-stop on the interstate, just before he strolled over and picked up the brochure for the train ride. As if somehow, without really knowing . . . he *knew*.

When we finally pulled into the Van Buren station, I found I didn't want to leave this man. The feeling grew stronger when the train actually stopped and people started getting off. My head had cleared a bit by then, and I remembered the seriousness of my predicament. I had nowhere to go if I left him.

"I think this is your stop," he said, watching me.

"I can't get off," I murmured.

"Why not?"

I looked up into his eyes. My own were beginning to fill with tears. "I can't leave. I don't know where my folks are."

He studied me a moment.

"Timothy Franklin," he said quietly, "this has been a happy time for me. Meeting you was . . . special." He paused, and I could see the deep concern on his face. "This sounds silly, but I think you were somehow . . . sent to me today. I think also—no, it's stronger than that; I *know*—that you have to leave me now. I don't know why, but I know you must."

The train, though still wheezing like a winded fighter, was motionless now. Passengers were filing past our seats and down the steps to the wooden platform of the station. Through the open window I could see a row of iron-wheeled loading carts lined up like parked cars against the side of the building. Bulging sacks of northbound mail were being hauled out of the station and tossed on board.

"But you don't understand," I pleaded. "I can't—"

"You must," he said, and then he did a strange thing. He pulled me to him and hugged me tight. I could feel his whiskers on my forehead, could smell his cologne. I hugged him back, and held on.

After a long moment we separated, and he smiled at me one last time. Though I wasn't sure, I thought I saw the sparkle of a tear in his eye.

And then, so quickly I could do nothing to stop him, he turned and marched down the aisle and out the back end of the coach.

I stood there a minute, my head spinning. At last, as if in a dream, I turned toward the doorway at the front of the car, not because it was what I wanted to do but because there seemed to be no other choice. It was almost noon. In a short while, Cecil Burnside had said, the train would take on freight and another set of passengers and head back north again. Though I had no idea what awaited me here at the Van Buren station, I felt this was where I had to go.

Then I saw the mail bags. For their trip north they'd been stuffed into a corner of the forward compartment, where only a few hours ago I had heaped my plate with goodies from a buffet table. There was no table in there now, buffet or otherwise. Just two brown canvas sacks filled to the brim and loosely bound with lengths of heavy twine. And just above the bags, on a waist-high shelf near the outside door, was a shallow box of supplies. Pencils, paper, string, ink, a bottle of glue.

I knew, without even thinking twice, what I had to do. I took a blank sheet of paper from the box, spread it flat on the shelf, and grabbed a pencil. In a hurried but careful hand I wrote:

TO MR. CECIL BURNSIDE:

ON THE AFTERNOON OF JULY 4, 1910,

OWEN LANGTREE AND HIS MEN

WILL TRY TO ROB THIS TRAIN.

THE TRACKS WILL BE BLOCKED

NEAR THE WHITE RIVER BRIDGE

THIS IS NOT A JOKE—

YOU HAVE BEEN WARNED.

A FRIEND

Breathing hard, I read over what I'd written. I realized it was a poor effort. My warning, if taken seriously at all, would be forgotten long before it would make any difference. But at least it was something.

I folded the paper once, pulled open the mouth of one of the mail bags, and stuffed the message inside with the other letters.

And then two things happened, almost at the same time. First, a tall black man in workclothes stomped in carrying a bucket and broom; second, I heard a BANG somewhere in the distance, and the muted sounds of cheering. I jumped, and the workman stopped and grinned at me. "Don't be scared, little buddy," he said. "That's been going on all morning."

"But . . . what was it?" As I uttered the words I heard another explosion, louder than the first.

"Just folks getting an early start, is all. Where'd you find them clothes?"

I frowned. "An early start? For what?"

"For the celebration." He gave me a long look. "It's Independence Day. You know, the Fourth of July?"

It took a minute for that to sink in. When it did, I took a step back and looked at the calendar, pinned to the bulkhead wall. "But it's May," I said.

The black man reached past me and tapped the calendar with an accusing finger. "Dunno why they don't throw this out. Guess they keep it 'cause of the pretty picture. Dern thing's two years old."

The words, at first, didn't register. Neither did the connection.

1908?

Plus two years . . . ?

The answer hit me so hard I felt my knees buckle. My heart froze in my chest.

This was the day.

"You okay, little podner?" the black man said. "You don't look so hot."

Even as I tried to calm myself, to formulate what I would do next, I felt the workman's strong hands helping me, steadying me, guiding me out the doorway and toward the steps.

"No!" I shouted. "I've got to warn him—"

"Come here, little man. Just two more steps down. We get you a drinka water, you'll be good as new."

"Wait!" I was struggling now, trying to pull loose from his grasp. "Grandfatherrrrrrrr," I yelled, as loud as I could—

***

And looked up into my father's face.

"Dad?" I mumbled.

He was standing beside me on the platform at the foot of the steps, and there were bright tears in his eyes. And more than tears, too—a look of shock and wonder and relief. Without a word he snatched me to him and hugged me as the conductor had done moments earlier, in another world.

"Timmy," he whispered into my neck. "Oh, Timmy."

And Mom was there beside him, hugging me also, and even my stupid sister. Off to one side, but watching me closely, was the modern-day conductor, Mr. Hardy. Not to mention about a dozen curious passengers.

"Tim, are you—are you all right?" my mother asked, sobbing.

"I think so," I said. I still couldn't quite put my thoughts together. Was I really *back*?

Jenny stuck her head between me and Dad, grinning. "You had us pretty scared there for a while, kiddo," she said. The crowd had built up around us now. I stared at them in disbelief.

"Will you still be needing a doctor?" the conductor asked my mother. I noticed he kept his eyes on me as he spoke.

"Yes," Mom said. She had stopped sniffling long enough to give me a worried look. "I think he needs to be checked out, at least. Don't you, Robert?"

Dad just nodded. Like Mr. Hardy, he was watching me with wary eyes, as if I might decide to sprout wings and circle the station a time or two.

"What happened to me?" I said, to no one in particular.

My dad drew a shaky breath and let it out in a whoosh.

"It was the tunnel," he said. "When we went through the tunnel near Winslow you . . . changed. After that, you didn't seem to see any of us, or hear us either. You kept looking around, and frowning. You looked scared."

"And that's what scared *us*," Mom said. "We tried to talk to you, and you just looked . . . lost."

That's because I was, I said to myself.

"And finally you started talking," Dad said. "Not in answer to anything we were asking, though. You just started rambling. Something about Rogers, and Van Buren, and other things that didn't make sense. Once you said your name. It was like . . . like you were having a conversation with somebody who wasn't there." He glanced at my mother, who was wiping her eyes with a soaked tissue. I noticed the crowd was dispersing now. The kid's okay, their looks said. Time to go see about lunch.

"And then," Dad went on, "you got up all of a sudden and walked over to the front seat, where Mr. Hardy had been sitting. You scooted right over to his window and looked out for a long time, just nodding your head now and then. You seemed to brighten a little, but you still wouldn't respond to us." He paused, and I could see in his face the stress he'd been through. "We started to take you off the train when it stopped earlier, but we were told there was no doctor there, so we waited till now."

I wasn't sure I had heard correctly. "When it stopped?"

Dad glanced at the conductor, who explained, "We had an unexpected stop, not far south of the tunnel. They think it was a problem with one of the isolator valves. We were delayed only a few minutes—you just sat and stared out the window."

"Mrs. Derryberry had to get off," I said dreamily.

Everyone's eyes narrowed at the same time. "What?" Dad asked.

I blinked and focused on him. "Nothing." I turned to my mother, who still looked worried. She kept reaching over to smooth my hair, or touch my face. "I'm fine now, Mom," I said, and forced a weak smile. "I really am."

Not that I actually convinced anyone, but they seemed to

accept the idea that maybe I wasn't as loony as I had first appeared to be—or at least that I wasn't about to lapse once again into a catatonic state. I wondered, as my family said their goodbyes to Mr. Hardy and got directions to the doctor's office (my dad said we'd rent a car tomorrow so we could retrieve our own car from Delores) whether I would ever be able to explain to anyone what had really happened.

And then a thought jumped into my mind. It had occurred to me before, back when we first boarded the train, but it hadn't seemed that important, then. It did now.

"Remember this morning," I said to my dad, "you were telling us about the train wreck? The one that killed your great-granddad?"

"What about it?" He and I were walking along together on the tree-shaded sidewalk. Mom and Jenny had gone on ahead, to look for the sign for the doctor's office.

"You said there were no survivors," I said.

"That's right."

"Well . . . if there were no survivors, there wasn't anybody around to tell what happened. Right?"

Dad stopped and looked down at me. "What are you getting at, Timmo?"

"Why did people think the wreck was caused by the Langtree gang?" I asked.

He frowned. "People didn't *think* so. They *knew* it was the Langtrees."

"But how? How could they be sure?"

Dad hesitated then, and I realized it wasn't because he didn't know the answer. It was because he was worried about me again, and wondering why I was so interested in this. And during that pause I also knew—I knew with a goosepimply, spine-tingling certainty—what he was going to say next.

"Because of the letter," he said.

I swallowed. "The letter?"

"They found a letter the next day, after the accident. In a mailbag that was thrown clear of the wreckage. It said the Langtree brothers were going to hit the train, even mentioned the time of day." He glanced up the street, where Mother and Jenny were marching back to fetch us. "With that as evidence," he added, "the Law raided the Langtrees' hideout, somewhere east of here. A month later all three brothers were hanged on the gallows beside the Fort Smith courthouse."

I felt my stomach flip over. *What had I done?*

But I couldn't let myself think about that. Not now. Right now, another question had locked into my mind, one even more important.

"But if the Langtrees were all hanged," I asked, holding my breath, "who murdered the kids at the Brineyville school?"

Dead silence. Even Mom, who had arrived in time to hear my question, looked confused. "Brineyville?" she said.

"What kids?" Dad asked. He and Mom and Jenny looked at each other, and that look—open and honest and impossible to fake—told me all I needed to know.

There had been no schoolhouse killings in Brineyville, Arkansas, in the spring of 1911. There had been no killings because the killers were already dead.

I must have gone really pale or something then, because Jenny's eyes widened and Mom rushed forward and Dad scooped me up in his arms the way he'd done when I was a baby and carried me to Dr. Edward Summerall's office.

Fifteen minutes later, after a great deal of parental and medical attention, I sat in my underwear on an examining table and listened as the doc reassured my mom and dad that I would in fact live to see tomorrow's sunrise. But I was only half listening.

Mostly, I was thinking. Not about the Langtrees and who

they might or might not have murdered, or what other changes I might have caused to the future of mankind—I would think plenty about that later. I never even stopped to consider, at that point in time, whether one of the future descendants of those kids at the Brineyville school might grow up, in this new and altered universe, to pilot a shuttle to Jupiter or become President or find a cure for cancer. Those things never crossed my mind. What I was thinking about was my great-great-grandfather.

I couldn't seem to get him out of my thoughts. His kindly face, his bristly gray mustache, the blue eyes behind his glasses, the smell of his cologne as he held me in his arms.

I found myself smiling a little, partly because of those images and partly because I knew now that they *were* real, and that I wasn't crazy after all.

The moment of truth had come only minutes ago, when the doc had asked Mom and Dad to get me undressed. Far more embarrassed by this than by my earlier behavior, I pulled away from them and informed everyone that I was quite capable of taking off my own pants. It was then, as I unbuckled my belt and stepped out of my jeans, that I felt it.

At some point, you see—probably when we'd hugged each other just before we parted on July 4, 1910—Cecil Burnside had slipped me a little memento. And I didn't have to take it out and look at it to know what it was, either.

Hidden in my pants pocket, warm now against my fingertips, was a fine old pocketwatch, with a copper case and a winding key and a long gold chain.

***

I thought about it all the way home.

A strange peace had settled over me. Something incredible had happened to me today, something unbelievable but true. I had the proof in my pocket. But should I tell anyone? I could only imagine the looks on my family's faces. Would they ever believe me?

No. Mom and Jenny wouldn't. But Dad would.

Finally, at about the time we pulled into our driveway in Nashville, I made up my mind. Dad would turn forty in a few weeks. My secret could wait until then.

I even smiled a little, thinking about it.

Birthdays were good times for surprises . . .